WATCH BY

MOONLIGHT

WATCH BY MOONLIGHT

A NOVEL

Kate Hawks

WILLIAM MORROW
75 YEARS OF PUBLISHING
An Imprint of HarperCollinsPublishers

HarperCollins books may be purchased for educational, business, or sales promotional use. For information please write: Special Markets Department, HarperCollins Publishers Inc., 10 East 53rd Street, New York, NY 10022.

FIRST EDITION

Designed by Jessica Shatan

Printed on acid-free paper

Library of Congress Cataloging-in-Publication Data

Hawks, Kate.
    Watch by moonlight / Kate Hawks.—1st ed.
        p.   cm.
    ISBN 0-380-81465-X
    1. Dorset (England)—Fiction. 2. Brigands and robbers—Fiction.   I. Title.

PS3557.O316 W38 2001
813'.54—dc21

                                         00-049113

01 02 03 04 05 RRD 10 9 8 7 6 5 4 3 2 1

To Terry and Debbie Bramley
and all the delightful folk
of the Milton Arms, Winterborne Whitechurch.

Bless all in the house.

To give the reader some idea of the buying power of the English pound and shilling in 1763, the pound was worth about fifty or sixty dollars in today's currency, the shilling equal to about three dollars. Source: *Rousseau and Revolution* by Will and Ariel Durant (Simon & Schuster, 1967).

PART I

The wind was a torrent of darkness among the gusty trees,
The moon was a ghostly galleon tossed upon cloudy seas,
The road was a ribbon of moonlight over the purple moor,
And the highwayman came riding—
  Riding—riding—
The highwayman came riding, up to the old inn-door. . . .

DORSET, ENGLAND, 1763

The night Jason Quick came into her life, Bess Whateley felt desperate enough to scream. But she'd wanted to howl out her frustration over a thousand and one long days beginning at dawn, trudging through the same round of tasks for the last seven years. She was a daughter, not a servant, though she slaved like one. Her father's public house, the King's Shilling, lay on the coach road from Blandford Forum, and so his business throve as hungry travelers stopped to rest and eat.

"Thriving, Reverend!" Jedediah Whately would boom of a Sunday to Pastor Cobbe of St. Mary's. "Truly thriving."

Aye, the King's Shilling turned a neat penny because Bess and her mother worked from daybreak to late night, the heavy days falling from Anne Whateley's life like autumn leaves and from her own even before they budded. Eighteen since St. Distaff's Day in January and *nothing* in her wasting life exciting or different. Come opening time Bess knew to the man which beer-swilling wags would try to pinch her bottom and which might leave her tuppence over the reckoning. Tuppence was usual but not always possible for poor Dorset farmers. Now and then travelers from Blandford might leave three or four pence, and five was sheer windfall. Bess saved what she could, heroically denying herself new shoes or a frilly shift even when she yearned for them. She wasn't sure just what the thrift was toward, but something important. Her hoard amounted to almost two pounds now.

This spring day began as countless others: Bess tended the cows, fed the chickens and geese, muttering back at the tedious crowing of their old rooster (bound for the stewpot soon), started the kitchen fires for her mother, then bathed in water gone tepid by the time she lugged enough up to her room. There had been Rose Allen two years ago—tawny Rose with her sly smile and man-knowing eyes and no better than she should be, Anne Whateley allowed. Certainly Rose knew more of men than Bess, but who didn't? Her mother's was a mild judgment in Bess's opinion. Rose was a right whore the way she carried on with loud-mouthed Willy Boston, and oh, didn't she know how to coax an extra tuppence out of men in their cups. Not only a whore but a thief; twice Bess saw her giving short change to a customer too drunk to notice. The first time might have been a mistake; the second time Bess told her father, and Rose was packed off home to Cheselbourne after cursing Bess in words the girl blushed to remember. But after Rose left, Bess had twice as much work to do.

Sundays were blessed respite. The inn was closed and she could doze politely through Reverend Cobbe's sermon at St. Mary's—that is, if Tim Groot, their stableman, didn't try to hold her hand or press his knee against hers. Every Sunday after services Bess prayed fervently in the little Lady Chapel for some miracle to transform her life, for a miracle seemed her only salvation from a future that promised nothing more than spinsterhood or Tim Groot.

Some nights in the Shilling weren't bad at all. On an evening when custom was slow, old Abel Gant who lived down Dewlish would tell her stories over his hot wine and lemon. Small and wispy, dry humor and dignity mixed, Abel Gant carried himself with the threadbare gentility of someone descended in the world from higher things. He'd been a schoolmaster in London, or so he said. No matter, Bess adored Abel, who always left her something on the table, and didn't he have a grand way with words! Sometimes near closing when the tavern was empty save for him, Abel would spin a tale for her, pausing now and then to knock the ash from his pipe, his dry voice wine-warmed to music, lulling Bess into her best-loved tale of captive Rapunzel in the tower and how she let down her long hair for the prince to climb. She reckoned all that tugging would hurt something fierce, but the story enchanted her. Like Rapunzel, she let her hair grow, not minding the weekly bother of washing and daily doing up. The thick black tresses hung down her back past her hips now.

By the open window in her darkened room, brushing out the long ebony waves, she often pretended she could hear the prince's horse drumming along the moonlit road to clatter over the cobbles beneath her window. Then he would lift his arms to entreat:

"Bess, my Bess, let down your hair."

Rapunzel and the prince became part of her heart's secret lore, the inn itself and her airless life the imprisoning tower. As for the witch, that could be ever-hovering Tim, who *would* not see that she didn't want him. More than once, rapt in dreams at her window, Bess caught Tim staring up at her from the dark stableyard, causing her to close the shutters and turn away. He was ever trying to catch her attention or asking to walk out with her after church, always *watching* her with that dull intensity. As if she'd squander precious free time of a Sunday on Tim when she had to be back in the kitchen come evening to help her mother prepare for the morrow. That Tim wanted her was flattering, she supposed, but there was something about the young ostler that made her skin crawl. Not his looks; Tim was well enough made, with straw-colored hair and a lean, strong body. Perhaps it was the flat, implacable purposefulness in his pale blue eyes set too close together, and the way he took for granted that Bess was his alone.

There were some boys at least. Last year she'd walked out some with Evan Bromley, who took her to the summer fayre at Winterborne Kingston. A fine husky lad Evan was, with a gentle way to him. He won the ax race by five strokes over the nearest contender, Bess cheering him on, but he was no match for Tim's cold fury when the ostler heard he'd asked Mr. Whateley for Bess's hand. Tim waylaid Evan on the Kingston road and thrashed him. He could have spared himself the trouble. Jedediah Whateley wasn't yet ready to lose a good worker, and in truth Evan stirred no more in Bess's heart than Tim. She wanted—she didn't know what, but something finer, a man to scale her bleak tower at least, one with some quality she could respond to. And there was much in her to respond, she knew, a bell waiting only to be struck for its pure note to ring forth.

Odd how she could talk more freely of such things with Abel Gant than her mother. Not that Mum didn't care. Sometimes on free Sunday mornings before church, Anne Whateley would bathe her daughter as she had when Bess was little, not talking much but her hand scrubbing, rinsing and drying with more eloquent tenderness than she could ever convey in words, and then patiently brushing out the lengthening hair with long, even strokes until it shone.

"It wants cutting, girl."

"No. I want to grow it long as I possibly can."

"Why? 'Tis bother enough already. 'Twill be snarling and the ends split."

Rapunzel, Bess remembered as her gaze and dreams sought beyond her window.

With old Abel like a second father, her bell could ring out at will. Ever since she was fourteen Bess often spent Sunday afternoons with her dear companion, astride behind him on his old horse, wandering over the broad downs south of the Dorchester road, and she would reach up into the bowl of the sky—

"Do you know, Abel? Sometimes at night I stretch my arms up so, and I can *feel* the sky like a river full of diamonds rushing past, and I wish I could write more than just my name so I could make poems out of all of it."

"No need, Bess"—tamping fresh tobacco into his dark-stained pipe—"when you are what poetry is all about."

Now there was a strange and thrilling thought. Bess would never have imagined such. "Me?"

"Bess," said Abel, "others have put it better, but you *are* poetry. And someday soon some fine young fellow with keener eye and sense than's common in these parts will make you believe it."

Oh, when would that be? If she was poetry, where was he that would make her rhyme before she faded to the worn look of her mother? More disturbing than that: In the last half year, though she favored Tim Groot not one whit more, his attentions bothered her less. She could even give him a smile and a friendly word as he hunched over his supper in the kitchen—until Bess realized with a shock and then a sinking heart that she was surrendering day by day to the inevitable, and what she dreamed for a future was happening now. With a dull horror her mind fled into that future. She would become like her mother, permanently bent over the same rolling pin, the eternal basting ladle and turning spit. She would never breathe air not thick with the smell of onions and turnips, salt beef and boiled cabbage, and when she looked up from endless acres of pie dough, there would be no one there forever but Tim.

So, this spring evening as she carried from kitchen to table the ten thousandth plate of bubble-and-squeak, Bess felt sure as Judgment Day that there would be nothing beyond this, on and on until the damp earth of St. Mary's churchyard closed over her. And for the ten thousandth time she screamed inside. *Let—me—out.*

But . . . Mr. Jellicoe wanted another warm wine with his supper, and as Bess bent to place the tin slipper in the alcove over the fire, she heard the tavern door open and close behind her and her father's unusually hearty greeting, the tone reserved for customers of obvious quality. "Come *in*, young sir. Come in and welcome to the King's Shilling. What is your pleasure?"

"Brandy, sir. A glass of your best if you will."

Some arresting quality in that voice made Bess straighten and turn. Without effort his voice rode clearly over the tavern buzz.

Bess stared at the claret velvet coat under his Inverness cloak, the
tailored breeches, the hair black as her own, falling over his forehead as he removed his tricorn hat—and her deadened soul
stirred and resurrected. He was only a year or two her senior, she
guessed, with the pallor of a city man, his thin face drawn too
tight just now, as if he were in pain.

Her father ordered, "Fetch the gentleman his brandy, Bess."

She hastened back of the bar, reaching at first for the usual
pewter mug but choosing instead one of their rarely used good
glasses and pouring it a wee bit fuller than her father would. He
was quite occupied with the stranger, who had seated himself at
a table in a dimly lit corner. The other diners were as curious;
even Mr. Jellicoe paused over his plate, while Jedediah Whateley
inquired in his best mine-host manner, "Have you journeyed
from Blandford, sir?"

"No, from Cheselbourne." The stranger took his brandy neat
and handed the glass to hovering Bess. "Another, please."

"Our Tim has your horse?" she asked.

"Yes . . . yes, I'm sorted out."

"Bess!" Mr. Jellicoe called plaintively. "I wish my wine warmed,
not boiled."

Oh Lord, she'd quite forgot. Bess grabbed the slipper from its
alcove and poured it into Jellicoe's mug. When she brought the
stranger's second brandy, Bess saw him wince slightly and ventured to ask, "Are you ill, sir?"

"Yes, actually." He sipped at the brandy and set it down, placing his cloak-wrapped left arm as carefully on the table. "But
most distressing. I met a rider who said the Dorchester coach
had been waylaid tonight and the passengers robbed. Does this
happen frequently?"

Now the tavern was all ears. Mr. Jellicoe banged his mug on
the table. "The Fleecer," he rumbled.

The young man looked up at him. "Who, sir?"

"A common highwayman, sir," Mr. Whateley called from the
bar. "Calls himself the Golden Fleecer, he does. A poor joke and

poorer for business on this road. Thank God he's not troubled us here in Winterborne Whitechurch."

"Indeed, a blessing." The stranger's eyes slid to Bess, and she saw the warmth in them, dark as her own. "Among many. Your brandy is excellent. Thank you."

He smiled at her and Bess gave silent thanks that her cap was freshly washed and starched, her hair beneath not completely askew. *If not a prince, he looks like one.*

Not all, though. His clean-cut good looks were marred by two scars across his left jawline, recent and still reddish. The liquor jiggled slightly in his glass. His hand was trembling.

"We've not seen you before, Mr. . . . ?"

"Quick," he told her. "Jason Quick."

A name to suit him, Bess judged. *Everything about him is sharp and fine.* "You're new to these parts then?"

"I was bound for Plymouth," he responded politely. "But your countryside is so beautiful it seemed a shame not to tarry awhile."

A clatter of horses in the stableyard, and then a plainly worried Tim Groot slipped into the tavern. "Mr. Whateley, there's soldiers come."

"Good God." Whateley came out from behind the bar; the other customers bowed heads over ale mugs and tried to be inconspicuous. Soldiers never meant anything but trouble, especially those of the Fifty-fourth Foot. Most of the regiment had been posted to Ireland, thank God, leaving a company in Dorchester and a smaller detachment in Milborne St. Andrew. Whateley could do without their trade, though a blessing they came seldom to Winterborne Whitechurch. The remaining troops were regimental dregs, ruffians, mostly pressed men from Dorchester slums or felons who took the king's pay to escape his prison. Wild Willy Boston had been one of them once, so Rose Allen said. When you saw their red coats with the broad green facing, you found urgent business elsewhere.

The door swung open and a beefy, red-faced sergeant shoul-

dered Tim out of the way, followed by three soldiers. The
sergeant's eyes swept the bar and dining room before settling on
Jedediah Whateley. "I'm Provost Hallow from St. Andrew," he
announced in a tone of clear no-nonsense. "You'd be the host?"

"I am, but it's late if you are wanting sup—"

"We don't," Hallow cut him off. "The Dorchester coach was
robbed tonight, got to St. Andrew just an hour ago. The Fleecer,
they said. Driver shot at him but probably missed. Bugger made
off quick. They said he rode this way. Any strangers passed or
stopped here tonight?"

Tim pointed at Jason. "There's him."

Bess couldn't help speaking up. "Surely not, sir. Why, this gentleman rode in from Cheselbourne only a few minutes past and
told us of the robbery."

"Cheselbourne." Sergeant Hallow planted himself over Jason
Quick. One of the soldiers leered invitingly at Bess.

"What's your name then?"

"Jason Quick, sir. Late of London."

"And now?"

"As the lady said: Cheselbourne. The Crown and Thistle."

"Not but one inn there," one of the privates volunteered. "You
know, Sarn't—where sweet Rosey works."

The sergeant inspected Jason Quick from the crisp white lace
at his throat to his polished boots. "What's a London macaroni
doing in these parts?"

"Passing through to Plymouth, sir. Outward bound to Virginia."

"That's true," Bess jumped in quickly. "He told us the same."

"And a gentleman right enough," Hallow decided with a
touch of dismissive contempt. "Got hands white as whey."

"I've not been well," Jason Quick told him. "My physician said
the city air—" He broke off, appealing to the room at large.
"Lud, but I just realized. That rider who told me of the robbery.
He barely stopped before dashing on. Do you think he might
have been the robber?"

"Could be," one of the soldiers allowed, yearning thirstily toward the bar. "Fellow nipped off this way for sure."

"He wasn't sparing his horse either." Jason Quick coughed delicately into a laced handkerchief. "Yes, very like."

The provost demanded, "What'd he look like?"

"Almost no moon tonight," Jason answered. "All I could see was his hat and cloak. He spoke with a broad accent. Welsh I should say. I was fortunate not to detain him."

"So you were." Hallow narrowed his eyes at Jason, studying him closely. "Aye, you look ill, right enough. Pale as snow."

"That and a narrow escape, sir. But it is reassuring that you and your men are so keen. Will you take a glass?"

"We've no time, thanks."

From the thirsty soldier plaintively: "Just one, Sarn't?"

"I said no. We'll ride on to Cheselbourne and perhaps stop for a glass there. You there." He jerked his chin at Tim Groot. "Give the horses some water first. Hop it."

The soldiers clumped out after the ostler. When the door slammed, the mood in the room relaxed like a fist unclenching. Jason Quick drained his glass and rose to depart. "Thank you for speaking out for me, lass. May I ask your name?"

Yet his eyes asked a great deal more. "Bess Whateley. 'Twas only honesty." *And my pleasure.*

"Indeed, Mr. Quick," Jedediah invited. "Please come again. I had rather the custom of one gentlemen like yourself than a hundred of their kind. We do fine roasts three times a week and close only on Sundays."

"You may be sure I will," Jason promised in that soft but compelling voice as he smiled again at Bess. "And since the good provost is suspicious of strangers, I'll most certainly be less of one. Good night." He looked again at Bess, repeating her name as if savoring it. "Bess . . ."

He'd left the reckoning on the table, but as Bess went to scoop it up, she blinked, wondering if she saw aright. Beside the price of his drinks there was a whole shilling.

For me. He left that for me.

And something else. Where his cloak-wrapped sleeve had rested on the table, there was a dark smear. Bess wiped at it. The smear came away red on her white cloth.

No wonder he was pale. *"Driver shot at him but probably missed."*

Bess wrestled briefly with God, conscience, and instinct. She'd damned Rose for a thief, but *he* never stole from her, and he was certainly generous. One didn't tell soldiers any more than needed. Or her father for that matter. And he would come again; Bess could read that much in his eyes. She knew his name and where he dwelt. She frowned suddenly at the thought of Rose serving him at the Crown and Thistle. Would that slut have the brass to give Jason Quick short change? No, she wouldn't dare. Well mannered and spoken he was, yet there was that in him too wary to be cheated.

He would come again. He simply must.

That night at her window, Bess gazed out at the Dorchester road and dreamed.

What Bess took for wariness in Jason Quick was steely will forged by deep rage that had scarred his young soul past healing. Jason was a have who, in one terrible year, became a pennyless have-not. The fall wrenched him, bringing out his best and worst, above all his determination that he and his ruined father would survive.

Jason had the manners and courage of a gentleman; however, the qualities were not inborn but learned. The son of Abraham Quick, a stationer who dwelt above his Cheapside shop, Jason was a true Cockney, born within the sound of Bow Church bells. More a lover of books than a man of commerce, Abraham was habitually in debt but managed to stay afloat, while Mirabel Quick put food on the table year round even if sometimes only cabbage and potatoes. Jason was allowed three years at a council grammar school and then, like most strapped tradesmen's sons, was needed in the shop, stocking shelves, cutting signatures of paper for the pamphlets his father printed and occasionally penned himself.

The poisonous mixture of fog and coal smoke that too often smothered London deepened Mirabel's wracking cough into a consumption that laid her in the grave when Jason was fifteen. He wept and prayed for her in Bow Church, while life went on in the shop where he now proofread and corrected the increasingly virulent Whig diatribes against the king's Tory government. While Abraham went deeper into debt, his creditors trusted his character if not his sense of business. Writers of every degree, from Edmund Burke and Dr. Johnson to the humblest scriveners, patronized Quick's. A born mimic, Jason heard the difference between their speech and his own jangling Cockney and practiced to emulate them. He read everything off the shop press, from political essays to satire and wretched doggerel verse. In 1760, when he was nineteen, Jason cried "God save the king!" as George III ascended the throne. Two years later, Abraham in debtors' prison and himself living by his wits alone, Jason's *save* soured to a bitter *damn*.

He came to hate the king but never his own London, where the very air was alive. Jason watched his city stretch, change, and grow even as he had in passing from childhood. As he delivered books for his father along Fleet Street, fashion and filth jostled him on either side. Along the Strand, where the rich could buy the best of the world and a burgeoning empire, he gaped at the courtesans stately in their sedan chairs—

"Fifty guineas a night, they tell me," Abraham declared.

"Garn!" Jason had never seen fifty guineas at one time in his life. "What's she do beside? Card tricks? For fifty guineas I could bed a saint."

"Better you do, be you ever so rich. Always go for quality,"

Abraham advised, thinking of young Mirabel with reminiscent pleasure. "But stay away from the doxies around here. Shilling and a pint for cost, and next week ten pounds to the surgeon to rid you of gleet or worse."

—and applauded the wonderful David Garrick and Kitty Clive in *The Provoked Wife* at the Drury Lane. From his one-shilling seat at the Little Theatre, Haymarket, he roared at the satire and mimicry of Samuel Foote. Hurrying home late after a play, Jason learned early to dodge the linkboys hired to light pedestrians home, for they often fattened their fees by informing thieves where to lie in wait. A dodgy business being out at night, but Jason knew every side street, court, mews, and alley between Cheapside and Westminster. A haphazard life but exhilarating to a youth whose world felt as solid and unchangeable as St. Paul's.

In 1762 that world collapsed beneath Jason. The obstinate young King George chose the Scottish Earl of Bute for his chief minister over the furious objections of the House of Commons and passionate Whigs like John Wilkes.

And Abraham Quick. "Bute, I ask you," he fumed to his son and customers. "Not only a Scot but a Stuart! 'Tis old King Charles risen up, by God. 'Tis ruin!"

As George and Bute proceeded to reclaim, act by act, the power won by Parliament after the Civil War, Abraham Quick grew angrier and more reckless. Already in theaters perform-ances were interrupted by protests against Scots in the stalls. Anti-Bute tracts and satires poured from Quick's press despite the warnings of cautious friends and, finally, Jason himself. Abra-ham burst into the shop one day, thrusting a sheaf of pages over the counter at Jason. "Here, my lad. Read this. Sell a thousand copies if one, it will."

Jason squinted at the single name beneath the title. "Who's Junius?"

Abraham winked. "That's for me to know and the king to pon-der. Bought me an excellent lunch at Child's this very noon. Junius, my boy, is that ubiquitous—" Pleased with the word,

Abraham savored it again. "That u-bi-qui-tous author Anonymous. Read, Jason, read."

Jason scanned the pages with growing dismay. Clever and comical, yes, but perilous as flame near gunpowder. Whig writers regularly lampooned the king as a clown, but this went leagues beyond license. He dropped the pages on the counter. "We cannot publish this."

"Not publish? My creditors will rejoice that I've been well paid. And God knows the substance may be true."

"Are you serious? Whatever the royals' sentiments, no one faults their virtue. George is the first king since Jesus who keeps no mistress. This Junius suggests that Bute not only has the king in his pocket but the bleedin' queen mother in his bed. Not satire or lampoon, Dad, but dangerous calumny."

"And who," Abraham persisted, "is to say it may not be true?"

"May not?" Jason looked after the bantam rooster figure of his father already bustling about the press, choosing among type fonts, and knew Abraham was capable of being both stubborn and perverse. "If I fire a pistol at your breast, it may not kill you, but how keen are you to find out?"

"Oh, tut. Come, read it again and make the corrections. He spells abominably."

"At least omit your name as stationer."

"I have always put my name to what I print."

"Junius bloody well didn't!"

"Jason, we are Quick's, stationers of Pancras Lane, Cheapside. So the work will state."

So it did. Priced at tenpence, Junius's scurrilous lampoon sold over a hundred copies the first week. Rubbing ink-stained palms together in glee, Abraham ran a second printing that sold as briskly. An early copy was bought by the Whig leader John Wilkes, and word of mouth spread. Once Quick's regular customers got wind of the pamphlet, Jason couldn't keep enough copies in stock. The general coffeehouse laughter was loud enough to reach the outraged royal ear.

One morning a carriage drew up in Pancras Lane and a lean little man in brocaded coat and satin smallclothes entered the shop.

"I am Mr. Beedle of the King's Bench." He dropped a copy of Junius's pamphlet on the counter. "Which demands the true name of this author."

"Sorry." Abraham Quick shook his head. "I respect my client's wish to remain anonymous. Who is asking? Bloody Bute?"

"Were it merely an earl, the Bench would not bother. Does this scribbler comprehend whom he has libeled?"

"I assume he does, sir. If libel it is."

"With no other name for this hack, Master Quick, one might assume, since you are known to have penned certain Whig tracts, that you yourself perpetrated this filth."

Listening by the press, Jason reckoned Beedle for an anonymity himself, scuttling on errands between chambers and court, never to do anything so definite as die but simply fade into the nearest wallpaper upon demise.

"Assume, sir?" he laughed. "You may assume I have a pound in my purse and turn it out in proof, but damme if you'll find more than sixpence. Mind the gutter as you leave, Mr. Beedle. The horses have been generous."

"Well, sir." Beedle settled his tricorn precisely on his head and tucked the pamphlet into a brocaded cuff. "What can I say but that you are criminally reckless." He turned abruptly and left the shop.

Abraham chuckled. "Now we know how far the voice of Junius carries."

The fact did not comfort Jason. "So we do."

"Tonight let's dine in some style," Abraham flourished. "Dolly's Steak House for the best dinner and ale."

"Aye, Dad."

Jason turned back to the press, worried from the start of this business. Beedle's visit didn't help, nor the seven eager customers who came in later asking for copies. Jason worked on through the day, then clapped up the shutters at seven and locked the shop, when he and his father departed for supper. They did not notice the five men idling on the walk some distance behind them.

Remembering later, Jason marked that May evening as the end of one life, the beginning of another. In the clarity of pain he recalled their supper at Dolly's and how they jested over beef and ale, Jason mimicking the dry-dust look and sound of Beedle; how they teased each other, as always, for opposite tastes in beef. Jason liked his barely seared outside and fairly raw within. Abraham merrily pronounced his son a damned cannibal and munched a blackened chop that might have been dragged too late from an inferno.

In an expansive mood they left a whole thruppence for the waiter and set forth to ale themselves home through the public houses along their way. Teetering down Queen Street on Jason's supporting arm, Abraham paused to sniff at the air. "Jason, wha'zzat?"

"What's what?"

"Smell smoke?"

Jason did. "And there's folk milling about in our street. Hear 'em?"

Turning into Pancras Lane, Jason's heart dropped into his stomach. The last smoke drifted through the smashed windows of their shop. People scurried this way and that, most huddling in front of Quick's. One man emerged from the burned-out ground floor holding a handkerchief to his nose, shaking his head. Another hurried toward the Quicks as they approached: Mr. Muggeridge the draper whose shop and dwelling adjoined theirs.

"Master Quick, it's your shop. We—we couldn't save—"

"I can see that," Jason snapped savagely. "Who did this?"

Muggeridge spread shaking hands in ignorance. "No one knows. We had to make sure it did not spread. We put it out before abovestairs burned, but your shop . . ."

The shop was a gutted ruin. Someone had scattered the lead type fonts all over the floor, ripped up paper, then broken their whale oil lamps over the mess. The stocks of paper were burned to ash, the press battered beyond repair, the lead type silvery puddles on the blackened floor planks. As Jason turned about amid the wreckage, he bitterly damned Junius, whoever the bastard was: He should have burned with his rotten screed. Jason's nose rebelled at the harsh smell of smoke and charred wood soaked down by frantic neighbors desperately trying to extinguish the blaze before it spread through their own tinder-dry houses.

He tried to keep his voice from quavering with panic. "What are we going to do?"

"Do?" Abraham salvaged and lit a heat-warped candle from a charred drawer. "For now we'll go to bed."

"Bed? Do you think I can sleep—?"

"I do." Abraham wove toward the stairs. "Will't be any the better if we worry all the night?"

There was his father for you, reckoning ruin no worse for a night's sleep. Once upstairs, Abraham wrestled unsteadily into his nightshirt and donned his nightcap askew, turning to Jason with an impish grin. "For all our misfortune, I allow we gave Georgie and Bute a proper kick up the strap, eh?"

"Aye, and broke our foot doing it."

While his father snored obliviously, Jason lay awake in the acrid stench of their burned-out life, trying to think clearly. Abraham was an optimist, praise be, Jason more an opportunist, but he could see no way out for them. They had no more than twenty-five pounds in the bank and owed ten times as much. His father's axiom: Put the money in the business, and the business will breed money. He had plowed every penny back into the shop. While he anticipated a sweeping profit on Junius, his loans were extended to their limit.

There was no business left and, God damn him, better if Junius had never written a line. The bastards who did for the shop had even rifled the till of the few shillings left there. Twenty-five pounds: The dismal litany repeated over and over in Jason's exhausted mind. Twenty-five ekcd out between all creditors. The house must go for whatever it would fetch. Tomorrow they must try to arrange something. Anything.

Twenty-five pounds. *Damn your easygoing pay-'em-tomorrow ways, Father, and damn me twice for not seeing it come. Sweet God, what are we going to do?*

Ruin was merely the beginning. Abraham and Jason watched their house and few possessions go on the block. All was sold and the pittance distributed to creditors, all but an old pike carried at Naseby against Charles I by another Jason Quick and handed down, father to son, with proud sentiment like an officer's sword. Jason sawed off the shaft close to the blade—

"To remind me that we will ever fight our own kings when need be."

— and packed the shortened weapon along with his clothes. They must vacate within the week.

Mr. Nightingale, whose wholesale house supplied Quick's with inks and paper, petitioned the Lord Chancellor on their behalf but to no avail. Nevertheless the decision of the Chancellor's commission stunned Jason when a sheriff appeared to take Abraham Quick into custody. Since he had no assets, he could no longer be considered a tradesman but merely an insolvent debtor. He was bound over to Old Bailey. Jason rushed frantically to Mr. Nightingale's home in Mayfair.

"This is *mad*, sir. They can't imprison him for the work of vandals."

"Calm, boy. Calm." Nightingale offered Jason brandy and a chair. "I have canceled my part of the debt; the others could or would not. The commission wouldn't hear of plain bankruptcy, nor are they convinced of vandalism over simple accident."

"Accident?" Jason's voice leaped up an octave in frustration. "Every damned lamp was out and the stove as well."

"Most unjust," Nightingale commiserated. "Indeed, it is as if they wanted your father in prison out of sheer malice. Someone influenced the judgment, I'm bound."

Jason recalled Beedle's clammy warning: *If it were merely an earl* . . . "Aye, someone who sits on velvet. And on our necks. The king's laws are pious wonders, Mr. Nightingale. Wages are kept down so profit stays up."

A humane man by any measure, Nightingale still felt the honest sting of that himself. "Jason—"

"No, damn them." Jason downed the brandy in one fiery gulp. "They look down at us through jeweled lorgnettes and judge that the poor must be kept poor for the betterment of their souls. Why give the buggers an extra shilling a week? They'll only drink it up. They may be turned out to starve or freeze to death in a doorway come winter, but the owners are marvelous moral."

"Jason, Jason," Nightingale interjected, "your family never starved. You were never really poor."

"Well, I'm damned well there now, aren't I? A nice distinction, sir: If my father had been dishonest or merely unwise at business—God pardon me, but he was that—the law would shelter him as a bankrupt. But if some lord sends gutter sweepings to burn him out, he doesn't stand a rat's chance in hell."

Jason buried his face in trembling hands. When Mr. Nightingale offered another brandy, he refused. "No, I—no thank you, sir. I must keep my wits about me. I must leave our house tomorrow. That will be hard. I was born there."

"Then take this." Nightingale pressed a five-pound note into his hand. "You'll be supporting yourself and your father."

Jason would have refused a week before; now there was no time or room for pride in a matter of survival. "You are kind, sir. I will consider this a loan."

"What will you do now?"

"I'll redeem his debts somehow."

"How, boy? I would help, but I've no position in my establishment I can offer."

"I'll get it."

Brave words but how indeed? All that week as his father awaited judgment, Jason trudged from stationer to stationer, but all had apprentices working for board and experience, and none were disposed to pay ten shillings a week for Jason's skilled work. Factory work would bring half that, and his father might be dead of jail fever before the debt could be erased. They died so every week in Newgate or lived in misery where every bit of food above tuppence worth of bread daily had to be bought from the jailors. He'd managed new linen and a decent blanket for his father, but even had to pay for light chains rather than the heavy irons clapped on paupers.

He found a cramped room over the Cross and Horn in St. Martin's Court off Charing Cross Road, blessedly shared with only one other young man, Owen Jones. Worst of all was to stand in Old Bailey and watch his father file into the dock with other ragged debtors who probably never saw a whole pound at one time in their lives. Abraham was a slight man, all heart but no heft; now he looked ten years older, dirty and unshaven in his shackles. At that moment icy rage darkened Jason's growing fear: His father was *not* like those others, *not* a beggar. Yet he slumped there, weaving on his feet without even the magistrate's nosegay of sweet herbs to keep the stench of the others from his nostrils. Jason's new catechism began to harden, and it had claws.

No, Nightingale, we never went hungry, not until now. But your father paid children pennies to slave twelve hours a day so he could send you to your beloved Harrow or wherever, while I had only three years of council school. Master Gant taught me reading; he said I was good at it, quick as my name. And my father worked six days a week all his life only to go deeper into debt. You are a good man, Mr. Nightingale, but pause on that when you drop sixpence in the poor box of a Sunday and go home to your port and roast feeling righteous.

Money ran dangerously low. Jason needed three shillings for his share of the rent; that left only two or three for his father if Jason went without a meal once a day. The cheery Welshman who shared his room, Owen Jones, was good about lending but couldn't be counted on forever. Jason bowed down day by day under a growing weight of hopelessness. The rank smell of St. Martin's Court offended his nostrils, whereas in Pancras Lane there had been running water piped in two or three times a week.

Still, things might be worse. Owen Jones was good company, always with money in his pocket to stand them both a drink, though he appeared to have no employment. Owen knew all the doxies who lived in the court, and Jason found them a good lot making the most of a hard life. None of them had ever known anything better, but Jason felt horribly displaced. Even drinking with them on Owen's generosity, one image never left his mind: the bars on the cells just below street level at Newgate, and the hands reaching through imploring a few pence of passersby. Pray God his father wouldn't come to that while Jason had a penny in his pocket one way or another.

Too soon, too cruelly it came to that. Passing the low bars on his way to give the jailors his last pence for Abraham, he tried to close his ears against the monotonous, whining pleas of the prisoners, when two chained hands thrust out to him.

"Jason!"

He stopped, praying to be mistaken but recognizing the filthy coat sleeve. Jason knelt by the bars.

Jesus have mercy.

Abraham tried to smile but his face had fallen in, all color gone. He coughed deeply before he could manage to speak. "Come this way from here out, to this same place. I'll watch for you."

Jason took his father's hands. "Dad, you're sick."

"Do you have some money for me?"

"Aye, but there's that I left with the jailor three days ago."

"Don't," Abraham rasped. "Never again, never with them. We never see it."

"They keep it?"

"Most of it. They aren't paid, so they live off us."

Jason could scarcely believe the inhumanity. On second thought he could. Bastards. Leeches.

"Come to these bars." Abraham broke off with wracking coughs deep in his lungs. Then his eyes brightened with a ghost of the old impishness. "We'll fox 'em, boy. I'll watch here every day at five. Pence, food, whatever you can fetch."

Jason ducked his head away. "God amercy."

"Now, now. There's those here far worse off than me."

Jason slipped the coins into his father's hand. It was filthy, the nails black. Abraham who used to fret at Mirabel when he didn't have clean linen every other day. "At five," he promised, pressing the hand between his. "Whenever I can."

He had to flee away, had to hide the flood of pity that burned hot in his eyes before it spilled over to shame Abraham's manhood and his own. He held back the tears until he was away from the bars, but when he turned back to see the large manacles hung over the prison entrance, what started as a snarl poured out in tears. Something died in Jason then, and a darker thing drew its first defiant breath. Jason flattened against a wall, no longer caring who saw his agony.

God save the king? He'd prayed to one and cheered the other, but what under merciful heaven did they want of a man? To break him, grind him into dust until nothing remained to defy either?

Someone tugged at his sleeve. Through a blur of tears Jason recognized Long Jane from St. Martin's Court frowning in concern. Owen it was who dubbed her Long Jane for her unusual height, tall as Jason himself. "Her father was a ship's mainmast," Owen swore, "and her mother a long country mile."

Of his own age, Jane had aged far more quickly, like most of

the shilling-and-pint girls off Charing Cross Road. While prais-
ing Jane's good nature, Owen had warned Jason away, as Jane
sometimes carried the gleet and possibly worse that would kill
her in ten years along with some of her customers.

" 'Allo, Jasie," she greeted him. "Whatever's got yer down,
want to come home wif me and talk about it?"

Jason wiped a hand over his eyes. "Good of you, Jane, but I've
only a bare sixpence for supper. Gave the rest to Dad in Newgate."

"Through the bars is best."

"Yes, else the jailors keep most of it, he said."

"Them," Jane muttered in contempt. "Always pass it straight
through the bars. Done it meself. Don't give them beggars nuf-
fin."

She glanced both ways along Newgate Street. "Well, time flies
as they say, an' ent gonter be angels pays my rent. Keep yer
pecker up, Jasie."

Long Jane moved away, easing into the hip-swinging saunter
that was part of her stock in trade, but turned back with a new
thought. "Yer a good lad, Jason Quick. Always talked to me like
a gennulmun. I'll be having a word with Owen. God bless."

His grief and rage exhausted themselves. Jason began to feel
hungry, though pride refused borrowing more from Owen Jones.
Only sixpence in his lean purse, but the Merry Grenadier in
Queen Street knew him and Abraham well. Perhaps the host
would go him a decent meal on trust. He trudged away down
the street.

No luck. The publican regretted but never extended credit
now, having been burned too often. Jason's few pence stretched
to one ale nursed over bread, a thin slice of cheese, and cold
bacon. At another table he saw the ample girth of Mr. Bottomley, who owned the poultry shop in Pancras Lane where his
mother had always bought their fowl. When Bottomley nodded
to him, Jason had a fleeting urge to ask him for a loan, but Bottomley went back to the last of his steaming roast. Jason

brooded over his own meager fare, too discouraged to pursue the thought.

"Finished then?" The young serving girl, Fanny McKinney, leaned over the table to him, reaching for his empty mug. "Another?"

Fanny's bosom hovered invitingly near, but Jason's hopeless mood smothered any interest. "No."

"Saving to get set up with a likely girl?" she teased. "Anyone in mind?"

The notion struck Jason as blackly funny. He stretched back on the bench. "Fanny luv, I can't even buy another ale, and even were the girl fetching as you, I couldn't afford to have her stand across the street and blow a kiss at me."

"I know, more's the pity," Fanny commiserated. "Rotten business about your dad. I prayed for him Sunday at Bow." She shot a quick glance at the unattended ale tap, moved away and quickly returned with a fresh ale. When Jason protested, Fanny just winked at him. "Drew it by mistake."

Jason drank half of it gratefully. "Come a pot of gold, I'll marry you, Fanny."

"When pigs fly." Fanny removed his empty plate. "Been a good night for me. Old Bottomley always leaves me tuppence, 'count of I always give'm a smile. Ah there, he's off."

The well-dined Bottomley sailed out of the Grenadier like an overloaded merchant ship. Jason finished his ale, regretting he couldn't leave Fanny something for her kindness but promising himself to leave a bit at some future date. Clearing Bottomley's table a moment later, Fanny snatched up a dark object. She snapped her head toward the door. "Mr. Bot—oh, he's gone and left his purse again. Forget his head one of these—here now, Jason? I'm wanted in the kitchen." She tossed the purse to him; it chinked heavily. "Catch up Mr. Bottomley and give it to him? There's a love."

Jason hurried out into Queen Street, looking northward after the portly figure of the poulterer. About to call out, he halted, silent. He stepped into a doorway and emptied the purse into his palm: over twelve shillings. *Just a bit he'll never miss, and I'm bound he gave my mother short weight on goose more than once.*

He taxed the poulterer modestly, only one and six, several meals for his father. Guilt twinged at Jason but only in passing as he remembered Abraham pleading through the prison bars. His principles had fallen through those bars and perished in the stink of Newgate. From this moment he would have few scruples over his own survival, over Abraham's none at all.

Now I'm a thief. Men are hanged for this. He pocketed the two coins, poured the rest back into the purse, and ran after Bottomley.

Jason sat in his room gazing at the coins in his hand. Not only thief but a hypocrite. When Bottomley wanted to reward him, Jason refused with Samaritan modesty. But there was the raw truth: He would rather steal then take charity from the Overseer of the Poor or surrender to the workhouse. Quicks were skilled tradesmen, self-sufficient and respectable. The king's law (and perhaps the king himself through the ferret Beedle) had torn him from his rightful place and cast him down into a hell he could not tolerate yet must to survive, like a cat forced to swim. The stinking world would not look on him or his father as beggars; by God they would not. To Jason that shame burned deeper than anything he must do to live.

Yet all came down to money. Without it a man was helpless, nothing possible. How subtle but vast the difference between enough and not enough.

His meager supper left him still hungry. Hearing Owen Jones's bounding step two at a time on the stairs, Jason hoped the fellow had brought something home.

The door burst open and Owen entered with a flourish. Like a herald unfurling his banner, he drew a headless fish from inside his patched coat. "Hot up the coals, Jason lad. We've mackerel for supper."

Jason took up the scuttle and poured coal into the brazier. "Don't fishmongers wrap them anymore?"

"The monger was busy elsewhere, and here was this orphan crying for a home."

"Crikey, you pulled it?"

Owen doused the coals with oil and hurried the flame with a bellows. "Rescued."

Jason smelled the mackerel and winced. "Not in time."

"Only three or four days at the stall. No matter. Lay on enough mustard and pepper, it'll be young as we are."

Young Owen was, threadbare but jaunty, his battered beaver hat worn atilt. With half his life spent in London, the Welsh lilt in his speech was barely audible. He still entertained Jason with renditions of the Glamorganshire accent, which Jason's quick ear could reproduce unerringly after a time.

Owen relished the mackerel, nodding with gusto. "Nothing like a spot of mustard. Hides its age as well as an actress."

Not to Jason, hungry though he was. After a few bites he pushed the plate toward his friend. "Thanks, but I've not much appetite after all."

"You're a toff, Jasie," Owen scoffed, piling the fish onto his plate. "Never worked hard in your life." He inspected Jason's hands. "Soft. Long Jane's are harder."

His critical frown turned thoughtful. "Small as hers too. Are they quick as well?"

"Quick as my name. I've set type since I turned fourteen. Dad never had to hurry me on."

Owen set down his fork. "Jane was speaking of you not an hour gone." He took another mouthful but spat it out. "Right you are; the monger should be ashamed. The landlord's cat would not have this."

Jason watched the energetic Owen snake into his shabby coat again, dropping his wallet into a side pocket. Rather a grand wallet for Owen's circumstances, soft pigskin lined in scarlet silk. "I'm bound for a drop and bite down the Cross and Horn. Come along, then."

"Lud, Owen, but I'm stoney."

"Am I asking you to pay?" Owen cocked the hat on his head and spread his arms to embrace Jason. "You are a dear lad but thick. Take a dram of wisdom from Owen Jones, who was wise enough to get out of the coal pits before he died of the black lung like his da. Never refuse a drink or a woman when either's free."

Jason hugged Owen close in return. "Or a temptation?"

"That neither." Owen hurled the door open. "Come on."

"So I am." Jason slipped into his worn coat, stopping Owen as his friend turned for the door. "What will you pay with?"

"No fear, there's five shilling in my—" Owen felt at his pocket, then dug deep. "Now didn't I just take the damned thing from that table?"

"Oh, this?" Jason tossed Owen the pigskin wallet, wiggling larcenous fingers at him. "Small and quick as my name."

"Well, if that's not enough to turn me from chapel back to Roman mass." Owen gave him an approving nod. "Long Jane had the right of you. Not a finger did I feel. Come, Master Quick!" He bowed Jason out with a flourish. "It is trade we will speak of and learning for you."

Through the early summer, under Owen's teaching, Jason learned the delicate art of the pickpocket. A "puller" could work alone, but more efficiently with a "pusher" whose job it was to jostle or distract the pigeon. String purse or wallet: First you found which the fellow carried and where. String purses were sliced free with a small razor. Wallets were easier. One quick dip and hand off to the pusher, who faded away in the crowd. To Jason's tidy mind the action resembled a precise dance.

"And your last if you be caught," Owen cautioned.

"A thinking man could turn it into a science."

"First comes skill. Look now."

Owen produced a handful of thin iron spits, each seven inches long, bunched them upright together, and sprawled them on the table before Jason. "Take them one by one from the pile—mind, without moving any of the others so much as a hair. If one moves or I hear a scrape, you're caught, and it's old Jack Ketch's gallows for you."

Deft as he was, Jason went to the gallows seven times before all obstructing spits remained unmoved and unheard.

"Now," Owen said, bunching and scattering the spits again, "do it at twice the speed."

Jason suggested working at night, especially when fog rolled up from the Thames. Time flew while Abraham wasted in New-gate. "Cut the linkboys in for a bit, they'll tell us where they're lighting a fat pigeon home."

"Linkboys? No," Owen refused from hard personal experience. "Look you, I come from honest folk and you from better. There's *degrees* to our calling, Jason. Linkboys, is it? They're low as the pimps who pull a man's wallet in the dark while the doxy keeps him happy. Greedy lot they are and unreliable. Greed costs you money. Unreliable can leave you shivering in the fog all night for naught. Or dead. Or a murderer if you use a pistol."

Owen studied the pile of spits before him and extracted one cleanly. "Some don't mind doing a man that way, but nothing's worth killing a man."

"Some men," Jason allowed with cold conviction. "Some who grow fat putting better men in prison."

"There's the English in you. Flat bloody-minded." Owen peered closely at his friend, suddenly dead serious. "And there's a darkness in you, Jason. Have I not seen it? Work clean. Carry this instead of a gun." He held up his well-thumbed Bible. "And we shall be strong in the Lord."

Though not in any way intended by Scripture. Appearance and deception were important to the cutpurse of quality. Their clothes brushed clean, linen washed, they ranged from Charing Cross Road across Leicester Square to Piccadilly and back, searching out likely pigeons in the bustling crowds while maintaining the appearance of threadbare but respectable students.

They sat on a bench in the tree-shaded square, Owen munching the last of a meat pie while Jason apparently absorbed himself in Holy Writ. Then Owen straightened. "He-ere comes fortune." Fastidiously he cleaned his fingers, flexing them in readiness. "Fat toff in the scarlet waistcoat. Mark him."

Jason closed the Bible. "The laborer shall be worthy of his hire."

"Amen."

Saturdays were always good for their vocation. Workers had wages to spend, and better-heeled tradesfolk were abroad to shop. Owen and Jason preferred the latter. Better chance of a good pull, beside being more of an honest lark than skinning some poor fellow who'd sweated all week for seven shillings.

"That one never sweated in his life." Like a shark scenting blood, Jason followed the progress of the scarlet waistcoat as the portly fellow halted at a baker's stall to buy a pastry. "Wallet left coat pocket."

Owen rose. "Shall we dance?"

"Delighted."

Owen sauntered obliquely toward the pigeon, Jason lagging behind, head lowered over his reading, to collide squarely with the man's ample paunch.

"Oop! 'Ere now, you watch it."

"Forgive me, sir," Jason apologized. "I am a divinity student, and I was quite absorbed in this passage from—"

"Bugger you." The plucked pigeon lumbered grumbling away.

"God be with you, sir," Jason called after him as Owen slipped the wallet under the Bible. They strolled by different routes toward Charing Cross Road. As Owen was fond of saying, a piece of cake.

Not until they were safely back in their room did they inspect the wallet's contents. "Only three and six," Owen groaned, scattering the coins on the table. "And paper."

"Paper? Show me." Like most poor folk, Owen didn't trust paper money, but when Jason spread out the heavy note, his heart leaped. "You bloody Welsh dunce, it's for ten pounds, Bank of England." Gleefully he grabbed at Owen and collapsed them both on the floor. "Ten *pounds*. What would you do without me, eh? Can't tell fortune when it waves in front of your face."

"Get off me," Owen protested, struggling. "They will never— Get *off*, you great clod! They'll never change that for silver. Suppose they have not got ten pounds they will part with for the likes of us?"

Jason rolled off his friend and sat up grinning. "Ye of little faith and less learning. I'm off to fetch it now."

"Here, just you wait a mo'." Owen's suspicion had the weight of Welsh history in dealing with the English. "Ten pounds is enough to lead a saint astray. How do I know you'll be back?"

Jason vented an exasperated sigh. "You are a trial, Owen. Come along then. Wait outside the bank and pounce the moment I come out."

"Just see if I don't." Owen rose injuredly, dusting himself. "Ten pounds is a monstrous lot of trust."

They prospered as a team and diligence reaped its reward. Owen the expertise and Jason the driving purpose, they ate and dressed better. Although far from well, Abraham was amply fed and supplied through the bars.

"Roast ham!" he exulted over the fragrant meat. "Glazed with honey and mustard. Must share this with old Liza; she won't last the winter, poor old thing. Bath cake and an orange! Lud, boy, how did you manage all this?"

"I find work here and there," Jason told him, coloring truth only a little. "Can I bring you more medicine for your cough?"

"Indeed you may." Abraham winked slyly. "But no fear, son. Your old fox of a dad has yet a card up his sleeve. How goes it with our debts?"

"I've thirty-five pounds toward. Would have more but I needed a new coat and breeches."

Only a small indulgence, Jason reasoned. His success as a pickpocket depended on not looking like one. More, his soul needed what good clothes represented, a tangible step in regaining respectability. In scarlet coat and buff breeches and with lace at his throat, he impressed even Owen.

"A gentleman head to foot. We'll be pulling in Belgrave Square yet."

Jason set the flat-crown beaver hat on his head at a dashing angle. "Not likely."

"And where's richer pickings?"

"In Drury Lane. And Garrick plays tonight."

"So do I," Owen sighed in anticipation. "Down the Cross and Horn and all night with Mistress Kitty Watts."

"Lazy lout: Rent paid, belly full, half a pound to spend and bugger tomorrow, there's Owen Jones."

Too often Jason had to crack the lash of ambition over easygoing Owen and he often bullied his friend into working the theaters in Drury Lane, Covent Garden, and Haymarket. When a wallet went missing or purse strings lightened, two presentable young men with subscription tokens to the plays were ever beyond suspicion.

"A science, Owen," Jason purred as they divided the evening's profit.

"And often a sin on my soul," mourned the Glamorganshire chapel boy.

"Not mine." Jason fluffed out the lace at his throat. "I don't feel a thing. We're for the Drury Lane tonight. Garrick is playing *The Suspicious Husband*. With Miss Louisa Payne."

"Ah, we've seen it twice in the way of business."

"But Louisa not often enough," Jason sighed on a note of amour.

Owen rose reluctantly. "Such as you are the curse of the working man. But Louisa is a charmer," he admitted. "Got the gentry bucks tied in knots, I hear. Bound to die rich, that lass."

Garrick's soubrette, Louisa Payne. Jason pleasurably recalled tawny curls, mischievous eyes, an upturned nose and a sensuous mouth made for kissing, hopefully soon by himself.

They made their richest pulls during popular comedies like *Husband*, when audiences were too convulsed with laughter to note agile hands at work. Riots were profitable but dangerous, as when Garrick ruled at this season's beginning that patrons would no longer be seated on the stage and all hell had broken loose. Now this night's performance had scarcely begun when one, then several, voices brayed out "No Scots! No Scots!" in objection to the presence of some of Lord Bute's friends.

A scuffle began among the middle benches and quickly spread through the audience. Benches were thrown and shattered, eyes blackened, noses broken or bloodied. Jason struggled through the surging crowd toward the stage. His pigeon already marked, Owen lost sight of his friend in the fracas. His eye now on the target like a hawk stooping toward quarry, Owen was struck from behind by something hard and went down, trampled under a dozen feet.

"Lord Jesus," he begged of heaven, "deliver Daniel from the lions. Jason! Where in hell are you?"

Fighting his way onto the stage, Jason had only one purpose in mind. He'd grown up admiring David Garrick onstage. These louts would not injure his idol, and *no* one was about to lay rough hands on Louisa Payne.

He slipped through the hastily drawn curtains and hurried into the wings to find Garrick and Louisa and two frightened actors he knew by sight, Holland and Fitzpatrick, huddled together while the stage door rattled under furious pounding.

Jason managed to bow with some panache. "Mr. Garrick, Miss Payne, gentlemen: Jason Quick at your service."

Jason was surprised to find Garrick smaller than he looked onstage, the marvelously mobile features now contorted in disgust. "Aye, bang on my door, villains, pound away! Sheridan's behind this. Scots indeed. That's his claque started this roil. Opened his own play tonight and wanted no competition."

The great actor seemed just then to remember Jason hovering close. "And you are . . . Mr. Quick?"

"Yes. Please, sir, and you, Miss Payne." Jason ventured to take Louisa by the elbow. "All of you follow me to the cellarage."

A fresh assault slammed against the buckling stage door. *"Down with Garrick! Down with Dreary Lane!"*

"There is no other way out of the cellarage," Holland protested. "We'll be bottled."

"There is a way." Jason glanced toward the stage door. "Will you trust to me or them?"

Louisa appeared delighted by the whole adventure, squeezing Jason's arm. "Well said, my gallant. Friends, shall we retire with dignity?"

Snatching a candle from its sconce, Jason led them down the cellar steps. In the farthest corner he heaved aside a long-discarded breakfront, dislodging a century of dust, to disclose a small doorway.

Louisa clapped her hands in delight. "Voilà! We are saved."

"Well, I am a Lichfield dunce," Garrick muttered. "Years I've owned this theater and never knew of this."

"Few did," Jason said. "It leads under Catherine Street to the cellarage of the Rose Tavern. Haste now: take the candle."

He ducked them one by one through the small door, hauling the breakfront back into place. Above, the stage door gave up the ghost and collapsed. Jason led the actors through the damp, cobwebbed passage, praying Owen had the good sense to be elsewhere by now.

They followed Jason in single file, sweeping cobwebs out of

their faces. The vaulted, brick-lined tunnel appeared to go on forever. Louisa gave a startled squeak and snatched her skirts higher as a large rat scuttled across her foot.

"Almost there," Jason promised. "Ah, here we are."

The passage ended at a short wooden stair. Jason mounted and pushed at a trap door, which swung up, rusted hinges wailing like the damned. One by one they emerged into a cramped space behind two huge hogshead barrels.

"Well, David." Louisa brushed cobwebs and dust from her costume. "We have made more graceful exits but none luckier."

Fitzpatrick spat out a strand of cobweb, listening to sounds filtering down from the tavern. "I'm for a drink to wash out the dust."

"Not here," Jason warned. "The Bow Street police have likely cleared the theater by now. If those are indeed Sheridan's claque, they're bound to come drinking in the Rose."

"Well bethought." David Garrick cast about for the cellar's outside door, found it. "Holland, you and Fitz get home by the back streets. We'll wait a bit and then make for the Strand."

"Good night, David." Holland extended a grateful hand to Jason. "And you, Mr. Quick. We are in your debt."

"Not at all, sir. You played well tonight."

"So I did," Holland beamed. "But damn that Sheridan. We never got to my best scene."

"Curse me if I don't serve him a bill for damages," Garrick vowed. "Hurry now, get you home."

When Holland and Fitzpatrick were safely away, Jason led Louisa and Garrick cautiously out into Catherine Street which was lit only by the lights from the Rose Tavern. They hastened south toward the Strand, Louisa clinging to Jason's delighted arm.

"I for one am starved," she declared. "And we must reward our savior."

"We'll not be niggard in that," Garrick promised. "To the Turk's Head. *Allons!*"

They stopped briefly at Garrick's house for him to change
clothes and for both actors to remove stage makeup. Then, over
oysters and a fruity white wine, Jason was made to feel like
Lancelot rescuing Guinevere. Louisa's unadorned features looked
older than by stage light, the fine lines about her eyes deepening
when she smiled at Jason. No matter; he was already vanquished.
Her femininity exuded that erotic mixture of innocence and sensual awareness that had robbed more than one devotee of sleep.
And her foot, minus its shoe, played with his under the table.

"But come, sir," Garrick pressed. "Your story. How did that
heaven-sent tunnel happen to be there, and how did you dis-
cover it?"

"Oh, that's a grand tale," Jason said, filling his glass again.
"When I was little, no bigger than a minute, my father had it
from an old man once employed as ratcatcher by Drury's former
owner."

True enough so far. "The tunnel was a guarded secret known
to very few, built by Charles II for access to his favorite orange
girl, Nell Gwynn."

"Old Nell!" Garrick hooted. "The king's sweetest dalliance, so
she was, and a saucy one. Go on, Mr. Quick."

"No more to tell, really. Nell Gwynn moved on to become a
favorite at the Drury, and in time the tunnel was forgotten."

"Except by you," Louisa breathed, her adventurous foot slid-
ing up and down Jason's lower leg. "When did you first find it?"

The delightful forays of her foot raised Jason's temperature.
He hoped it didn't show. "Tonight, Miss Payne."

"Wha-at?" Garrick spluttered. "You didn't *know* 'twas there?"

Jason prayed the flush on his cheeks would pass for modesty.
"No, but was it not an excellent time to find out?"

"By God, sir." Garrick pointed to Jason's plate. "Investigate
your oyster shells upon the instant! There will surely be a pearl,
for you have the Devil's own luck."

Not exactly. He and Owen had been forced to flee to the cellar during the riot over seating onstage, when Jason uncovered

the legendary passageway. What Garrick didn't know would hurt no one in this case, and Louisa was here and close.

"Do I?" Jason appealed to her. "Am I lucky, Miss Payne?"

"Louisa. And yes." Her husky laughter caressed his ear as she laid her hand over his. "Mr. Quick will have luck in any pursuit he undertakes."

The invitation was plain. A few moments later when Garrick rose to speak to a friend at another table, Jason whispered quickly to her, "If I dared pursuit now, might I have the pleasure of calling on you soon?"

"Oh, there." Louisa sat back with a sigh of relief. "I thought you would never ask. This Sunday at one? I live in Henrietta Street by St. Paul's. Ask the sedan bearers; they all know my house."

Rendered even more gallant by fascination, Jason promised, "I'll be there though hell should bar the way."

As he walked home the joyous swelling in his chest threatened to burst and flood him through with a happiness never known before. Jason inhaled deeply, and the thick fog rolling up from Thames carried, for him, the scent of roses.

For all the healthy urgings of his twenty-one years, he had avoided the doxies of the town because of his father's grave needs and because London sickened with more pox and gleet than a stray dog carried fleas. But now Louisa rose up pristine and glorious in his sight as sunlight after a month of rain. Pigeons might go unplucked this Sunday, for Louisa's invitation would surely lead to more than tea and chat.

He found Owen sitting on his bed, cold compress in hand, nursing a large bruise on his cheek. "Rum evening this was, Owen. Pull anything?"

"Only this." Owen uncovered his injury. "Very scientific, Jason. Where in Christ's world were you?"

Jason flung himself down on his bed, hands behind his head. He recounted his adventure and the invitation from Louisa.

"Oho. A conquest?"

"Hardly. She lowered the drawbridge herself."

"Take her in armor, Jasie."

"Why? She's no common doxy."

"Nor do you want her leaving a baby basket at your door. Armor, boyo. I will furnish the first fish skin myself."

"No need. You're a cynical and randy Welshman."

"Am I?" Owen swung his feet to the floor. "I am serious: caution with that one. I hear a word now and again. She has a 'patron.'"

The quotation marks were too pronounced to ignore. Jason sat up. "How do you know?"

"Wall-Eye Mags, the serving girl at Child's. He usually takes Louisa there after the theater. In a sedan chair, no less."

But she was so open, so eager for me to come. "Who is this man?"

"A widower, a real toff. Solicitor on the King's Bench, very grand. And very hard smitten, Mags said. Word is he means to marry her."

Not before Sunday, by God. In his happiness, Jason hadn't considered any rival. "His name?"

"Sink me if I remember. Needle . . . Beagle."

Jason stiffened. "Beedle."

"The very same. You know him then?"

"I've met him." Jason sank back on the bed, not trusting himself to speak further. Beedle, that bloodless little weasel who helped put Abraham Quick in Newgate. A year ago Jason could not have thought with such calculating clarity. Now he saw vengeance distilled to its purest and most poetic form. Jason relished the double delight of loving Louisa and tasting that exquisite dish before she reached the shabby table of clammy, gray Beedle, if she ever did.

As he fell asleep, Jason dreamed his way toward his own fate.

For a week London lay under fog, but for Jason the sun never set on his paradise. Spruced, brushed, giddy with anticipation, he was hard put not to present himself too early on Sunday. He arrived around the corner from Louisa's house as church bells chimed quarter to the hour, and paced Bedford Street back and forth, waiting for the blessed time to ring, scraping the mud from his shoes and composing what he might say to Louisa, how he might declare himself to her.

The quarter hour dragged by like a century. Jason knocked and was admitted by a stolid young maid with a German accent. Gisela was a Bavarian immigrant, he later learned, Louisa's maid of all work. Her taciturn discretion, which Jason grew to value, came equally from common sense and a meager understanding of English. While Jason waited for Louisa to appear, Gisela laid an exquisite Wedgwood tea set on the table and retired.

His first afternoon with Louisa was a time Jason could later recall in every detail, even the china decorated with parrots and bluebirds, rimmed in gold, and the exact pale rose hue of the French chemise dress she wore. While waiting for her to join him, Jason noted that the appointments of her parlor, the drapes and furniture, seemed far beyond the means of an actress. The dingy spectre of Beedle rose up before him -but then Louisa came in to greet him, and he forgot all else.

In daylight she looked older but if anything more beautiful, much of which came from her poise and ease of manner. They spoke of the theater season. Jason complimented Louisa effusively on her performances, while she thanked him again for their lucky rescue through his courtesy and daring. Jason, who could catalog and reproduce any accent heard, detected in Louisa's trained speech the same hint of North Country he'd perceived in Garrick's. And overall he warmed to the unspoken invitation in Louisa's manner, the sense of an intimacy promised between them. "You are a man of parts, Jason. In the excitement of our escape through that wonderfully sinister tunnel, I quite forgot to ask your profession."

Jason improvised rapidly. "I have been left a modest patrimony. Presently I'm seeking a position."

On the other hand, sincerity in moderation might serve better than an outright lie. "My father was a stationer and something of a pamphleteer."

Louisa's smile was provocation itself. "Modest, you said."

"Sufficient to keep me humble. I occasionally work for stationers about the city. You've no idea how many scribblers have more money for publication than wit to spell aright."

Louisa set down her teacup like one turning to delayed business. "You are far too modest altogether. Did I not prophesy success in any pursuit?"

Her tone and luminous smile sent a flush through Jason's whole body. *Dare*, it urged. "Not too modest to tell you what I've felt since we met."

He went dumb for a moment, waiting for Louisa to draw back, keep him at arm's length. Had he gone too far too fast? Yet he saw only *yes* in her eyes and remembered her questing foot at their supper. He needed such words as *enraptured, impassioned, enslaved*, but even these would ring hollow beside the tumult he felt, and the past year had sharpened his open nature on the stone of caution. "You must know how much I admire you."

Louisa said simply, "Yes, I do," and bent forward to cover his hand with hers, surrendering to that endearing giggle. "And I have been wondering why you sit so far away. Faint hearts may be wounded in retreat, but heroes only on the front."

The door was open. A moment came when a man claimed his own or lost it forever. "Then I'll put modesty by awhile."

"But not manners," she warned gently. "I have a taste for gentlemen."

He came around the table to her. Louisa lifted her lips to his, then rose, still locked in his embrace.

"Bitte, Fräulein." Gisela stood in the doorway, stolid as a Rhine castle. "You are with the tea finished?"

Louisa disengaged herself, one hand straying casually over her dark blond hair. "Yes, I should think so."

As the maid cleared the table and departed, Louisa murmured to Jason, "I don't play tomorrow. Come to supper at seven."

He arrived the following night promptly upon the hour. Her maid might have been in the house, though she was nowhere in evidence. Louisa herself opened the door and led him to the dining room, where, by soft candlelight, they dined on sweetbreads in eggplant and pepper sauce, new carrots, and a pleasant white wine.

In this soft light as on stage, Louisa radiated enchantment. Her table manners were fastidious but direct. She ate rapidly and avidly, relishing a portion of something not on his own plate.

"Tripe," she said.

Jason yelped. "Ye gods—tripe?"

"I love it." She forked another mouthful. "It gives me a feeling of security."

"Good lord." He and Owen would rather eat raw parsnips and stale bread than the chewy lining of an ox's stomach that took hours to cook and even then had little flavor.

"Each to his own liking, Jason. It is an early taste I never lost. More wine?"

"I think not."

"Some brandy then?"

"Perhaps a sip."

Louisa took one light from the table candlelabra. "Will you fetch the decanter?"

With brandy and two glasses, Jason followed her. She did not turn into the sitting room but led him wordlessly up the stairs to her bedroom. Jason's heart pounded; while he could hardly believe a gratuitous miracle, he was not about to question one. He wanted Louisa painfully.

A good fire had been laid sometime earlier and glowed now as embers. Louisa set her candle by the bed and quickly turned down the covers. Jason's whole body burned as she came to wind her arms about him. For a moment desire paralyzed him. He mumbled something idiotic but grateful. "Well."

"Well," Louisa echoed against his cheek. "Surely we do not need Mr. Garrick's direction here."

She let him undress her, making him take his time. His hands trembled with excitement, fumbling at hooks and buttons until the last petticoat dropped rustling at her feet, and Louisa stood thrilling as discovered El Dorado.

"My God," Jason choked. "You're so lovely."

Louisa slipped the coat from his shoulders and undid the stock at his throat. "Let me," she whispered huskily as her hands worked faster.

She was both fierce and yielding, sensually wise. The sight of her half covered in a bedsheet, the caress of her unbound hair across his loins, or her breasts lightly brushing across his chest could rekindle passion in Jason only moments after exhausting it. When he half lay over her smooth, conquered form, more conquered himself, a possessive frenzy took him as he gripped her to him.

"I'm jealous of any man who ever touched you."

And when Louisa drew him down and into her again with kisses and husky laughter, Jason could almost make himself believe, against all obvious proofs, that none ever had.

Yet he could scarcely help wondering why neither Louisa nor her house gave any hint of Beedle's presence, not a dressing gown, slipper, razor, nor even a telltale snuffbox. Did she hide them? His puzzlement over the absence of these articles and his anguish over the thought of Beedle touching Louisa were as constant as a dull ache in a back tooth. Evenings in a row now there would be a message for him at the theater regretting she could not receive him as planned, and then came the night when Jason narrowly missed being seen by Beedle in Catherine Street as the solicitor handed Louisa into his coach. When he called next forenoon knowing full well she would be home, he was told by Gisela that she was not. That night, with no further word from Louisa, Jason heard the reason from Owen Jones.

"Wall-Eye Mags served them supper at Child's. Beedle's been away, but he's back. Mags guessed trouble between them—aye, and nothing small either from the lady's distress, and Mags said Beedle didn't leave her the usual tuppence."

Alone downstairs at the Cross and Horn, Jason brooded over brandy and his barely tasted soup, no longer able to delude himself. Beedle away: that was why Louisa's time was so free once and so scant now. No longer an ache, Beedle was an agony. The early pleasure of poaching on the royal ratcatcher's preserve became gnawing jealousy and loss.

Enough and more than enough. He would confront Louisa. He would name Beedle and know once and for all her true situation and where he stood.

By next noon Jason knew. As he and Owen shared breakfast before a profitable sweep of Covent Garden, light footsteps pattered up the stairs followed by an urgent rapping at their door. Jason opened it to the maid Gisela. She was urgent and distraught.

"*Bitte*, Jason." She thrust a sealed letter into his hand. He recognized Louisa's stationery. "Herr Beedle is come," Gisela said, struggling with English. "*Er ist*— He knows. He has seen you. *Alles kaputt*. Fräulein Payne is very sorry."

The girl bobbed a curtsy and scurried away, leaving Jason to fumble at the letter's seal in a cloud of misgiving, while Owen tactfully gave his attention to rum-laced coffee.

Jason had to read the letter twice for understanding, his emotions confused as Louisa's must be to judge from her writing. Her smoothly rounded hand was here jagged, *i*'s undotted, *t*'s uncrossed, some letters omitted altogether in her nervous haste. But the impact of her words hit Jason like a fist in his stomach.

Beedle, she wrote, had directed that her house be watched in his absence, for her protection (he said). Jason had been observed coming and going very late and very early and identified as one with whom Beedle had dealt before.

> I cannot describe my feelings or his rage when he charged me with faithlessness. Such a scene would be unplayable onstage as it was unbearable to my heart. It was torture to confess what could not be denied. But, oh my dear, to learn of your true circumstances and those of your father only aded to my pain.
>
> You must come no more, Jason. It is far too dangerous for both of us. Forgive my silent lies as I forgive yours a thosand times, for not a moment in your arms was a lie.
>
> —Louisa

"Owen." Jason set the letter by his plate. "You must work without me today."

"I did not think 'twas good news, but was it that bad?"

Jason pushed the letter toward him, forgetting that Owen couldn't read much more than numbers and tables of fare. When Jason read it to him, the Celt in Owen Jones admired the turns of phrase but shook his dark head over the import. "There's pretty but sad. Here, such news wants more rum in your coffee. Come out with me."

"I'm in no frame of mind for business. I'd get us both pinched."

"Then how can I leave you so? I will not," Owen vowed. "Today we will spare the pigeons."

A few minutes later another step thudded on the stairs, heavy and deliberate this time, then three peremptory raps at the door. Owen opened it to look up at a tall, portly man with the determined expression of an unpaid landlord. He entered and glanced about with distaste, moving no farther than necessary into the untidy room, as if it might contaminate him. "I am Mr. Redding." Like Gisela he bore a letter for Jason Quick. "From Mr. Malcolm Beedle."

"Busy post we have today," Owen quipped. "There he stands, sir."

Jason read the note; a glove whipped across his face.

"I am his second," Redding said.

"Second?" Owen blurted. "Holy Jesus, what is this?"

"A challenge." Jason found he could afford Redding a cold smile. "One should not think things can't get worse. They always will."

Beedle's handwriting was precise and chill as the solictor himself.

I need not explain the obvious. I knew from our first unpleasant meeting that you are a brash and foolish young villain surely to end like your father. But that you are pennyless I would sue in court for gross alienation of the affections of one dear to me and soon to be my wife, but my impending station demands satisfaction. The gentleman who bears this will arrange particulars of our meeting.

From worse to catastrophic. "A duel?"

Redding nodded. "To that end."

Preposterous; he'd never fought a duel in his life—yet something ignited in Jason at Beedle's slighting of Abraham. His father loved words, wit, and life, while life—and Louisa—were prizes Beedle could only buy. Jason's soul stiffened its shoulders. "Mr. Beedle surprises me. He might simply have had me beaten by the kind of men who burned our shop."

His acrid comment was lost on the impassive Redding. "Mr. Beedle is shortly to be knighted. He extends to you the courtesy usual among gentlemen. Rather generous, I would say."

"So little Sir Malcolm can do for me himself."

"To that end, I gather. He is not of a forgiving mind in this."

"Nor is Jason, by Saint David," loyal Owen snapped. "And him burned out and his good father broken and convicted."

Redding ignored him. "Will tomorrow morning be convenient? Early is best. There should be sufficient light by eight."

"I imagine so," Jason agreed. "I'm new to such dealing."

"We will await you on the turnpike at Tyburn Tree. The pistols will be Bladburys, quite new and accurate. A doctor will attend."

"There's careful," Owen piped up. "And we will ask mutual inspection of weapons."

"Of course. And who are you, pray?"

"Owen ap Robert. Mr. Jones to you." He pointed to Jason. "*His* second."

"Very well." Redding chopped his head curtly and opened the door. "Frankly, Quick, we expected you to decline."

"Frankly, sir, were it any but Beedle, I would be happy to."

Redding's mouth curled in a wry smile but his eyes remained cold. "He said you were too glib for your own good."

"Inspection of weapons." Jason sank down in his chair as the heavy man's tread receded on the stairs. "And my second? What do you know of pistols?"

"Bladburys? I've seen them loaded."

"There's a world of comfort."

"Well, more than seen. I have handled one." Owen poured himself a rum without benefit of coffee, turning serious. "Give ear, Jasie. Bladburys have a cursed hard trigger pull and heavy recoil."

His moment of pride and anger past, Jason faced the clammy prospect of possible death. "You said you never carried one."

"Never in the line of business, but I have fired one. Not a thing I like to speak of."

"You were good to stand up for me. Damme if I'm not feeling very lonely just now."

"I know," said Owen. "Once upon a time there was a girl like Louisa—darling and plump she was, with dimples—and some trouble with a second suitor like Beedle. We could have just knocked each other about the noggin, but like Beedle he fancied himself gentry and wanted to impress her. I was more frightened of her thinking me coward than I was of him."

Owen chuckled over his drink. "I can still sweat thinking of it. Both of us so terrified and shaking we both missed by a mile, and the two of us almighty grateful. The girl married a butcher."

Owen leaned forward to Jason, his smile older and harder than his years. "And that, my dearest Jasie, is why I sort with the honest likes of Kitty Watts, bless her obliging hide and heart. What she advertises, she delivers. Now, about pistols. Squeeze the trigger, don't jerk. If you do, you'll pull your aim to the left. . . ."

The tarnished denizens of St. Martin's Court avoided authority whenever possible and never reported anything. When Owen confided the challenge to the publican of the Cross and Horn, who was also their landlord, he knew the matter would stay within the tavern doors. The weather had turned colder, with the smell of snow in the air. Knowing Jason had no warm coat, the publican donated an old greatcoat and three shillings for coach fare, plus a blessing:

"Shoot a Tory for me."

Their coach started for Oxford Street before light. In his nervous state Jason's eye and senses caught details vividly. New snow brightened London for a few hours before turning to gray slush and trodden mud. Jason had never fired a pistol in his life, much less faced a man over one. What did it feel like to be shot? To die? If it must be, let it be quick.

"Owen, you've done this before. Can you advise me?"

"Only what I've told you. Don't be nervous."

"There's a world of help."

"And do unto Beedle before he does for you."

"Believe me, I will try."

Oxford Street became Tyburn Road and then the west turnpike as they neared Tyburn Tree. Not long now. The coachman opened the trap to call in: "That your party waiting up ahead?"

"It is but no need to haste," Owen instructed. "They're not friends. Let them shiver."

Jason's mouth was dry. "Mind, Owen. If—if this goes badly for me, there's my father—"

"Jesus, don't be burying yourself before the dying. If you're frightened, I'm bound wee Beedle is terrified. I'll lay ten shillings you both miss. Done?"

A better prospect than anything Jason had heard in days. "Done."

I dare not be afraid, at least not too much. I must survive. I will survive because Dad needs me.

Nerves pitched high, his mind raced, lit by a thousand brilliant lights. Jason remembered how angry he had become when Abraham defeated him time and again teaching him the intricacies of chess. *You lost because you became angry and reckless. Make your opponent lose his temper. Turn your blood to ice. Dad said that's the way to win at chess, arguments, politics, and war.*

Three men waited by Tyburn Tree. In the gray half-light their coach reminded Jason of a hearse. Owen poked his head out, calling to Redding. "Where is it to be, then?"

"Follow us," Redding directed.

"They've laid on the niceties," Owen said. "Him with the bag I take to be the doctor."

Another quarter hour jolting over the unpaved road. Dwellings were few this far west of the city. They followed Beedle's coach off the road and onto a narrow lane which took them into a large stand of silver birch reaching winter-bare branches to heaven.

Like dead men's arms beseeching God, Jason thought bleakly. *No, think ice. Chill your soul with it.*

Beedle was born cold. How could he be made to boil?

By the time they arrived, he had his answer. Of its own will his hand opened the door, and he descended to face Beedle flanked by Redding with the pistol case and the third man with the countenance of a dyspeptic hog who shivered within his greatcoat as if long unused to being abroad in such weather.

"Dr. Pettibone," Redding introduced him. "Surgeon."

"Your servant, Doctor," Jason nodded. "My second, Owen Jones." He tried at a glance to gauge Beedle's mood. Was Owen right? Was the man as scared as himself? He could read nothing in that characterless face—no, wait. Beedle evaded his eyes; he didn't do that in the shop when he was preparing to burn them out. Use it. Goad him.

"Good day, Beedle. How does Louisa?"

The smaller man glared. "You are not fit to speak her name."

"Louisa thought so."

Before Beedle could retort, Redding came forward, pistol case under his arm. "This is not the time for words but determination. Before I offer arms, I must ask if any reconciliation is possible."

"None," Beedle spat. "I have been too deeply insulted."

"And you, Quick? As the wounding party, will you offer apology?"

Looking at Malcolm Beedle, Jason could see only his father's hands reaching to him through Newgate bars, and however he'd soiled the man's dubious honor, apology stuck in his throat. "No."

Then to Pettibone, who huddled like a discomforted bear in his coat, "Pray you're proficient, Doctor. I can't abide the sight of blood, especially my own."

"Ha!" Beedle yelped. "A coward with candor."

"Known for candor, sir." But Jason heard how the man's voice pitched unnaturally high. "Beedle—"

"*Mister* Beedle, damn you!"

"Can we not conclude this absurdity one way or another?" the doctor protested grumpily. "I'm chilled to the bone. Get on, get *on*."

"It is a small man who cannot forgive when this day is all profit to him," Jason said. "If you leave this wood alive, you'll be marrying the best tumble in town."

Beedle's lips disappeared in a thin, hard line. *Press him now*, Jason prayed. *It's your only chance.* "Indeed, Louisa's been topped so often, it may truly be said you marry beneath you."

Beedle's colorless cheeks went even paler, eyes blazing. "You—" He faltered back a pace. "Pistols!"

Blowing on his cold hands, Owen stepped forward to inspect both weapons. Satisfied, he offered one to Jason. "Try the trigger pull before we load."

That done, he and Redding loaded flint, primer, powder patch, and ball.

"The grievous nature of this quarrel dictates the shortest distance between you," Redding intoned. "On my count you will take ten paces and halt. At my word, cock pistols. At my next, turn and fire. One shot at will. Gentlemen, remove your coats."

As Beedle slipped out of his coat, Owen removed Jason's greatcoat and drew him a few steps away. "It is fine you're doing, Jasie, and wee Beedle's not so grievous insulted he has no care to living. These are small-bore pistols. The ball might plow a flesh wound in a fly, but it is only a brave gesture he is making."

Not very comforting. "I hope Louisa appreciates it."

"To hell with that." Owen embraced Jason suddenly. "Look you now, we've come a long road in a short time, but you're the best friend I ever had, bloody English though you are. *Squeeze that trigger, mind. Don't jerk. And make the bastard bleed."*

Jason's own blood roiled in his veins, every sense heightened as he stood himself back to back with Beedle. He could scarcely feel the cold as Redding's sharp voice pierced his ear.

"One!"

His feet moved of themselves to the count. Condemned men must feel much this way climbing a gallows toward the rope.

"Nine . . . ten. Halt. Cock pistols!"

Jason's finger trembled in the trigger guard. *Take up the slack as you felt it before.*

"Turn. Fire at will."

As Jason turned he saw Beedle's weapon come down level on him, saw the primer flash into flame, heard a nasty *bap!* as the ball ripped the air past his ear. What happened next was not clear. He must have aimed, must have closed his finger about the trigger. The barrel flashed and Beedle staggered, slumping into Redding's arms as the second rushed forward to catch him. Then Owen was before him, eyes shining, wringing his hand. "Fine, Jasie. Just fine."

Pettibone knelt by Beedle, removing his bloodstained satin waistcoat. The ball had entered under Beedle's arm but angled toward his back before exiting. He shook his head. "Not serious."

Jason surrendered his pistol to Redding as Owen draped the greatcoat over his shoulders. Beedle stared up at him, eyes dull with shock but still full of hate. "I am not satisfied, Quick."

"No. Into the coach with you," Pettibone ordered. "I must clean and dress that wound."

"I am not satisfied."

"You must be, Malcolm," Redding insisted. "One shot apiece, nor can I call any foul against Quick."

Time returned and with it the knife-edge wet cold crept into Jason's limbs. He found his voice. "I am satisfied, Beedle. Not for her but for my father. We are done."

"We are not." Beedle hissed.

"Come, Owen." Jason led the way toward their waiting coach, his friend loping at his side like an excited hunting dog. "God my witness, I've prayed more this hour than in the whole of my sinful life. But there you stood calm as a corpse."

"Calm . . ." Jason stumbled up into the coach, trying to fasten the coat about him, but his hands refused to work. Owen had to secure the buttons as Jason's whole body began to shake violently.

Two nights later Owen awaited Jason downstairs in the smoke and din of the Cross and Horn. Outside in the court a cold rain had fallen since early dusk. They'd promised to meet for supper, but six came and went, seven, and then eight with no sign of the man. Owen ordered a meal finally, premonition nagging at his Welsh soul and robbing food of its relish.

I am not satisfied.

Little Beedle—aye, little he was, so scant a man he needed that *Mr.* to lengthen his name so as not to disappear altogether. But a long arm he had for all that. *Jason, where are you?*

Each time the tavern door opened, Owen expected, then hoped, then desperately prayed to see Jason. Opening again now: He swiveled his sight toward the door. No, only Long Jane shaking the rain from her shabby coat. She searched about, found Owen, and pattered over to slide onto the bench opposite, reaching for his whiskey bottle and belting down a hearty swallow.

"Eh, Jane. Have a good night then?"

"Bugger that. It's Jason."

"Jesus, did I not feel it? What of him?"

Jane gulped another large swallow. "No trade out tonight," she wheezed, "so I pack it in for home. I'm leggin' it down Leicester Place toward the square, and I hear someone moan all weak and pitiful. God amercy, there's Jason stretched out by a cart 'n not half blood, his face all sticky wif it. Good job Kitty warn't by; she'd be sick for sure. Beaten half dead he is, and no tellin' how long he's laid there in the rain. Fetch'm, Owen."

"Right, I'm off." Owen threw on his coat. "But no doctor will come for the like of us this time of night."

"I know one who will." Jane wrapped the ragged muffler about her head and throat. "Lives up Long Acre Road. He's rid me of troubles one time or another and got paid prompt."

"Then bring him quick. Tell him I'll make it worth his while."

Owen strode out of the tavern, running down the court and across Charing Cross Road through pelting rain.

He barely remembered being half dragged on Owen's wiry arm but must have lain for hours crumpled by the cart. He'd wanted to be alone for a time that evening, his mind still unsettled by the searing experience of the duel. To join Owen at supper pure chance turned him off Lisle Street into Leicester Place, huddled deep in his greatcoat and deeper in thought. He didn't notice the three hulking men who crossed Lisle behind and followed him into the shadows.

They went on beating him forever, battering his face with ham fists and, when he fell only half conscious, with their boots. One pain worse than all the others lanced like a blade through his right side—then nothing, only shock and silence and rain spattering over the sticky mess of his face.

The doctor who attended him with taciturn efficiency was evidently well known in St. Martin's Court. Gruff, shabbily dressed, he nevertheless quickly diagnosed Jason's condition.

"Could be far worse," he grunted as he bound the rib cage tightly. "Not broken, just cracked. Broken you couldn't move. They'll knit, but you must lie still."

The bruises about his eyes and cheeks would fade, but the deep gash along his jaw, made by a crushing fist wearing a heavy

ring, would scar him always. Long Jane brought him soup from
the Cross and Horn, while Owen journeyed every few days to
Newgate to see to Abraham's needs.

When the doctor returned on the third day after the beating,
Jason shook with fever. His whole upper body ached, and
breathing tortured him. The doctor frowned over his patient
and sent Owen scurrying to the nearest apothecary for colts-
foot and hyssop.

"Not the bones now, but pleurisy," he worried. "Chilled
through lying wet in that damned alley. I'll be looking in every
day for the time. If this deepens into pneumonia, the lad's a
worse fight on his hands than he took before. Haste, Jones!"

The fever finally broke, the cracked ribs knitted, but in the
end Jason's salvation was no more than his vital youth.

"Marvelous thing to be young," the doctor opined, removing
the bandage from Jason's jaw. "Had you been ten years older, this
might have gone into pneumonia with the devil to pay. Twenty
years older, and you'd be dead."

" 'Rejoice, young man, in the days of thy youth,' " Owen
sang out.

Too weak to rejoice, Jason could not sit up without considerable discomfort until after New Year's. He wondered how Owen
had managed all those weeks. "What did the doctor cost us?
How much left?"

Feeding coals to the brazier, Owen waved the subject aside.
"He's been seen to."

"With what? You didn't use the money for my father's debts,
did you? If you have, Owen Jones, you'll get a hiding worse than
mine."

"Not a penny, old son. Don't get into a state now. Mr. Garrick
covered the bill."

Garrick? Now why would he—? Jason lay back on the pil-
lows, wondering if Louisa had aught to do with the generosity.
Garrick owed him nothing.

"Mr. Garrick is an artist and a gentleman," Owen declared

with genuine respect, adding his ultimate accolade. "I would not pull his purse were it lined with a thousand pound."

He set the iron grill over the coals with a pot of stew to warm. "He'll be to visit soon, says he. Wants a word with you."

The actor-manager of Drury Lane appeared next morning while Owen was out on his rounds, which would include, hopefully, a profitable hour in Covent Garden before replenishing Jason's medicine and a few shillings to Abraham in Newgate. Garrick shed his heavy cloak and drew a stool close to the sickbed. "How goes it, Jason? Mending well?"

"Tolerably, sir. Good of you to come. I regret I can't entertain you in a manner—"

"Bother that." Garrick's dark, commanding eyes riveted Jason. "I've news of a sort."

Jason had to ask. "How is she?" He thought of Louisa's touching letter still kept, hoping it wouldn't be her last. "Did she send a message?"

"In a way. She's—um—she married Beedle two weeks ago. Yes," Garrick put answer to any unvoiced question. "I'm quite sure she knows he had you beaten."

"As if I could prove that."

"No chance; resign yourself to that." Garrick drew a banknote from his waistcoat. "She sent this with her sympathy."

Ten pounds. No letter, just money as if she were letting go a redundant servant. Jason wadded the note and thrust it back at Garrick. "Declined with cold thanks. I should be paying her for services rendered."

The older man's mobile features melted into gentle compassion. "That's harsh, lad. But you're young."

Am I? Nothing feels new or young anymore.

"And the young can be cruel when hurt," Garrick added. "I lived with a good woman for years without benefit of clergy before marrying elsewhere. We're still friends. One learns to say goodbye gracefully. To let go, Jason." He dropped the banknote on the blankets. "Take it. It's really Sir Malcolm's money."

"In that case, with pleasure. He owes me that much."

"He's yet the delirious bridegroom indulging her every whim. And I fear Louisa will be most whimsical."

"*Sir* Malcolm you say?"

"Oho, did I not!" Garrick bounced up, too vital yet in his forty-fifth year to sit still for long. "You'd think Arthur himself laid Excalibur cross his shoulders. Beedle is out-Heroding Herod this month. Puts on airs finer than the king's. A week after the wedding, Louisa asked me round to tea."

Nose in the air, Garrick struck a haughty pose, rolling his *r*'s with comic effect. "And *Sir* Malcolm informed me from his g-r-reatly elevated position that *Lady* Beedle's station r-r-rendered impossible—nay, unthinkable—any further appearance on the stage. Louisa sat there demure as a portrait and myself feeling I ought to genuflect."

He slapped his sides in finality. "And there it is. We need a new soubrette. God's truth, how I hate auditions."

Jason stared at the banknote. "So she married . . . that."

"No surprise there," Garrick allowed cheerfully, seating himself again. "But I would not judge her too severely."

"Severe?" Jason burst out, paying immediately with the pain in his ribs. "Between the two of them—"

"Listen to me," Garrick commanded. "Hear me. This is really why I came. I knew her father in Lichfield. A millworker, five shillings a week with as many children and a wife. Louisa told me she used to stand with her brothers at the butcher's alley door and fight cats and dogs for scraps to take home. She could barely pay for a room in that house until Beedle bought it to keep her."

And indeed she had loved tripe. "I see. Value given for that received."

"The way of the world." Garrick shrugged. "Beedle's cursed fortunate to be alive. One hears you're an excellent pistol shot."

"Luck of a novice, sir." Yet the pistol had fit into his hand so naturally.

"Beedle's luck seems to hold everywhere," Garrick reflected. "But then he works at it. He's far too well off for a solicitor, wouldn't you think? Lord Eglinton says 'tis an open secret in Lords and Commons alike. Beedle, it seems, has a certain grimy talent—magic if you will."

"Yes. My father and I have felt his wand."

"For his betters and a price, he removes obstacles and makes embarrassments disappear. An indiscretion with a woman of no consequence, say, producing an inconvenient child. That got his knighthood. And Louisa."

The actor's smile softened with reminiscence. "She was a starveling when she came to me at the Drury, hoping I remembered her father. But I saw her talent. Lord, how she worked to get the sound of Lichfield out of her mouth; hard as I ever did. I think I bought her first good meal. She asked for more, then wrapped it to take home."

Jason remembered Louisa at table: absorbed as a predator at her food. "I understand."

"Do you?" Garrick challenged. "I wonder. I don't think you've ever been that poor or hungry. It twisted odd warps in Louisa. She buys twice as much as she could possibly need of everything for fear of going without. I've seen her eat herself sick not out of gluttony but the *fear*, Jason, the terror of being hungry again."

Garrick offered Jason his hand and rose to put on his cloak. "If I know aught of women, leave judging or even forgiveness. Her most earnest wish is that you be happy and able to think well of her in time."

In time perhaps he might. At the moment Jason felt nothing but a sudden need to rise from his bed, never in his life so tired of anything before. His whole young, healing body cried to move again, to act. When he sat up, his ribs didn't ache quite as much as before. "You were kind to pay the doctor, sir."

"Oh, in heaven's name don't noise that about," Garrick protested. "I will deny it. I have a reputation for being mean with money and prefer to keep it. You wouldn't believe how many

actors come moaning to me near penniless the day after I've paid
them."

Garrick slid another ten-pound note from his wallet, pressing
it into Jason's hand. "Not a word of this. For our rescue from
Sheridan's henchmen. I must remember that very convenient
tunnel. God keep you, Mr. Quick."

His legs weak from disuse, Jason managed by stages to rise,
bathe himself, and dress, but the effort drained him. At least he
had some appetite. Gathering himself, he crept slowly downstairs to the Cross and Horn to order soup, only to have hunger
vanish after a few spoonfuls. The stairs back to his room might
have been a mountain. He collapsed on his bed and slept most of
the afternoon.

Owen's step on the stairs brought Jason fully awake. The fire
had gone out, and the room was cold and dark. Owen's usually
bounding ascent was now slow and deliberate.

"Jason, you're dressed."

Jason swung his legs to the floor. "You saw my father?"

For answer Owen only shoveled coals onto the brazier. "Cold
in here."

"I said what of my dad?"

Owen didn't look at him. "He's gone, Jason."

"Gone? What the devil do you mean?"

"Did I not say? It is gone I mean, him and a hundred others.
Transported to Virginia."

Jason tried to comprehend but could not. "They don't transport debtors. You think I don't know that much law?"

Owen still couldn't bring himself to face his friend with cold
truth. "It's the jail fever. Very bad this time with Newgate sore
crowded." Owen sat down and slumped over the table, obviously weary. "And with the transport contractor there at the first
whiff of profit, mind, they were not particular about whom."

"And my father?" Jason agonized. "Does he have the fever?"

"Not when I last saw him," Owen reported honestly. "But he looked far from well. They were dying four and five a night, he said."

Jason screamed at him, his voice cracking with weakness, *"Why didn't you tell me?"*

"What would that help, man, and you too sick to rise from bed?" Owen turned away, face shadowed as his thoughts. "The smell of that place. It rises up through the bars . . ."

Jason fell back on his bed with a moan beyond weakness or despair. Owen came to sit by him. "Listen, Jasie, there's hope still. The jailor, God rot his festering soul, tells me of a letter— but oh dear, he must have mislaid it. And all the while rubbing thumb 'gainst fingers for a hint mild as a cannon burst. The dishonesty of this world surely weighs heavy on the heart of Jesus." Owen took a folded paper from a side pocket. "Cost two shillings to clear his feeble memory."

Jason snatched at the letter. "Fetch the lamp here."

The message had been written on a fly page torn from Abraham's Bible. His father's writing was neat and clear, the hand of a man used to making precise notes in margins.

> Jason, I am not transported against my will but by my wish. When Jones told me of your troubles and illness, I could not burden you further but must go now when good fortune affords opportunity. Old Liza passed away last night, and I felt sure to follow her—

Jason flung an arm over his eyes. "Oh God . . ."
"Easy on," Owen soothed. "Easy, lad."

> Mister Andrew Reid, the contractor, is glad to get a skilled craftsman. Thus seven years indenture is in truth salvation. Did I not say I was the fox? My thanks to Owen Jones who helped me out of his own pocket all

these weeks. God willing and the luck of the Quicks holding good, we will meet again, and so may God bless you.

—Your Father, A. Quick

Jason read the last lines through a film of tears. "You fed him
with your own money."

"Ah, naught to mention. Two good nights at Sheridan's theater. Did that man's evil not deserve it?"

"Forgive my shouting at you. You're a decent man, Owen
Jones. Let me up now."

"No. Lie back and rest."

"Let me up, I say. It's time to move. Time to do."

On his friend's arm Jason rose shakily to his feet.

"God damn the king and damn his rotten, foul laws that do
this to us." He swayed and might have fallen, but Owen held
him tight.

"Get back in bed now. Please, Jason."

"To hell with that. Let me *go*."

But Owen's grip was firm. "Before God I'll hoist you up and lay
you to rest myself, so I will."

Jason's refusal was cold steel. "Before God? When God made
England, chapel boy, he must have slunk away in shame from
such work. This fox has no love for the farmer, only the pickings
from the henhouse. Get me to the docks, Owen. Perhaps the
ship hasn't sailed."

"Two days ago," Owen said. "Weighed anchor and gone. I've
just come from the Customs House. Legged it all across London;
had to hire a chair home, I was that cold and tired. It's over and
done, Jason."

"No, not done." Jason husked. "If you know when it left, you
know the ship and destination."

"Aye, the *Tryal* under John Errington, Captain."

"And bound?"

"Alexandria."

Yes, that seemed logical. Alexandria was a main market for

African slaves and indentured servants alike. "At least I know where to look and whom to see. Andrew Reid or his agents in Alexandria. I'll find a ship. If I've not got enough for passage, I'll get it."

Jason snatched up his greatcoat. "I can thank Beedle for one thing at least. I take to a pistol like bloody mother's milk. Come on, let's eat."

"Eh, you've an appetite at last?"

"None, but I'll stuff it down for the strength." He yanked the door open. " 'Struth, I wish I'd blown Beedle's head off."

"God might well have forgiven you that."

"I don't need forgiveness, friend. I need money and a ship— and you didn't turn me out a good puller for nothing."

To leave an England he could only despise was no harder for Jason than letting go the thought of Louisa, for whom his passion had congealed to cold pity with amazing swiftness. To find his father was everything now, though two days' scouring of shipping offices gleaned disheartening news. Felons and indentures might be transported in any weather, but paying passengers, facing two or more months at sea, preferred later months and calmer weather. No ships were listed to sail from London before April. By then Abraham would be nearing port if not already landed and sold.

There was the *Caroline* sailing from Plymouth to Boston in late February with a cargo of hardware and tea. A long way from Alexandria, but the soonest passage Jason could hope for. Plymouth it was, then.

He had almost seventy pounds but felt a twinge of bourgeois shame that his father's creditors, even good Mr. Nightingale, must go unpaid. To have such scruples after his supple morality of the last year seemed coldly amusing now. But there was the acid truth: Most men's morals were a matter of circumstance.

Well fed and solvent, theft would be abhorrent to them, forbidden by the Commandments, but Jason knew the desperate walked with the Devil.

But debts of kindness must be paid. Jason returned the landlord's greatcoat, pinched a little from his hoard for an Inverness cape, and went to supper with Owen and Long Jane at the Cross and Horn. It was a mixed occasion, both convivial and regretful. Hearing Jason was off for America, neighbors paused at their table to wring his hand and wish him Godspeed in a land where men could evade King George easily as missing church of a Sunday.

Long Jane, suffering a cold which kept her from profit that night, presented Jason with a much-used portmanteau for traveling and would take no thanks.

"Lumme, you'd think I'd laid out for it. 'Twas just found, more or less. Oh, but see what Owen has for you."

From beneath the bench, Owen produced a fine but somewhat battered cherrywood case containing a brace of silver-mounted pistols with all accoutrements, pewter powder flask, bullet mold, shot gauge, flints, and tools.

Jason could hardly find words. "Owen, where in the world—? You should not have gone to such expense."

Over his fourth ale, Owen returned a foam-flecked grin. "Who said I did?"

True: Initials inlaid in silver under the case latch proclaimed an A.D. as owner.

Long Jane hiccuped and snuffled. "Anno buggerin' Domini."

The pistols had been much used but were of expensive craftsmanship. Owen now wore the Cheshire smile of a cat fallen into Devon cream. "Jasie, do not leap down the throat of a gift horse."

"Just that you've always hated guns."

"So I do." Owen raised a hand to heaven. "I have not your good aim nor your violent nature, man. One of God's runaways you are. I made up a rhyme about'm, Jane. 'How his sainted mother must've wept/To bear a son in whom the conscience slept.' "

"Bravo!" Jason applauded. He drained his ale and rose. "Thanks, friends, but I must be packing."

"Stay," Jane invited. "It's early yet."

"Not for me, lass. It's gone ten and my coach leaves Southwark at six in the morning." He kissed Jane's lips. "Good night, fair Juliet. And you, brave bard, don't fall over the furniture coming home."

Owen rubbed his eyes and watched Jason depart, drawing Jane close to him on the bench. "You're a good woman, Jane. He'll need the traveling bag."

"Didn't cost a brass farthin'. I pinched it same as you did them pistols."

"Still," Owen sighed, "it is the generous thought that counts. I'm thinking he'll need them too. I've said it to his face: There's something dark in Jason Quick that don't forgive. I didn't teach him that, but born or learned, it is there."

For two days the coach jolted southwest, stopping overnight at Winchester and this last night at Blandford Forum. February morning was dark and cold when Jason turned out of the lumpy inn bed to swallow oatmeal, ham, and strong black tea, and climb back into the coach with his fellow passengers.

Five in all: Mr. Kidwelly, a maritime assurance agent, and his loquacious wife Josephine, both portly enough to command one whole seat between them. Swaddled in a fur-trimmed pelisse, Mrs. Kidwelly chattered on in tediously graphic detail of her digestive ailments, fluttering or wringing pudgy fingers flashing with too many rings. Jason sat beside two young newlyweds, Ethan and May Fields, just returned from a larking honeymoon in London to set up housekeeping in Dorchester, where Fields was a greengrocer. In her broad-hooded traveling cloak, May

Fields reminded Jason of a contented kitten peering from beneath a blanket. The gold ring on her left hand still shone with its original luster.

"And you, Mr. Quick?" Josephine Kidwelly chirped over the creak and rumble of the coach. "Are you married?"

"No, madam."

"There's a pity. I am enough your senior to say you are far too handsome not to be."

"Stuff," Mr. Kidwelly harumphed. "And what is your occupation, sir?"

Jason neatly abridged truth by half. "A printer, sir. My father is a stationer in Boston. He writes that we will surely prosper there. I'm off to Plymouth to join him."

"Not many ships out of Plymouth this time of year, young sir. What is your vessel?"

"The *Caroline*."

"*Caroline?*" Kidwelly's jowls waggled with emphatic denial. "I think not."

"She's listed to sail on the twenty-sixth."

"Was," Kidwelly rumbled. "She took a frightful pounding in a storm off Bantry Bay. Barely limped into Plymouth. My company covers her assurance. I'm bound there to inspect her myself. One mast sheared, bilges like a sieve, the report said. You'll be fortunate if she refits before May. And why the colonies, pray? Each year they support the Crown less and clamor for more rights. I've heard that some Whig fools are talking openly of nothing less than separation from England. 'Pon my word. Plain traitors, nothing less."

The stout Tory, Kidwelly launched into what must be his favorite sore point, the festering discontent among colonials these days—"Half of 'em dumped out of English prisons"—and their preposterous demand for representation in Parliament.

Jason hardly listened. The *Caroline* unable to sail? What else would warped fate throw in his way? He wondered if even God was against the Quicks. They were well west of Blandford now, the morning lightening only a little under heavy gray clouds. Suddenly the coach braked hard, lifting young Fields out of his seat. He called out of his window, "Coachman! What in thunder is it?"

The answer came as a warning. "Stay inside, sir."

Then a different voice, harsh and singsong. "No, put 'm out. Put 'm out. I've business with all."

"My God." Fields threw a protective arm about his bride. "He's masked. We're about to be robbed."

While Mrs. Kidwelly went white and wrung her hands, Jason sat back with a fatalistic sigh. *And I had to ask what else could bloody well happen.*

The highwayman's demand came again. "Throw down the box and be quick about it."

They heard the two coachmen protest; there was no money in the box.

"I'll see to that. Down I say and no fancy notions. My hammer locks be filed fine. Takes but a touch on these triggers."

Evidently the post box was empty. They heard him curse and kick it aside before the scarf-masked face appeared at Fields's window. "Right, my lambkins, out you come. Stand and deliver."

Jason had time to thank the foresight that stuffed half his money in one boot. Then he stood shivering with the rest as the bandit swaggered before them. He spoke with an accent reminiscent of Owen's Welsh but far more pronounced. A smallish man brandishing a brace of pistols. Over the scarf that covered his lower face, the upper part of a broken nose lay flattened and twisted.

"For them what's never heard of me, you're the guests of the Golden Fleecer, known as I am from Blandford to Dorchester and all in between, taxing the king's roads."

He flourished a cocked pistol at Kidwelly. "You seem well lined, and that's a fact. Your purse."

Kidwelly coldly handed over his wallet. "Much good may it do you."

"Always does." The bandit turned his attention to Jason. His eyes were blank, dull as pieces of slate. "Now you."

Jason surrendered the wallet, his heart sinking even lower than before. This would set him back weeks or months, possibly forever. "Take it and be damned."

Unperturbed, the Fleecer relieved Fields of his money and turned his attention to the two frightened women. "I'll be troubling you for the rings."

He grabbed at Mrs. Kidwelly's hand, but the rings, squeezed around the fat of her fingers, required force to remove. Cursing under his breath, the Fleecer jammed one pistol into the waist of his breeches and tore the ring free.

Shaken and scared, Jason could still not believe how clumsy and careless this bandit was. He wasted time boasting, jammed a cocked pistol into his britches and could have blown his privates off, incredibly turning his back on two coachmen who might well have been armed. To a puller trained to speed, deception, and a light touch, this so-called Golden Fleecer gave banditry a bad name. He tore two more rings from Mrs. Kidwelly's hands, then turned on May Fields. The girl thrust her left hand behind her.

"Please, it is my wedding ring."

"I'll fit it to a proper bride." When she still hung back he warned, "My girl, it is growing light and I'm hungry for breakfast. The ring."

When May didn't move, he reached to twist it off by force, but Fields flung his arm away. "Leave her alone, you scum."

What happened then wrenched Jason's life from one course to another, the final twist in all that began with Beedle and Louisa. He'd known cold violence in his own beating but never seen cold murder. The Fleecer clubbed Fields across the face with his pistol, putting too much inadvertent pressure on the filed trigger. The gun discharged in a spray of fire, smoke, and blood. Fields was dead even as he fell and May screamed, half his head blown away.

May covered her eyes, shuddering. Perhaps shaken himself, the Fleecer backed away, covering them with the other pistol. "That's a pity, so it is and never intended by me. Keep your bleedin' ring."

He tucked his loot into a saddlebag and swung astride the brown cob. "Go on!" he roared. "Tell them in Dorchester you saw the Golden Fleecer himself."

The four passengers huddled outside the coach in gray morning, too stunned to speak. Then Kidwelly helped his still-whimpering wife into her seat while Jason did what he could for little May Fields, feeling sick himself. They couldn't just leave the body. One of the drivers threw down a canvas from the baggage rack. He and Jason wrapped Fields's body and laid it on the coach floor.

"He rode southwest," the driver guessed. "Toward Higher Whatcombe or perhaps Dewlish."

"Or Cheselbourne," his companion driver ventured. "Folk tell of seeing him thereabouts."

Jason seethed but tried to think clearly. The highwayman was a bungler destined for rope or bullet soon enough. But Jason's ear would detect that voice when heard again. He would recognize those flat slate-colored eyes and the dilapidated tricorn hat with its hind flap fallen down like a collapsed roof. And the brown cob horse with a lopsided star blaze on its forehead. The man couldn't be so far or Dorset villages so large Jason wouldn't find him.

"Tell me," he asked of the coachmen. "Where are these places?"

As always, all came down to money. With no other choice, Jason took a modest room in East Dorchester and rented a horse and saddle, not the swiftest mount but sturdy, reliable, and gentle in manage. All through February and part of March, Jason scoured the region around Dorchester from Cerne to Charlton Down and all the public houses in between, always recounting the story of the robbery. The Golden Fleecer was indeed known throughout his boasted hunting grounds, but none could put a name to the man or where he went to ground. The days dropped from the calendar like funeral knells, taking Abraham Quick closer to bond servitude and farther from Jason. Some nights, weary from a long day's ride, he came close to despair. A scant year ago he was an honest man. If he were one yet, he would give it over and find work to keep him until he'd recouped his losses.

Then he would jingle the coins in the purse lifted yesterday in High West Street. *Lord forgive me or not, but I've no more time for that virtue, no more honest than the Fleecer, just more skilled, but he killed more than poor Fields with that single, careless shot.*

Jason kept his resolve. Each morning as he loaded the pistols and tucked them into a saddlebag, he reviewed his catechism of common sense. The Fleecer had to rest, sleep, and stable his horse somewhere. He was miles from clever, just lucky; wouldn't last two minutes in London. If he had half the brain of an oyster, he'd change lodgings frequently. If he stayed in one place, he must have someone close and trusted as Owen Jones for aid.

Jason took his supper in Milton Abbas one evening, standing a round of ale for several farmers. He found Dorset folk more open than Londoners and agreeably talkative. One of them allowed he'd heard—"Just heard, mind"—that the Fleecer had been seen more than once riding into Cheselbourne. The coachmen had said as much the day he was robbed.

Jason had ranged through dismal Cheselbourne the week before, a few cottages strung along the road to Dewlish, and one dismal inn, the Crown and Thistle. What would draw a wanted outlaw back to a place in the middle of nothing? Perhaps just that. Perhaps Jason underestimated his quarry, but instinct said no. The man was a braggart in love with his own image; he must advertise his name. What else? Family, a wife or mistress? Oh, very scientific. The Golden Fleecer's sheer ineptitude might do him in before Jason ever recovered his money.

He moved from Dorchester to the village of White Lackington, only two miles from Cheselbourne. Two or three evenings each week he rode to take his meals at the Crown and Thistle, carefully noting every horse in the stable before entering. He took care in his dress always, coat brushed, lace at his throat, a London gentleman pausing in the shire before sailing for America. So he came to know Rose Allen, the tawny-haired, big-bosomed serving girl. Rose had a provocative manner with customers and a way of catching one's eye that reminded Jason of Long Jane. On slow nights Rose liked to chat, glancing frequently to the door as if expecting someone. But her eyes glowed with honest enthusiasm when Jason spoke of America.

"I'll be there," Rose vowed. "Right enough and not long from now."

On the twentieth of March the hard night wind drove rain in from the sea, and custom was light in the cramped little Crown and Thistle. Jason regretted coming even the short way from his lodgings. He'd be wet through going home. Two weeks of the inn's greasy fare was not dining but penance, and the information given him proved fruitless. No one resembling the Fleecer had shown himself.

Jason pushed his plate away and was about to call Rose for another brandy when the stableman clumped in for his supper, slapping rain from his hat. He gave his usual greeting to Rose as he lumbered toward the kitchen. "Oy, girl, and have they kept it hot?"

"Yes, yes. Go along."

"Eh, your Willy's come."

In his dark corner to one side of the fire, Jason saw Rose brighten visibly. She straightened her linen cap and gave her hands to the swift feminine gestures of primping before drawing a large whiskey and setting it out on a table. As she did, the door was hurled open.

"Evenin', all," the newcomer boomed. "William Boston, late of His Majesty's Fifty-fourth Foot, at your service on a foul night, and God bless you, Rose luv."

Rose squealed with delight and ran to kiss him, taking his wet greatcoat while, at the table next to Jason, a farmer muttered to his drinking companion, "Ah, shit now. Wild Willy again. And we was prayin' for a quiet night."

Jason's stomach contracted as he leaned back into the shadows again. He might be mistaken in the voice, but the ruined hat and broken nose were a beacon. He lowered his head, watching Boston as the man lordly spread his squat bulk on a bench and downed the whiskey in one gulp with a gustatory sigh of pleasure.

Right. I've got you.

Unarmed and unmasked, the Fleecer looked more brass than gold. Of any age between thirty and forty, the man's face had been mauled through his years. Beneath the broken nose, wide gaps showed between his remaining teeth, and one ear was pounded shapeless. The eyes, as Jason remembered them, were flat and dull.

So it's Rose he comes back for.

"Sweet Willy," she called from the ale barrel. "Where have you been? I've missed you that much."

"Where've I not?" Willy boomed. "Trying to make an honest living, now and again doin' the Lord's good work."

Rose winked at him. "Was the Lord grateful?"

"Never fails me." Willy banged his mug on the scarred table. "I'll have another, luv. Just to keep out the cold."

Jason set aside his brandy glass and signaled Rose. "A pot of tea, please. Black and hot."

He dawdled over his tea while Rose served supper to her

Willy, the two of them whispering and laughing, though precious little whispering the Fleecer did when he could bray.

God alone knows how you've lived this long, Willy. You'll die on some road with a ball in your guts, but first you'll pay me back.

The hour neared nine. Jason drank tea while the Fleecer finished his supper and brought out his string purse, spraying money over the table with a grand gesture, like a farmer sowing seed.

Now.

Jason quietly paid his reckoning and slipped out, squelching through rain to the stable. By the lamp, among the several hulking shire horses, the brown cob with its jagged blaze was easy to mark. He took the pistols from his saddlebag, removing the cotton patches from muzzles and priming pan as Owen taught him. On nights like this, dampness could easily cause misfire. He primed both.

The duel with Beedle had taught him brutally how little real stomach he had for violence. At the sight of the man's blood crimsoning the snow, every sermon in Bow Church rose in his gorge. He would not kill the Fleecer, only threaten. When his hands trembled loading powder and ball, he made himself remember young Fields and his wife.

He led his horse out of the stable and to a place across the road from which he could observe Willy Boston leaving. Rain fell steadily; the Fleecer still didn't appear. Jason huddled in his cloak and cursed the man, unable to quell his mounting tension. *Damn you, come out while I've yet the nerve for this.*

Even with the thought the inn door opened, spearing light into the stableyard. Jason recognized the ostler and the shorter figure hulking behind. They disappeared into the stable and, several minutes later, the rider came forth, reining his horse onto the road for Dewlish. Jason counted off seconds, reviewing each move as he and Owen always did. Just like a pull in Leicester Square, he told himself; no more than that. Piece of cake.

Fifty-nine . . . sixty seconds. Jason turned his horse onto the dark road and into a fast canter to overtake and pass Willy Boston. In a few moments he saw the dim blob of horse and rider ahead—then suddenly nothing. The gravel voice came out of the dark, startling him:

"Hold up there! Who is it?"

Jason's heart thudded in his chest. Was there a pistol leveled at him? He swallowed hard and decided to brass it out. "No fear, good sir. Just a plain chapel boy going home, and God be with you on this dark night."

He barely slowed, bent forward over the horse's neck and expecting a bullet any moment. Blessedly none came. He urged the cob faster to put distance between him and Boston. Just a little farther . . .

Jason reined to a halt in the middle of the road, listening for the slower duh-duh-*duh* of the other horse's canter. When the dark shapes were discernible against the night, he drew one pistol, aimed, and fired close as he dared to the tricorn hat.

"Stand and deliver!"

Opening his cape, he saw the other horse rear and dance. As he hoped, Boston was caught off balance. Anyone understood a bullet whistling by his head. Out of the darkness: "Who's that?"

"Just the chapel boy again. Reach for anything, best be your purse."

He heard the hoarse cackle. "You'd try to rob *me*, chapel boy? That's a laugh, that is."

Jason felt for his the other pistol butt, voice steadied only with an effort. "I gave up laughter for Lent. Drop your purse in the road and be thankful that's all I take."

"Well, if this world ain't turned bottoms up." The dim figure leaned forward in his saddle. "It is a novice, by damn, out to rob a man on a night so wet your primer's soaked through by now. Give way before I'm angry."

Jason saw clearly enough now to discern definite movement.

He drew the loaded pistol and cocked it beneath his cloak. "I said the purse, you murdering son of a slut."

"God damn all fools. Your powder's wet, else I'd be dead."

Jason's eye caught the arm movement. Whatever Boston drew forth, it wasn't his purse. Jason didn't squeeze his own trigger until his aim came up centered on the man's chest. The flash of his discharge, then a sound tore out of Willy Boston, half cry, half grunt as he arched backwards and fell heavily in the mud.

I didn't want this, but what's done is done, and he would have killed me. Yet I pray my supper will stay down.

The wounded man was moaning, writhing weakly in the mud. Jason took the pistol from his hand as one might take a dangerous object from a baby. With his pocket knife he cut the string purse from Boston's belt and felt for a wallet. There was none, but his hand, after brushing across the man's wool waistcoat, came away sticky.

"I can't help you, Willy," Jason said, and he was God-honestly sorry. "You'd best pray for both our souls."

And there, dearest Bess, is the ballad of my woes. I killed a man who stole from me, but his theft, like Beedle and Louisa, set me on the road to you.

I know the risks and the wrong in what I do, even sometimes the futility, but I try not to think of that. Willy Boston must have had a lean week ere I found him. His purse held less than a quarter of what he robbed from me alone. The pious would say 'tis God's punishment—and yes, I could labor in some Dorchester print shop for six shillings a week, but for how long? My father is fifty-two years of age. How long can he live in bondage? How long before I could give you the life you dream of?

The shot that killed Willy put me in his shoes and his price on my head. There it is and so be it, but neither you nor I nor Abraham Quick will ever be poor again. In less than a year, brief as this last that turned me thief, we can sail free to a new life. Then there will be time to be honest and even ask forgiveness of God, but for the moment—to work.

"Easy, Jones." Jason steadied the big Cleveland bay as the Royal Mail coach rounded a bend in the road. "We're novices no longer. Easy now."

In the last of the spring twilight he checked his own pistols, then the brace taken from Willy Boston. They were less accurate than his own, and the filed hammer locks made them treacherous. He usually fired one or both for warning shots before drawing his own.

In his first weeks working the Dorchester road, he garnered less money than hoped but vastly improved his technique over that of the bungling Boston. He memorized the coach schedules between Blandford and Dorchester, where each would be and when. The horse he rode stood over sixteen hands high, a fine jumper, long-legged and swift enough to leave any pursuer behind. Jason had rescued the gelding, as Owen might say, from a well-to-do squire at Milborne St. Andrew with whom he drank one evening, thankful the man's eye for good horseflesh exceeded his taste in spirits.

As he'd worked with Owen, in robbery Jason wasted no time. The box was thrown down only when unlocked by one of the coachmen. Men only were ordered out to render wallets or purses. Jason seldom bothered with money belts and no mucking about with women's jewelry. To his middle-class sensibility and divisible scruples, robbing women was not quite right. Besides, they tended to hysterics, distracted one from business, and jewelry was cursed hard to dispose of. If robbery was a sin, a thinking man could indeed turn sin into science. One's work should be clean as his linen.

The coach neared. Jason slipped the black neckerchief over his nose and mouth, drawing and cocking Boston's pistols. At just the right distance he spurred out of the trees and fired two shots to frighten the coach horses. Of the two drivers, one would be busy steadying them while Jason leveled the other brace at them.

"Open the box and throw it down," he barked in the Welsh singsong now practiced to perfection. "Gentles, you are the guests of the Golden Fleecer. Stand and be shorn, my lambs."

PART II

He whistled a tune to the window, and who should be waiting there
But the landlord's black-eyed daughter—
  Bess, the landlord's daughter—
Plaiting a dark red love-knot into her long black hair.

She'd done her mourning, seen poor Willy into his grave in St. Martin's churchyard while the rector hurried his service in the morning fog's chill and the sexton waited with his shovel to bury Rose Allen's hopes along with Willy, who went to heaven or hell with no music but the damned *hoo-hoo*ing of a stupid wood pigeon.

Rose had no real women friends she could confide in; to understand how she felt when Willy was found dead in the Dewlish road with a ball in his chest. There was one pain; another was how she missed his body. In the red fever of their lovemaking, Willy's body always paid her to live. 'Tweren't the money he spent on her but the *zest* in Willy that set her aquiver when they stole down the side road with blankets for a tumble in the woods. His hairy back was ridged and honeycombed with whip scars from when they flogged him for stealing in the Fifty-fourth Foot, but she clung to him as Willy loved life itself. No, the stupid farmwives of Cheselbourne wouldn't understand. They already thought her a slut, and perhaps she was, but God rot them all. Rose would weep alone.

Oh, Willy, Willy—a rogue and a bastard, but you've left a hollow in my heart. Would to God I knew who done you. I'd tear out his eyes and his liver, for he's not only taken your life but your name and fame and making free with it.

She and Willy had a dream. When there was enough money they'd be off to America, to Boston or New York. They might have gone before this were Willy not such a fool spendthrift who couldn't keep hold of a penny if 'twas buried with him. He didn't have a brass farthing on him when he was found, and Rose knew damned well he'd a full purse that night, flashing it about, making sure they all knew he had plenty. Whoever did for Willy picked him clean. Rose herself paid for his meager laying out and sat alone in St. Martin's Church most of the night with the plain coffin. She paid the sexton's fee for the burying, as low as she could haggle down. Wild in love as she'd been with Willy Boston, Rose was nothing if not practical.

The week after Willy died, Jason Quick took a room at the Crown and Thistle. He was Willy's opposite in every way, much younger and handsome as they came, with good manners and a quietly impressive air. A gentleman he was, and private where Willy had been open and roaring; didn't tell much about himself. Once or twice when he first came, Rose crept from her room to his when the inn was closed and dark—

She found him preparing for bed by lamplight. "The fog creeps in very cold before morning," she murmured. "Brought you another blanket."

Jason smiled at her from the bedside, removing one shoe. "That's kind of you, Rose."

Not only handsome but a way with him of saying a woman's name with music in it. "You're from London. I can tell."

"Yes."

"Used to see Londoners sometimes when I was in service down Whitechurch." Rose hovered, her invitation plain. That first time she went to Jason because the loss of Willy ached in her and she couldn't bear to be alone. She needed what a man could do for her simply to feel alive. "And what else might y'need?"

Jason removed the other shoe with a sigh—an odd answer out of a man so young. The clean line of his jaw had two large scars laid over an expression curiously older and hard as herself. She heard that hardness in his voice. "What else are you offering?"

She moved to blow out the lamp.

Rose hadn't been a virgin since the age of fourteen when she gladly traded that useless virtue for a tumble with the son of a drayman. Save for Willy like a fire in her blood, love was no great matter since. She found Jason fresh and hot, if not very experienced. Then—Rose couldn't remember just when—she felt her old dream stir in Willy's coffin and revive. She was bold enough; she dared to dream again. Jason Quick might serve— aye, why not? He was bound for America. When the time came she'd go with him and be a wife good as any, come to that.

Queer though; she didn't know just how, but even tumbling Jason there was something elusive in him that Rose, whom life had taught to bite every coin for the feel of lead, could not quite grasp. Of late he spent his evenings away, and all Sundays down at the King's Shilling, preferring Mrs. Whateley's cooking, at least so he said. But the King's was closed Sunday. Rose hoped the lure was food and not that ninny Bess who got her sacked, the bitch.

Dear a-down daisy, Rose complained to any gods who might listen: What a woman went through just to get on in life. She thanked Providence and her own clear eye to profit that she was no dreamy little Bess. She had no time for stories from wheezy old Abel Gant nor built air castles on the reality of America. Rose Allen simply set her well-worn cap for Mr. Quick and her sights on her goal.

Jason came to the King's Shilling for the first time a week after taking lodgings at the inn at Cheselbourne—in some haste and with the king's men not far behind, but from the moment he clapped eyes on Bess Whateley, let Rose Allen set her sights or her clock for him, her chances were stillborn. Abel Gant, with far more than book and chalk dust in his vibrant blood, understood without words the alchemy that left some men and women indifferent to each other and bonded others in a potent compound. As Long Jane might have put it, "Some folk gets in each ovvers blood."

Which said it all. Jason had lain awake during his interlude with Louisa, but that never put off sleep when his healthy young constitution cried for it. The image of Bess robbed sleep so completely that Jason heard the tedious clock below stairs sound one and sometimes two of the morning while he tossed or stared, troubled, at the ceiling overhead.

Disturbing and faintly frightening. Time and again he reminded himself of his resolve and where and why he must go, but always clear determination dissolved and shifted to the picture of Bess: How she moved with unconscious grace about her tasks, a certain glowing softness in her eye when she glanced his way or served his supper. What *was* it, Jason stewed, in a certain woman's manner, in the *self* of her that slipped into a man's guts and stayed there? No, he resolved; the girl was lovely and plainly inviting him in her innocent way, but he had responsibilities— not to mention the risk in achieving them—in which Bess or any woman could play no present part. And yet . . . there she was, and here he lay awake feeling his granite motives turn to mud.

She had no education, couldn't read, and yet the quality of fineness stood out in her. Her even features had character in repose, her happiness a charm and a kind of promise that wrung a pang from Jason's heart. And she sought him; she wanted him. He knew that keenly as thirst under hot sun.

Were he jaded the matter might have become annoyance or even boredom—Botheration! Take a yes or a no and be done with her—but at twenty-two, despite the brutal lessons of London, Jason's blood still rioted with life. There was excitement and intoxication in mere breath. He didn't really believe he could die ever. Every morning was promise, and any evening— *this* evening—beckoned with such possibility that he could break into a run with the sheer thought of the girl and being alive.

Jason walked the road between the Crown and Thistle and St. Martin's Church talking to himself and to the thought of Bess,

saying *no* with male decision, only to admit *yes* as he returned to
the inn, preoccupied over brandy and a puzzle to Rose Allen,
who had all the intuition of a stone. To hell with it! If he couldn't
conceive of a future without Bess, she must be part of it. He
would ask to take her to church Sunday next and hopefully walk
out with her afterward.

When he asked, Jason was surprised at how pleased Bess was
and her mother too. Jedediah Whateley inspected Jason pater-
nally up and down before deciding he made a suitable escort for
their daughter, the flower of Winterborne Whitechurch. Tim
Groot the ostler glowered balefully as Bess and Jason sat apart
from the family at service, sharing a hymnal between them.
Irregular at worship since his mother's passing, Jason was
touched by Bess's faith. The girl didn't spout religion and need
not, for she lived the quality, part of her hands as she worked,
evident in how she stayed after services to say her private
prayers in the little Lady Chapel to one side of the nave.

Later they strolled up St. Mary's Lane, their progress halting
and tentative as their thoughts as Bess began shyly to share her
personal history with Jason, including her walking out with Evan
Bromley. Much as Jason excited her, it wouldn't do to let him
think she'd not been sought after before.

"We only went now and again to the Kingston fayre and such.
Not there's ever that much time with the work to be done."

Bess fell silent, and Jason sensed an ellipsis like a writer delet-
ing a thought he chose not to confess. "And what came of that?"

"Oh—Tim. Had a proper set-to with Evan, the stupid lout."

"Very possessive of him," Jason commented, wondering how
she felt about the ostler. "What sort is he then?"

"Tim?" A world of dismissal in the name. Bess's nose wrinkled
in distaste. "He's been here forever, and much I care. I couldn't
fancy him did the king himself command."

They walked on in silence for a time. The physical awareness
of her next to him was like a weight in Jason's loins. He took to
whistling to appear casual.

"I know that tune," Bess chirped brightly. " 'Seventeen on Sunday.' "

"Aye, a favorite of mine."

"So's it mine." She hummed a snatch of the old song. "And you?" she ventured. "A printer in a fine London shop. Must've been proper exciting."

Jason tried to describe the work he did, mostly an enthusiastic description of bustling, energetic Abraham, but that was not really what Bess wanted to know. Walking on, looking resolutely ahead, she asked (a little too offhandedly) if he had a lady in London.

"Years and years ago."

"Tosh! As if you're that old."

He couldn't tell her of Louisa, whom he could no longer separate from the dingy image of Beedle. Better something older and innocent. "There was a draper's shop next to ours in Pancras Lane. Mr. Muggeridge, and his daughter was named Patience."

"Mug-ger-idge." Bess giggled. "Sounds as if't tasted bad."

"Oh no. Patience was lovely, sweet, and proper. We were sixteen and swore eternal love, even gave each other horsehair rings to seal the pledge." Jason kicked a stone out of his reminiscent way. "But along came a solicitor's clerk who wooed and dazzled her with his prospect of rising to as much as nine shillings the week someday."

"So much?"

"Enough to dazzle her father as well. Patience was regretful but firm. She returned my ring and asked for hers. And there, as my friend Mr. Garrick might say, is the tragic tale of me br-r-roken heart."

Bess seemed to digest that in satisfied silence. At length she remarked, "I'll wager she had seven children and got fat."

"Eight. And enormously."

They laughed together and walked on.

"Will you be in for supper tomorrow?" Bess asked.

"Not tomorrow, I fear, much as I'd rather. I have to catch the early coach for Blandford."

"That's a pity. We're serving roast goose."

"But look for me Tuesday," Jason promised.

Tomorrow was Monday, and Tuesday was more distant than Bess would wish. "What takes you to Blandford then?"

"Oh—banking, more or less."

Bess hoped it was that, remembering the blood he left on the table the night they met.

She was enchanted by him. His Inverness cape swirled through her thoughts and dreams at night. He was a prince from the far lands Abel told her of, and the second time they walked out after church, his hand brushed hers and clasped it as if it were the most natural thing in creation for them to be joined.

Bess noticed the smallest details about Jason. His habits were, refreshingly, those of a gentleman; he never appeared in the King's Shilling unbathed or unshaven, his linen and lace jabot immaculate. Of the fact that Rose Allen was paid extra to do his laundry (and labored so with motives of her own) Bess knew nothing. Unlike the young local farmers toiling the year round and seeing no more than they needed to see, there was an alertness to Jason. He listened to more than he told, and if he was a highwayman, there was no brag or swagger to him. Rather an elusive quality that fended off questions by turning the conversation to herself, which at once frustrated and drew Bess to him. Perhaps there were hurts given him once that he couldn't speak of yet but would surely share in time.

Bess warmed herself at his humanity and drew him out to share his dream of America with her. It was good to meet someone who had the heart to wish and want keenly as she did and, even more winning of her trust, a man who didn't come the smooth London seducer looking for a quick country tumble. Jason was as considerate of her in private as in the Shilling. Bess might be virginal, thanks to Our Lady and common sense, but a

long way from a dunce about men. Most of those encountered in
her eighteen years had no notion of how a woman came to love,
and likely didn't care. For them there were the realities of hus-
bandry and children, and mating was as simple and abrupt as a
bull: See the cow, bellow and mount. For a woman love rose
gradually as one of her mother's perfect loaves in the oven, all the
mixings kneaded to proper consistency and slow-baked until the
nourishing bread rose to a flavor and rich fragrance of its own.

Yet always there was that evasive thing in Jason. They were in
the kitchen yard after church, and Bess made up her mind to
confront him with the question that nagged beneath her happiness. They must be open with each other, but there was that
locked room in his life that she feared and feared for. Soldiers
prowled the shire day in and night out hunting the Fleecer, the
reward on his head already high enough to tempt angels. Diffi-
cult for Bess to believe their quarry stood that close to her now,
examining one of her few treasures, an ancient coin Evan Bromley had unearthed with his plow and given to her.

"Silver, Dad says, but so old and black you can't make out the
king's face. Here, look."

Jason turned the coin over, squinting close at the barely discernible human profile. "Not a king, Bess. Not an English king. A
caesar."

"What's a caesar?"

"A Roman king from long ago."

"God amercy! And there it was in Evan's field all this time."

Jason made to hand it back, but— "Oh, pardon. I dropped it."
He stepped back to search the ground about them. "Now where
in the world—?"

"Oh, please don't lose it."

"But I can't see—no, wait." He straightened up. "There it is."

Bess saw no coin, only Jason smiling at her with impish tenderness. "Where?"

"Behind your right ear."

Her hand flew up. "Where?"

"Right there." Jason stroked her ear and, as he withdrew the coin, one finger trailed lingeringly across her cheek. He closed her hand about Caesar. "Hold it tight, love."

Now how did he do that? "Was that magic?"

"No, that was deception. When I pretended to drop the coin, you didn't see me palm it away."

"You old mountebank, you—"

Then her mother called from the kitchen door with some errand, and Bess's question went unanswered still.

That night before she blew out her candle, Bess drove the brush slowly through her unbound hair, gathering and brushing the ends as she wondered. *De-cep-tion. He said that's making what isn't look like what is. Like Jason himself.*

Like that something in him she couldn't fathom or hold.

Like the first time he kissed me in St. Mary's Lane. Not hard or hungry but finding me. Then he looked down at me there in the moonlight, and I could tell there was that he wanted to share but somehow couldn't. I think I know, Jason, and 'twill have to be said between us by you or me. I want to tell Mum how I feel, but not yet, not even dear Abel. For a while this is mine alone to keep and share only with the Blessed Virgin.

She raised her head at the sound of shod hooves on the cobbles below, and then heard his soft whistle from beneath her window, the first seven notes of "Seventeen on Sunday." Bess sprang to the casement and leaned far out—and, oh yes, there he was, reaching to touch her long hair as it cascaded down over her shoulders.

"Don't wake up Mum and Dad," she cautioned in a whispered rush. "What is it then?"

"What indeed."

"Hush, you'll wake them."

"Is that any way to greet a suitor come to ask your hand?"

"My . . . ?"

"Marry me, Bess, and be my bride in Virginia."

She felt suddenly light-headed.

"We'll sail for Alexandria," he said. "And beyond if need be, until we sail off the world and tumble into Paradise. Will you, Bess? I've been wanting and needing you—I'm not complete anymore, only half without you until I can't go another day without knowing."

Only one moment's joyful confusion quickly passing to sureness. "I would go anywhere with you, Jason. But we can't tumble off the world, you great fool. 'Tis round."

"A comfort to navigation, I'm sure, but on such a night with the moon bright as a new sixpence, would you deny a man in love his poetic licence?"

She knew there couldn't be a giddier, happier girl in Dorset. "Do you love me, Jason?"

"Need you ask?"

No, not really, not if he felt half what she did. "But you'll be asking my father?"

"I will."

The practical working girl surfaced in Bess. "Why are you riding so late?" And on a fine horse much larger than his old cob.

"Only to have your yes and to say good night." Jason stood in the stirrups to bury his face in the dark waves of her hair. A rush of tenderness brimmed in Bess. She leaned farther out to take his hand. Their fingers laced together.

"I wish it were only good even and you coming in the door. You'll be here tomorrow?"

"Could I stay away? I love you, Bess."

She held tight to his hand and his promise. "I know. I take you forever, Jason Quick."

"Not a day less."

"My friend from Dewlish should be in tomorrow. Always comes when we've roast of beef."

"Until then, Mistress Bess Quick."

A few moments after Jason departed, blowing out her candle and slipping into bed, Bess sighed with enough contentment to make her feel downright sinful. She lay with hands clasped on the pillow beneath her head.

Mistress Bess Quick. There's fine. I, Elizabeth, take thee, Jason. Just as I dreamed before he came: riding to claim me under my window, his face so white in the moonlight. It's true what Abel used to say when the brandy made him fanciful. The sun is an angry old man burning heedless across the sky, but the moon is a woman and knows my joy.

On this soft morning, Tibbs and Horner, relief drivers for the Royal Mail, rose as usual an hour before sunrise and yawned over breakfast while the Blandford inn ostlers hitched fresh horses to their coach. The Mail did not believe in overpaying its drivers or in allowing them more than a pittance for their accommodations. Tibbs and Horner had to share an uncomfortable bed with the RM money box locked and stowed beneath.

As lately ordered on the Dorchester line, they were armed. Older Tibbs dutifully carried one pistol, but young Horner, excited by the prospect of capturing the Golden Fleecer or any robber, decked himself with two at the line's expense and felt quite formidable. He imagined himself accosted but cool in the face of danger, dispatching the villain with one swift, unerring shot. ("Poor beggar didn't have a chance against Tommy Horner.")

Tibbs had three children and chafed at his low pay. Horner never had a decent pair of breeches or shoes until the RM employed him and so basked in occupational clover.

As the passengers for Dorchester straggled down to breakfast, the two drivers lugged the money box out to the waiting coach. The ostlers yawned loudly and went in to eat themselves. In the foredawn dark, Tibbs barely made out a slender figure loitering by the rear wheel.

"Who's there?"

His answer came in abrasively nasal Cockney. " 'Allo, mates."

"Who're you?" Horner challenged.

The Cockney sauntered closer, dressed in black with a wool

cap pulled low covering his hair. What they could discern of his features was adorned with a thick, flaring mustache of the style favored by fire-eating guards officers. " 'Ere now. This the road to Dorchester?"

"Aye, it is," Tibbs responded. "You wanting passage?"

"Nah, nah, got me own good 'orse. Cor! That box don't look 'alf 'eavy."

"Heavy enough," Horner grumbled. "Make way; we got to put it up."

The mustached and curious fellow didn't move. " 'Ow's it open then?"

"We don't," Tibbs snapped. "Key's in Dorchester. Out of the way."

"No fear." In the dark the movement was only a blur of hands as the Cockney swept his Inverness open. Tibbs and Horner found themselves looking down the even blacker barrels of two pistols. "Got me own key. Set the box down quiet like and back away."

Tibbs complied so quickly that the box tilted away from Horner, throwing him off balance and jarring him with a sickening discovery: At that moment he wouldn't touch his own guns for a hundred pounds.

"Now we wants no violence. Too fine a mornin' for the lettin' o' blood." The Cockney bent in one fluid motion, pistol to the lock, and pulled the trigger. The ball shot away at a fiery angle as it ricocheted from the shattered padlock. Quickly the robber wrenched the box open, rummaged briefly with a practiced hand, and extracted a thick sheaf of banknotes.

"I'll not bother with silver and such since time's short and greed's a sin." At his piercing whistle a large bay horse trotted obediently out of the shadows by the stable. "Gennulmen," he saluted them, mounting. "The Golden Fleecer bids yer Godspeed."

All had happened so fast that the robber was gone in mere seconds after blasting the lock. Tibbs and Horner stared into the dark after the receding hoofbeats as the innkeeper and curious passengers peered timidly out the door, wondering at the gunshot.

Horner hissed fiercely at Tibbs. "Why didn't you *shoot?*"

The phlegmatic Tibbs had sound, conservative reasons. "Why didn't you? I've a family. They don't pay me enough to die for. Well, let's turn 'em out and be moving."

As the loaded coach rolled out of the yard, Horner cursed the Fleecer and mourned his own aborted heroism. But *next* time— no, flat honesty shamed Tom Horner. Next time would be like Tibbs said. Weren't their own money, and no reward was worth dying for nohow.

Bess flew light-footed through the evening's work, beaming at customers and serving with more than her usual efficiency. This night would be special. Her friend Abel was returned, having been away for some time, and Bess was burning to tell him of Jason at last. In a fit of good will, Jedediah Whateley declared Abel's first brandy compliments of the Shilling, served with a flourish and a welcoming kiss on his lean cheek from Bess.

"We've missed you, Abel. Wherever have you been so long?"

Abel Gant ran his fingers through silvering hair unthinned by time or decayed circumstance. "Just to Dorchester, dear." He took an exploratory sip of brandy. If not the Shilling's best, at least it was free. "A delay in my, uh, pension. Lord, but don't you look happy tonight! Bright as Christmas candles."

"I haven't told you," she said, glowing. "I wanted you to meet him first."

" 'Him'? Bless me if my Bess isn't blushing. This sounds like serious matter."

"Oh, he's beautiful." Bess heard herself gushing and didn't care, for just then she saw Jason enter, his scarlet coat bright against the muted interior of the inn.

"Jason!" she trilled happily. "Come meet my dear old friend."

Jason started eagerly toward her, then halted in the middle of the floor, mouth open in astonishment. "Mr. Gant!"

Abel rose, arms outstretched to greet him. "Boy? Is it really you?"

They collided joyfully in a pounding of backs while Bess looked on, glad but bewildered. "Do you know him, Jason?"

"Know him! Lud, Mr. Gant was my old schoolmaster in London."

"And here's my quickest pupil," Abel vouched. "Learned to read faster than ever I did."

"Quick as my name." Jason pumped Abel's hand as if to wring it dry. "Well met, sir. Well met. Have you supped?"

"About to."

"As my guest," Jason insisted. When he turned to Bess, his smile seemed to light the entire dining room. "Oh, Bess, what a smashing gift to me. The two of you here . . ."

The two men drank and dined together, chattering at each other thirteen to the dozen, and Bess didn't mind being forgotten in their spirited cameraderie. Her heart overflowed; she *shone* as she served customers or drew from the tap. Spring had turned soft, summer coming in, and her dear friend and dearest love were here and united with her. She felt somehow like a contented mother, and life was and would be ever rich.

"Amazing!" Jason enthused over the onions and potatoes he peeled with Bess for next day's bubble-and-squeak. "I walk into the Shilling, and there sits Abel Gant. And you *know* him."

"He's in two or three times a week. Likes his wee drop, knows everything," Bess declared. "Tells marvelous stories."

"Didn't he always. When he read to me from *Oedipus*, I couldn't wait to find out what happened."

"Eedi . . . ?"

"Oedipus. Greek king who married his own mum."

"Go on with you." Bess was more puzzled than shocked. "No one marries their mother. How could he?"

"Well, that's the story. He didn't know. It's like a mystery tale. Abel taught me to read and made it exciting."

Jason plopped the peeled onion into the bucket and attacked another. "Old Abel. His hair's gone gray but still shoots up wild from his head like silver fireworks. Same old spectacles and clay pipe. His cottage has only two rooms, and I'm bound he never sweeps them out save perhaps Christmas or Lent, and what isn't bed, table, or hearth is books, mountains of them. Oh, it's grand to see him again."

More than grand. For Jason, this spring, though edged with constant danger, was like sudden harmony after long discord. The past year had been a roil of peril and passion. Finding Bess presented joy and problems alike, but eclipsed his brief, meaningless dalliance with Rose Allen as if it had never been, and even Louisa was long ago. There was only Bess, but she and Abel together were unbelievable good fortune. Abel had been a fine teacher for the child Jason. Jason the man now detected in Abel a shadow of the weary cynic.

He felt in excellent spirits this afternoon. They'd been to services at St. Mary's and walked out together up the lane toward Winterborne Kingston, and he'd put Bess up on his stoic old cob when she tired in the afternoon heat. Mr. and Mistress Whateley had invited him to supper. They approved of him without reservation, so it mattered not at all how Tim the ostler scowled. As Jason watched Bess's willowy form bent over her peeling, he wanted her poignantly—wanted all of her from her strong young body to her trusting, serious nature flushed now with all the noble and sensual urgings of a young man discovering that love is truly spelled with more than four letters.

So often in London, risking his neck with Owen, he'd thought of marriage. What a blessing just to come home to someone each night. No dodging the Bow Street Runners or always looking over his shoulder. Just a good life with a wife and children. But then again he would have been married four years ago save for the cost of his mother's last sickness, the burying, and if Abraham's business been sounder and money not always owing. Then he'd never have come to Whitechurch and Bess. As fortune turned out, on this lovely Sunday with Bess so close, Jason reckoned himself full satisfied.

Sometimes of late Bess's white forehead furrowed with anxiety. Often she seemed on the verge of saying something but quelled the impulse at the last moment.

Her suspicions were the only unshared thing between them, and Bess hated it. She watched Jason's hands with the knife: small and precise, wasting no motion. Something new to her to be so sharply aware of a man's body, his hands and the muscles moving beneath the skin with that still angry-red laceration below his left elbow. But his coloring was so much like hers that Bess could picture the look of the children they would have.

She listened to Jason talk of Abel but worried to herself. She was new to concern like this; it made her feel so much older. And her glance always returned to the scarred arm and what it confirmed for her. That sergeant from Milborne St. Andrew— Hallow, his name was—came and asked more questions, nailing up a new notice only last week offering a higher reward, thirty pounds on the head of the Golden Fleecer, and the drivers of the Royal Mail coach now rode armed at all times.

As her feelings for Jason deepened, Bess doubted less and less what she suspected. His clothes were too good, he had too much money for this part of the country, even for the son of a successful stationer. Soon or late that provost would reason the same.

"So," Jason was saying, "between Abel and my own dad in the shop, reading came easily."

Bess dropped the peeled onion into its bucket and made a decision. Jason loved her; she trusted that, and since she felt the same twice over, there must not be any lies between them, not the smallest. He was speaking now of his father prospering in

America and how there was always work in cities for skilled printers—

"Jason." She looked up suddenly. "You're not a printer."

"What? Well, I am. Didn't I just—?"

"I mean not now. We should be honest with each other. The first night you came, and then the soldiers, I saw the blood from your arm on the table."

His hands paused at the peeling. "Oh?"

"You'd been shot."

Bess wondered how Jason would take the bald truth and searched his face for his heart. It was out. She couldn't take it back and was glad. His eyes, like hers, were so dark brown they seemed black in the late afternoon shade.

"Yes," he said finally. "Pained like the very devil. I was lucky that night. I supposed you of all people would have to know soon or late."

Her heart squeezed tight as it would many times later. Lucky for how long? "Why, Jason?"

He reached for a new onion. "Because you've become part of it all."

"No. Why did you—? Don't think I'd ever tell, not even Papa or Mum. On Cross I won't. But why?"

Jason gave his attention to the peeling. "The Fleecer robbed me on my way to Plymouth. I didn't have enough money to go on. He killed a good young fellow, too. I returned the insult."

Bess stared. "You killed him?"

"God knows I didn't mean to, didn't want to. He was a fool. For the rest, ask the king and a knighted snake name of Beedle. Damn it, Bess—" Jason flung the onion across the kitchen yard. "No, I won't lie to you. My father's no printer now. Don't know where he is except he's a bond-servant out of Newgate. Indentured to Virginia because he was a brave, hotheaded Whig who printed a damned foolish satire about the wrong man. Would he'd been wiser, but I've got to find and redeem him, and I *will*. As Abel might put it, some are born destined, some achieve des-

tiny—and some have it shoved down their throats. The difficulty is . . . now there's you, Bess."

Further, taking the Fleecer's mask and mantle brought its own
problems and expenses. Somehow there never seemed to be
enough money for what he'd sworn to do. He wouldn't go poor
to America with Bess. He told her of his father's plight in prison,
omitting his time with Owen and how they lived. Sitting here
by the kitchen door in the soft country air, that life seemed inex-
pressibly shabby now.

Mrs. Whateley came out to pull a few radishes and leeks from
her garden, set down a few scraps for her old mouser, and to
beam contentedly at Bess and her gentleman. "Supper soon,
Jason, and remember you're to stay."

"Thank you, ma'am. I'm getting hungry already."

Mrs. Whateley disappeared into the house again.

"But, Jason, it's all so dangerous."

"No fear, love. Willy Boston had no talent for the calling. I'm
more cautious than bold. We'll get there with money in our
purse to buy Dad's freedom and set us up properly. How will you
like Virginia, Bess?"

"Oh." She ducked her head over the knife and onion, fear and
happiness clashing in her. Virginia sounded far away and
enchanted like the stories Abel told, but Bess would like the distant magic uncommonly fine so long as Jason was there.

"Bess? You're weeping."

"Just the onion." Bess wiped her eyes with a white lie good
enough for now. But he shouldn't tell her not to fear. "Jason,
promise me."

"Aye, anything."

She halved the last onion furiously and threw it into the
bucket. "Never tell me where you—when you're not with me.
You understand?"

He did. "Promise."

That must content her. After all her dreaming of the prince,
was this how it really felt to love someone completely, to be

filled with longings, to dream of beginnings and fear endings in the same heartbeat?

Anne Whateley warmed to the sight of them from a kitchen window. Bess had at last found a proper young man of substance, if not a moment too soon. While they looked heavenly together, she couldn't know how closely their young heaven was hedged by hell.

Furious pounding at the door roused Abel Gant from a dream of being accepted by the Royal Academy. Muttering choice curses, he stumbled out of bed to light an oil lamp from the dying hearth. The urgent pounding came again.

"Yes, yes. I'm coming."

From long practice he skirted around a pile of manuscript on the floor, his never-finished monographs on Hadrian and the decline of English learning under Hanoverian kings. Abel unlatched the door, lamp held high.

"Jason? What brings you here at this hour? It's past ten."

Jason brushed quickly past him and closed the door while Abel set the lamp on his decaying table and bellowed the hearth fire into new life. By lamplight he blinked at the outlandish sight of his former pupil. From wide-brimmed hat to stockings, Jason was dressed in black, a bandanna of the same hue about his throat. Four pistols protruded from a broad black belt.

"God's body, you look like an armed Jesuit."

Jason fell into a chair, visibly exhausted and shaken. "Not far from the mark, Mr. Gant."

"Four pistols?" Abel threw a split log onto the reviving fire. "One for protection perhaps, but four is ostentation."

"Not when one needs them all, sir."

"Just Abel will do." Jason's erstwhile teacher found his spectacles on the mantel, polishing them on his nightshirt. "I left 'sir' in London with the rags of reputation."

Jason dropped five silver shillings on the table. "I've put up a bay gelding in your shed. With your permission I'll be stabling him here, for it's too dangerous at Cheselbourne. Grain and water him well. I'll pay the costs. Do you have any brandy?"

Abel heard the fatigue and strain in the young man's voice. "No, more's the pity. Jason, what is happening here?"

The answer was muffled. "They almost got me."

"Who?"

"Patrol from Milborne St. Andrew. Bloody Hallow's lot. Lovely man he is, never gives up. Been riding or hiding since seven. Only thing saved me, they don't ride all that well and the horses are a scratch lot. But I couldn't—God, I'm tired—couldn't've lost'm did I not double back here. I regret putting you in danger, but my horse is spent as me."

Abel sat down opposite his old pupil, inspecting the coins. "These are freshly minted."

"From the army pay, Fifty-fourth Foot. Hadn't time to bag more than a few pounds before the road was alive with the bastards." Jason closed his eyes. His whole body sagged. "Abel, not my wish to put you in danger, but I have to trust you."

"One of the few who always could, boy. An honor of sorts."

"You can guess my occupation."

"Well." Abel tamped shag tobacco into a dark-stained clay pipe and fired it from the lamp. "I know of only one wayward soul hereabouts with a price on his head. The Fleecer?"

Jason's head moved slightly in affirmation. "Only while I must."

"But that scut was here before you came."

Jason spun one of the shillings on the tabletop. "He was retired. Forcibly."

"I see."

"You are shocked, Mr. Gant?"

" 'Judge not lest ye be'—et cetera. Our king has a laissez-faire notion of free enterprise. Why shouldn't I?"

"Bless you, Abel."

"Hardly."

"I can't say I'm sorry," Jason pondered wearily, "but how in hell did I come to this? Or you? Why is a man of your abilities buried in Dewlish?"

Abel rose, pipe clenched in his teeth. "I'll make you some tea, which I do miserably, but it's all I can offer."

He poured water into a kettle and hung it over the fire. "Pray you won't be shocked either. Being a man of parts, not all of mine are sterling. I am here by what is called remittance, a polite term for being paid to stay away from London."

There was a woman, Abel recounted, wealthy but parched in a marriage best described as an interminable yawn. Her husband was a member of the peerage. All quite civilized in the resolution. The baronet feared less the loss of lady than her loot. He proposed through his solicitor a modest sum to Abel each quarter. Despite the lady's anguished letters, and as a matter of reason and economics, Abel vanished.

"Not all men are so civilized," Jason remarked from hard experience. "It sounds like a novel of romance."

"Well, not entirely," Abel confessed. "There was also a matter of ten guineas missing from certain school funds."

"No! Surely not you."

"*Mea maxima culpa*, Jason. I grew tired of threadbare clothes, shoes worn through, a tattered gown, cloddish children to teach, and never enough of anything in return. So why should I be appalled at my brightest pupil gone the same way?"

Abel puffed placidly at his pipe. "I knew Abraham Quick, and damn them all for what they did to him. Be the best of brigands, I say, for we're birds of one tarnished feather."

"Wait." Jason shot erect in the chair, then sprang to the door. "Cover the light."

He opened the door only far enough to slip out. Abel followed to find him listening intently. Distantly they heard the jingle of harness and gear. The sound faded. Jason relaxed a little. "Hallow's patrol. Still looking."

"We're well off the road," Abel assured him. "They could not see this cottage from there of a sunny noon. Come have a cup of wretched tea and sleep by my hearth tonight."

Jason didn't move. He uttered the words like a doom. "They'll keep looking. There's thirty pounds reward. Every bastard in the Fifty-fourth will want a piece of me. That's why I live at Cheselbourne and not Whitechurch. If they catch me, I want Bess out of it. God help me, Abel, but she's the best thing my life has ever known."

"Aye, there are yet a few bright corners in my sooty soul," Abel Gant acknowledged, "and young Bess is one of them."

Jason looked off toward the dark oaks that hid them from the dangerous road beyond. "She has changed everything. Were't just me, I could get to Virginia in a ship's bilges. But not Bess. She goes as my lady, proper dresses with stomachers and paniers and hats in her trunk."

"Admirable, but don't hurt the girl in the getting."

"I could not ever." Jason's voice went tender, as if voicing inner thought. "Strange: I was bound for Plymouth, no thought but to sail. But the ship would not be waiting, as if God plucked me bodily from one way and set me on another to her. Do you believe in fate?"

Abel winced. Young lovers always believed their conjunction to be fate. Later it just felt relaxed and good. "Occasionally. Come, have some tea from very used leaves and then get you to rest."

Whether he was calm or choleric, drinking or dry, Sergeant Roddy Hallow's whiskey-rouged complexion always appeared apoplectic, but this month's shade was no counterfeit. He was a man under pressure from above. After a brief respite earlier in spring, the Fleecer haunted the roads again, and Major

Sedgewick himself roared down from Dorchester like a thunderstorm to impress his point on Roddy Hallow.

"Thirty pounds, Sergeant. I know the lot I've put under you. Sell their mothers for a piece of that. Find him, you hear? *Find* him. Scour the villages, post the reward everywhere. He has to sleep and eat somewhere. Someone must know something. Get him and you'll be sarn't major in Dorchester when Beckwith retires next year. Lose him and—well, don't even imagine losing him, Private."

That from a man who had bought his commission and every rank since, while Roddy Hallow had eighteen years coming up through the ranks. The prospect of regimental sergeant major could inspire any old soldier; the alternative was not worth thinking on.

But hell take all, how and where did you snare a highwayman when no two witnesses agreed on his description? He sounded older—he sounded younger. He wore a scarlet coat—no, he did not. 'Twas in black he was when he held us up. A Welshman by the sound of him. Nay, thee's daft, for he ent no taffy but Yorkshire. Do I not hail from Durham myself? Well, *I* hail from London, by damn, and he's pure Cockney or I'm a stuffed goose. . . .

So it went wherever Hallow tried to form any solid picture of the Fleecer. Either the man had three tongues in his head or Dorset was afflicted with three different bandits using one name. Not a possibility the beleaguered sergeant wanted to ponder, as it tripled the difficulty of capture.

They almost had him last week. For reasons of security against the Fleecer's reputation, the paymaster met the Royal Mail coach at Winterborne Whitechurch, where travelers paused to rest and eat. Hallow and his detail rode out from St. Andrew to escort the coach to Dorchester. Just the Fleecer's blind luck to strike west of Whitechurch, just Hallow's that his patrol hove in sight of the stalled coach while the dirty bugger had the pay box open on the ground. He didn't get away with much and wasn't far ahead of them when he did.

Roddy Hallow considered gloomily. He didn't have the best men or horses, damned sure nothing to catch that big bay. They settled in to wear the Fleecer down, but twilight deepened to dark, one of his corporals took a bad fall jumping a hedge, and one horse threw a shoe. He'd be chewing royal arse off the garrison farriers for that. They lost the bastard. Lost him this time. There would be others.

Roddy Hallow was not an agile thinker. He plodded, but plodding got a man where he must go sooner or later. For a time last year he notioned Willy Boston for the Fleecer, but Wild Willy was found dead and robbed himself, and maybe 'twas the Fleecer done him, none could say. None would weep Willy's passing save maybe that wench down Cheselbourne who sobbed and swore 'twas the Fleecer's work sure. No matter. Roddy Hallow would see him swing or dead on the road.

Regimental sergeant major: A rise in pay, a good living in Dorchester, and then a sweet, biddable widow with a bit put by. At least some woman who didn't smell of cow shit or silage. All he had to do was find one man. Foxes were wary, but foxes got caught by hounds who sooner or later ran them to earth. Roddy Hallow would run or plod as needed, but dead or alive he would bring in the Golden Fleecer. Sodding Major Sedgewick would likely want the whoreson dead, save them all trouble. Fine.

Bess looked up from scrubbing the inn yard tables as the patrol from Milburne St. Andrew clattered by, grateful they didn't turn in. Was it her new and constant fear for Jason or plain truth that they seemed to come more often and closer to Whitechurch than before, like hawks wheeling above sure prey?

Compared to this, the old Fleecer had been no more than normal bother to the provost's men who rooted about with the usual questions and went back to St. Andrew. But now, as the word got about from farmers and travelers along the Dorchester road, the Golden Fleecer had become their main business. All of them against her Jason. Imagination festered in Bess. She was certain that provost sergeant suspected more than he spoke, and that soldiers stopping in for a drink eyed Jason more closely than was natural.

"More than thirty pounds now," old Mr. Jellicoe declared to Jason over his supper. "Thirty guineas, sir; more than thirty-one pounds on the villain's head and likely to rise higher if he's not caught."

"It seems exorbitant," Jason observed mildly. "Still, whoever finds him will be a made man."

Oh, Jason, Jason—and Bess would turn away to the kitchen, noting by the clock how long till closing time when they could be together. The constant sense of danger charged their time together with a sweeter urgency, though when Jason was with her he was all tenderness and gaiety, full of plans for the future. To Bess the monotonous swaying of the pendulum, ticktock back and forth, was no timepiece but scissors snipping seconds one by one from their life. She wanted their future and forced herself to believe in it. . . .

But what if this was the future? What if now was all they had?

In one of his many moments of whimsy, Abel posed her the question, "What if you had to live all your life, all your years in one day? What would you do with it?"

"One day? That's flat foolish."

"Of course, but still?"

"What could I do with one day?"

"The most important thing of all." Abel smiled. "You'd find what your heart wants more than anything else. And unless you're an utter fool, you'd run to it."

Bess thought of that often now that Jason was all of her life. All her span in one day, a handful of days with him? She would run after her heart and marry him on the spot——or, aye, give herself to him without reckoning the cost, and if she had a child— well, her country common sense allowed, more than one shire marriage was blessed five or six months after the wedding with a miraculously full-formed infant, and more girls than herself whispered secret prayers in Lady Chapel.

Bess would know when that was right for them.

At twenty-four Tim Groot had been a stableman half his life. Like his father before him, he never talked much; as he saw it there never was all that much to talk about. That did not mean that Tim didn't think. His mind, like his deceptively strong body, moved slowly but with sullen purpose. Tim Groot settled on a notion like an oyster mooring itself to rock, not easily dislodged.

Bess. She was a child when he came, and Tim grew used to her being there. Gradually, as he pieced out any thought, his ambition firmed. Only natural he should marry her, and someday he would see part and then full ownership of the King's Shilling. Jedediah wouldn't live forever, and Mrs. Whateley would welcome a man to manage things.

Tim disliked strangers, especially men who looked to Bess. They interfered with his right way of things, like that Evan Bromley down Winterborne Kingston he had to teach a lesson. Bess should know by now they were meant to marry. Flighty and dreamy she was, but he would set her straight once they were bound.

For a time this year he thought Bess was coming round and warming to him, but then comes this Quick, pretty as a girl, all soft city talk and white hands, and Tim might be a mudsill for all Bess noticed him since. That weren't right. Plain she didn't know what was good for her or flat going to be. Given the chance and proper time, he might have to teach the Bromley lesson to Quick. When he was host of the King's Shilling and Bess in the kitchen or tending their babes, she'd have no time for such foolery.

Beside the matter of Bess, Tim had another good reason for disliking Jason Quick. That night when he first showed his pale face, the night the soldiers came, he insulted Tim Groot, so he did. When Quick came to the stable for his horse, he mounted in an odd, awkward manner, grasping the pommel with his right hand instead of the left like sensible folk.

"You don't know much about horses," Tim snickered, "mounting with the off hand like that."

Quick casually tossed him a sixpence. "Why not? I'm dreadfully right-handed."

When Tim digested that, it was clear the toff was making fun of him. Some men shrugged off irritation; in Tim Groot it simmered toward boil. Not that he ever showed his temper; he was too shrewd for that, at least not until it was time to get even. Tim did that proper, the way he forked hay, no hurry, every forkful in its place.

He glowered now at the harness he was soaping. Sunday again and Bess to church not with the family but in the Lady Chapel with that Quick again and wheezy old Gant. And after, they'd be walking out. Quick had grown to a serious bother, one Tim Groot could hate.

Sometimes the vague thought struck him uncomfortably: He disliked or hated a great many things in the life given him. The notion never stuck long, being outside his hard, narrow purposes. He cursed Quick under his breath and rubbed the soap hard into the leather with steely fingers, as if he were strangling it.

Of a summer Sunday then, Abel on his old cob, Bess regally astride Jason's, lady's sidesaddle be damned, and he leading their meandering way across the downs south of the Dorchester road where the ancient hill fort loomed up before them. London-bred Jason had never seen one, but Abel said the huge earthwork was older in England than the English.

Bess scoffed. "No one's older than us here."

"Oh, many," Abel insisted, ever the teacher. "There were the

Britons under great Arthur. Why, this might be the famous
Badon Hill where he beat the Saxons back for a full generation.
And before the Britons were the fairy folk, so legends tell."

His arm swept up toward the terraced heights. "Look there.
Who knows how many glorious battles were fought here
between one tribe and another? See? There's the causeway
going up."

In his shirtsleeves, Jason breathed deep, turning his face to the
sun's warmth. "What a sight. And what a splendid day for it."

Abel trotted out a little way, suddenly young as his friends.
"To arms, Bess! Queen of Amazons, give the order to charge. Let
us take Badon again for the English."

And off they went, Bess's high, sweet voice urging Abel on,
Jason shouting "Hi, wait!" in their wake. They cantered up the
causeway to the first, then the second level before pausing.
When Jason reached them on foot and panting, Bess was already
laying out their lunch of ham, cheese, bread, and beer.

After eating they lay back, content in the sun to gaze on the
gentle swell of downs before them, like the breasts of a woman,
Abel thought. When Bess nestled her head into Jason's shoulder
and they settled back on the soft grass, he deemed it time to
leave them alone. "I'm for exploring the top."

Jason yawned. "What in the world is there to find?"

"Oh—perhaps a flint, an old spearhead, a bit of rusted sword."
Abel mounted, giving free rein to an imagination ever too lively
for a schoolteacher. "Perhaps the footprint of an ancestor. Hi!
Gee up!"

For a while Jason and Bess lay together, the sun warm and
their close-nestled bodies warmer, building fantastic castles and
countries from cloud shapes drifting over them. They hardly
spoke at first, coming to enjoy the way they could be quiet
together without the need for words. Later they would remember this day as a talisman of all the best they shared.

"And Rapunzel let down her hair . . ." Bess dreamed.

"Mm?"

" 'Tis nothing. What's that cloud up there?"

"That," Jason estimated grandly, "is a rich county in Virginia, and in the very middle is a large house of stout timber and white frame where we live. And there be broad acres around where we grow tobacco."

Bess shifted drowsily deeper into his neck. "When, love?"

"When we have enough money."

She accepted that without detecting the anxiety in his voice. "Will you be by the Shilling for supper tomorrow?"

"No, there's . . . business in St. Andrew."

With their understanding silences they evolved a code based on the promise wrung from Jason not to tell her when he rode. "St. Andrew" was their white flag to change the subject. To assure her he'd be with her or safe at home: "The weather bodes good."

She didn't tell him but only Abel: Sometimes she worried so much that Bess all but expired in the effort not to ask. Not to know. Virginia was a beautiful dream, but when? Their dream required money, but how much? Could she help? Precious little she knew of money beyond a pound or so, let alone the price of a new life in a strange land halfway round the world.

"How much will we need, Jason?"

"More than we have."

Now indeed she caught the bleak, hard note. "Well, I've been putting by before you came, and do you know, Master Quick? I have a full pound ten, if that's any aid."

Jason rolled up over her, and the sudden tears glistening in his eyes surprised Bess as he covered her mouth with his. *What is it? What did I say?* But he had never kissed her before with such lingering tenderness. "Thank you," he whispered. "Thank God for you in my life."

"And mark you," she went on, "I can shave a penny here and there. There's them so drunk of a Saturday they'll never miss one from a shilling."

"No." Jason frowned. "Bad enough to do what I must, but not you. Shortchange your father's trade?"

Earnestly: "Oh, just now and again. A penny is a penny, Jason. And don't look at me like a magistrate."

"Well . . . it's dishonest."

"Stuff. Is it now?" Bess nipped at his nose. "Rose Allen pinched enough whenever she could. Got sacked for it."

"Could you honestly do that?"

"Not honestly—no more than you."

"Don't say that. I know what I do."

"But we've a good cause, and it won't be forever. And I'll pray in Lady Chapel. She'll understand." At least Bess hoped so.

As for Jason, he found indigestible the idea of Bess working a pigeon, no mind for how little. "What would your good father say? If you do, don't tell me, mind. And promise: Never take from Abel."

"Abel? I'd rather die."

"And no one you respect."

"Never," she vowed, knowing the field she sowed. "There's plenty I don't." She pulled his mouth down to hers again, grateful to God, the warm sun, and what life had given her after so long yearning for it. Jason had truly awakened her, and he was the first. Like Rapunzel she woke from girl to a woman's unselfish dream of love in a rush of giving. She trusted Jason would die for her and she as willingly for him. In this growing togetherness Bess warmed herself at a steady fire that would blaze up soon to join and consume them, but for now she rested content to lie with her head on his shoulder, tracing futures in clouds.

For Jason, this girl was a tiny bird fluttering in his hand, to be sheltered and never harmed. As Bess hummed softly, his own thoughts darkened with realities whose dim conclusion refused to come clear. There *had* to be more money, much more as the dream grew legs and ran more swiftly before them, threatening to escape. No fever of greed but the need to give Bess and Abraham the life they deserved, and that meant riding and thinking faster than Sergeant Roddy Hallow. As the risks grew greater and the odds rose, his caution turned to audacity bordering on recklessness. Sometimes, with a kind of black amusement, he wondered what banality of fate made him an honest stationer's son in a shop where his mind alone went into his work. The very marrow of him thrilled to robbing the king's money. Owen taught him better than he knew.

Pay boxes yielded the most profit, passengers less, beside taking time, which increased danger. Enlisted soldiers got their pay in silver, far too much and too heavy for any speed if he was pursued; that lesson had been learned almost fatally. But for convenience in large amounts, officers of the Fifty-fourth now received their pay in banknotes. The first problem was to find out where and when. Naturally there would be an escort, perhaps even a special coach.

Logical problems must have logical solutions. There must be a way out of any maze, simply because there must be a way in.

He'd been silent so long that Bess stirred and sat up, straightening her hair. "Take a penny for thoughts?"

"Not worth a farthing, love."

"Here comes Abel."

He'd walked along the top of the hill fort, dreaming on ancient battles while his more pragmatic horse grazed. Remembering the book of sonnets in his pocket, Abel leafed through a few of his favorites, savoring the exquisite pentameter before leading the old cob down terrace by terrace to the young people.

They must leave soon. Bess would be needed to help prepare the kitchen for the morrow. To Abel she glowed with the contentment of a woman opening to love for the first time. He'd been years too weary and jaded to succumb but could still appreciate the magic love wrought in young, growing things. His own wife saved him only from his own cooking before he abandoned her; afterwards his liaisons were sweet and brief. Now the prospect of love lured him no more, if as much, than that of a good night's sleep, but suddenly he wanted to embrace Jason and Bess together, shelter them both in any way from any harm.

Jason sprang up to greet him. "What a wizard day it's been, Abel. Bloody marvelous!"

Not bloody, Abel prayed, knowing the perverse determination in his friend. *Please, Lord. They are too beautiful both to ever have blood on them.*

Jason avoided Rose Allen when he arrived at the Crown and Thistle that night. The afterglow of Bess in his arms lingered, and there was the new challenge of his next business to be met. He needed no maps now. Every dip, rise, and escape route off the Dorchester road was familiar to him, but Hallow's persistence presented an increasing hazard. It could be fatal to underestimate the man. By lamplight in his room, Jason's mind revolved on the problem. When Rose Allen tapped on his door and entered familiarly, she was the last person he needed to see. More than that, she looked downright accusatory.

"Where've you been all the day, Jason?"

Sounded that way too. "It's late, Rose," he sighed. "I was about to retire."

She was not to be put off. "You didn't say where you was."

"I dined at the King's Shilling with Abel Gant."

"All day was it?" she challenged.

"We were out riding on the downs." Jason stood up, yawning. "I'm cursed tired, Rose. I want to go to bed."

"No." She sat down determinedly on his bed. "Seems you been too late or too tired for weeks now. Ain't I—amn't I good enough for you anymore?" Her accusing tone darkened. "Or perhaps you get more than dinner at the Shilling."

Oh God, not now. Invention deserted Jason for a moment as he realized uncomfortably that difficulties in courting the right woman were nothing beside those in gracefully leaving the wrong. He regretted having bedded Rose, no matter how casual at the time. How would Abel, in his wry wisdom and slant morality, handle such a situation? How to be shut of Rose without hurting her?

"Rose, listen to me." Jason sat beside her, drawing her close, relying on instincts now a little sharper from experience. Louisa had taught him feminine practicality and Long Jane how women with nothing need something *now*. In their hand. Though they'd never spoken of Willy Boston, that might be the key to his way out.

"Rose, I never looked into your eyes without seeing pain there."

She twisted around to him, surprised but still expectant. "Pain?"

"Yes. Somewhere I feel you lost someone. Don't deny it; I read the wound so clearly."

She looked away. "There was someone. Willy his name was."

"I hope I don't rake up hurtful memories, but only one who has suffered can truly appreciate suffering in others. I think any tenderness you showed me was for the memory of him."

"Did you know Willy?" she plied eagerly. "He and me was going to America. He was going to buy me passage and new dresses."

"And he would have, I'm sure. I never met the man—"

"But y'did," Rose plunged on. "You supped here the very night he . . . his last night. And God blight the bastard what done for him. It hurts terrible when I remember."

Then she could all the more read the same loss in Jason (who was conscious of more Garrick than true pathos in his fabricated tragedy). "There was a girl in London. We were to be married, but where we planned a life together, I had to sit by her bedside as she wasted away with consumption. Oh God, Rose, so much of me died with her."

"But she's gone," practical Rose argued, "and so's my Willy. There's still us."

"You don't understand. There can never be anyone else for me. God has drawn love out of me like a dead tooth. Wherever I go,

I must go alone. You're a good woman, Rose, but I can give you nothing. Leave me now and go to bed."

She rose, disappointed but still hopeful. "I'd be good for you, Jason. I know what a man needs, and you need more than most. You ain't hard like me and Willy. I know my way about a town. Ain't many sharp dealers sweet Rose can't see through. You'll need someone like me in America."

Jason vouchsafed Rose a look he hoped conveyed unutterable sadness. "I still wake weeping in the night."

She clutched at his hand, tried to embrace him. "Oh, Jason, let me—"

"No, I beg you." Jason extricated himself, rose, and firmly guided her to the door. "I tried to forget with you as you with me, I'll warrant, but that's not possible. She will be with me until I join her in the hereafter."

"Oh, you fool!" Rose shook him off angrily. "You weak ninny. Willy was ten times the man you'll ever be. Whoever she was, she's dead. I'm alive and here."

"That makes only one of us, Rose."

"Think again, Jason Quick," she purred, sure of herself. "I know men. You'll see it my way. You'll need me. You'll come round when the sap rises in the tree again."

When he finally managed to close the door on her, Jason expelled a deep breath of relief and some repentance. *Were I Catholic,* he observed to God and whatever saints were listening, *I'd swill out my mouth with holy water.*

Recounting the incident to Abel later, Jason marveled ruefully at the ease of his deception. "I know I'm an outlaw, but when did I turn so *dishonest?*"

Bess happened to be in the stableyard just before dusk when Sergeant Hallow's patrol rode past the inn. She reported the sighting to Abel and Jason at their corner table over an after-supper game of chess.

"They turned off for Winterborne Kingston," she said before hurrying to take Mr. Jellicoe's order for supper. "Reckon they'll be back this way."

"The road is damned busy this month." Jason moved his knight. "Check."

Abel moved his king to safety. "Give it up, Jason. Give it up now. Marry Bess and forget the rest."

"Forget my father?"

"Very well; take Bess and go, but get out of here."

"There's not near enough money."

Abel rested on his folded arms, regarding his friend. "More and more you say that. You've got enough to get you there and then some, and four good months of sailing weather from Plymouth. You can find employment."

"Abel, it is not enough for what—I—*need*," Jason ground out stubbornly. "For what Bess needs."

"Have you asked her all of what she needs?"

They fell silent for a time over their game. "Seems all life can be likened to chess," Abel mused. "Some play for position. Others go for whatever pieces can be snatched up. They get greedy and don't see the pattern closing in on them."

Jason understood the allusion, but the wisdom deflected off the armor of his determination. "Bess wants what I want. I've tasted too much dirt. When we go, it will be the cream for us."

"Not tonight." Abel moved a bishop aslant, discovering an inescapable threat to Jason's king. "Checkmate."

Halfway through their second game, Bess passed their table again. "Didn't I say as much?" she whispered anxiously. "Hallow's coming in and three with him."

Jason slipped two shillings into her hand. "Tell'm compliments of the house and keep them at the bar."

Sergeant Hallow and his patrol gusted into the King's Shilling

KATE HAWKS

like a strong ill wind. Roddy Hallow bore a printed notice which he directed Jedediah Whately to post immediately in the main room, as Bess, all sugar and smiles, treated his men in the bar. Mr. Jellicoe and the other locals mumbled uncomfortably into their ale mugs while Hallow downed a quick whiskey.

"Bless me," Abel muttered to Jason. "Do you see that notice?"

Jason studied the chessboard. "I did."

"Thirty-five pounds on the Fleecer now. Five added by the Royal Mail—and what is so amusing about that, pray?"

"Just ruminating," Jason chuckled. "Might there be a way for me to collect the reward and get away both?"

"I'd give odds against."

"You there! Macaroni!"

Roddy Hallow loomed over Jason, ruddy face still sheened with perspiration from a hot ride. "You're the sick fish off to America, wan't you? Still here, eh?"

Jason responded with a wan smile. "Convalescing, thank you, sir. What brings you to our hamlet?"

"Nothin' out of the way. Heard a rumor that Fleecer's been seen in Kingston and Dewlish."

Hallow's attempt to be casual was transparent. Jason wondered how much the provost knew or suspected. One might profit from a trip to St. Andrew, buying the man a few drinks and taking his measure.

"Dewlish is the Mecca for rumors," Abel volunteered. "Last week I heard that *I* was the Fleecer."

Hallow snorted and slapped Abel's bony back. "That's capital, old fart like you."

"I do my banking in Blandford," Jason said earnestly. "I was planning to travel there this week." He paused to cough delicately into a scented hankerchief. "But are the roads safe enough, you think?"

Roddy Hallow caught the perfume from that handkerchief with a pitying smirk. "Safe enough even for you, little mouse. The Fleecer, he goes most for pay boxes, and the regular coaches don't carry them anymore. Your old mum'd be safe enough here to Blandford. You buggers in the bar!" he roared at his men. "Drink up and put your bums in the saddle. Time to go."

Hallow started to turn away, then regarded Jason. "Your name would be Quick, right? Jason Quick, aye. Queer how I'd remember. But then Whitechurch don't get many new folks to stay." He strode away after his men.

"Third time this week they've patrolled this close," Jason murmured.

"Positively salivating for that thirty-five pounds." Abel's hand hovered over a piece. "Should make a highwayman feel truly sought after."

"Indeed," Jason agreed. "Lionized."

"I didn't like the way he looked at you. The whole affair's become far too hazardous. Joshua might tumble city walls, but even with the help of God he couldn't take a farthing on the Dorchester road."

Perhaps Hallow told the truth about the pay box, perhaps not. If not by Royal Mail, then it must come by special army coach. The route was no problem. No matter if the box came through Shaftesbury, Winchester, or wherever, the only road to Dorchester from any of them lay through Blandford Forum or close by. The idea actually gave Jason a thrill of challenge. Hallow was surely thorough and searching in all the right places but would never be looking under his very nose.

"Abel, aren't you off to Dorchester soon?"

"I am. To collect the wages of sin. My remittance, you know. Very punctual man, the baronet."

"When?"

"Oh, tomorrow or the next day."

"Make it tomorrow. You can purchase a few trifles for me."

Corporal Daniel Winner wiped the sweat of July heat from his cheeks and finished his beer. Despite his surname, Winner felt no part of one. He'd planned to be in Dorchester today frolicking abroad and abed with obliging Alice Mulgrew, but Hallow had posted him to command this coach detail with privates Bell and Soames. All the bloody way to Blandford St. Mary to meet the paymaster. So here he sat, sweating in a miserable way-station pub, drinking weak beer while Bell and Soames munched the worst pork pies in Dorset, all so's the bleeding officers of the Fifty-fourth could be paid prompt.

They had the leather pay pouch and saw no reason not to pause a bit before bumping back over the long, hot road to Milborne St. Andrew, especially when the beer and pies were paid for by the most ridiculous figure of an officer Winner had ever set eye to, a new lieutenant posted to the Fifty-fourth.

"Subaltern Barrett-Smythe," the apparition introduced himself, presenting his orders for the corporal's inspection. "Gazetted to Major Sedgewick's command."

Winner could barely read. The lack embarrassed him, but the orders looked official enough, and he could make out familiar words like *adjutant* and *C'mdg. Gen'l*, signed by a name too exalted in rank to bother with legibility.

Winner suppressed a sardonic smirk. Barrett-Smythe was a twit if ever one was born, in a fussily curled wig, with too-prominent upper gums that bucked out his front teeth, reminding Winner of a confused squirrel, and further diminished his scant dignity with a silly lisp. To compound the absurd image, a large cloth bandage swaddled his conspicuously swollen left cheek.

"Demmed toothache, don't y'know. Need a surgeon straight. Positive agony."

Barrett-Smythe produced a small bottle of clove oil and liberally swabbed far back in his mouth. That done, he opened an ornate snuffbox and gave a pinch to each nostril, fastidiously brushing flecks of snuff from the veritable geyser of lace erupting from his waistcoat. Winner was hard put not to laugh, but he'd seen green officers before. Young toffs with cheeks smooth as a baby's arse and no more notion of soldiering than a ribbon clerk.

"You seconded from another regiment, sir?"

"What? Good heavens, no." What Winner could see of the bandage-swaddled visage frowned with offense around his toothache. "Bought my commission like a gentleman should."

"Beg pardon, sir."

"Barrett-Smythe," the subaltern repeated. "My father is Baronet Barrett-Smythe. Surely you have heard of him."

"Oh yes, sir," Winner fabricated quickly with a polite nod. "Him."

The lieutenant negligently dropped loose change on the bar. "You and your men may have more beer. No need to travel straight off. Positively sweltering day, what? Drink up, you fellows. The colonel, my grandfather, always used to say, 'Take care of the ranks and the ranks will take care of England.'"

Doubtfully, Barrett-Smythe inspected several pork pies set out on the bar. "I say there," he called to the bored barman. "Do you think your kitchen might have a bit of squab?"

"Just what you see, laddy," he was told. "Meat pies."

"No venison?"

The barman went back to contemplating the view beyond a window.

Winner, Bell, and Soames ordered a round of beer and another after that. Over their drinks they watched the toothached popinjay seated loftily apart from them.

"Good job we're not cavalry," young Bell said, winking at Soames. "That one couldn't find either end of a horse."

By three o'clock Winner decided they could delay no longer if they were to make Milborne St. Andrew by supper time. Soames climbed onto the buckboard, while Winner and Bell sat inside the coach with the suffering subaltern who seemed to have no luggage apart from a small leather bag.

"Where's your kit, sir?" Winner inquired.

"Not ready. Orders came down before Gieves finished tailoring me. Demmed nuisance."

The coach lurched and jolted along for most of an hour while

Winner and Bell shifted about in growing discomfort, regretting not having relieved themselves before setting out. Finally the corporal opened the trap and called for Soames to stop.

"Out you go, Bell. Soames, you need to unload?"

"I surely do," came the reply. "My back teeth's floatin' away."

Winner leaned across to Barrett-Smythe who huddled, head in his hands. "Sir, do you need . . . ?"

"No," the subaltern lisped wanly. He swallowed hard several times, a man obviously fighting nausea. "But all this bouncing and jouncing about has got my innards in an uproar. I'll remain here."

Winner piled out of the coach behind Bell as Soames jumped down from the buckboard. Perfect place to stop, not a house or soul in sight. They moved a few steps off the road, unbuttoning breeches flaps. In the pleasure of relieving themselves, they didn't hear the coach door open and shut quietly behind them, only the whip crack and hearty "Hi! Up!" Winner spun about in dismay to see Barrett-Smythe waving farewell from the buckboard.

"My compliments, gentlemen. And thank you!"

Soames made a desperate run but caught no more than the coach's dust as it dwindled westward. Their muskets were inside and—Winner went gray with the realization—the pay pouch.

It all happened so suddenly that none of them comprehended the full enormity at first, just stood there in the dusty road, finally remembering to button their britches.

Soames said it first. " 'Twas him. Couldn't be none but him."

"Who else?" Winner grated. They'd been had like green recruits. If there were a jot of charity in his soul just then, he might admire the Fleecer's guts. "I seen men with brass in my time. Seen men bet their last shillin' blind before turning up a single card and then win the lot. But *him?*"

Winner fell silent under an agony of humiliation. The Golden Fleecer under their noses. Thirty-five pounds reward so close they could have scooped it in without bending an elbow. Instead they drank his beer and laughed up their sleeves at the silly ass until he was damned well ready to shear them. And Roddy Hallow said he'd have that bastard before the leaves turned? Danny Winner would give him long odds on that, but he didn't relish thinking on Hallow just then. They might well be flogged for this. At the very least Danny Winner would lose his stripes what took him years to get.

"Well, don't stand there with your thumbs up your arse. Come on." He started down the road, waving Bell and Soames after him. "Bound to be a farm where we can get the loan of horses."

Daniel Winner sweated as he walked, his lower lip jutting out in cold determination. Let them take his stripes. Come to that, he'd take the flogging if that was his lot. Only let him have the Fleecer cold over musket sights once before he died.

Jason pushed the wagon team at a gallop, putting distance between himself and the soldiers for some minutes before easing them down to a comfortable trot for the next half hour, waving cordially to the occasional farm wagons lumbering toward Blandford. A few minutes more and he sighted the stand of trees where Abel Gant waited with Jason's own cob tethered close by. He reined the team off the road to a halt and sprang down as Abel cried, "How went the day?"

"Most wonderful! But hot as perdition." Jason threw away the foppish spray of lace, stripped the padded kerchief from his face, hurled the wig as far as it would sail, and removed the cotton wadding from his upper gum. "Mr. Garrick himself would have applauded, but sink me if I ever incinerate my head in a wig again. Thunder, but I'd give five guineas out of this pull to see Hallow's face when he gets the news."

"Oh, worlds of fun. I've been here for hours, sweating and praying. You're not hurt?"

Jason winked at him. "Never better."

"Was there trouble?" Abel asked anxiously. "Surely they're coming after you."

"On foot, you worried old nanny." Jason clapped him on the back. "Oh, I had pistols in my bag but never had to show them."

Indeed, to Abel, Jason looked hale and even exhilarated.

"Only three soldiers." His old pupil laughed. "I poured them so full of beer they had to stop for a Jericho. Out they tumbled, fumbling with buttons, and while they were communing with nature, off I went. Oh, but I'll miss Barrett-Smythe," Jason confessed, wiping his sweaty forehead on a shirtsleeve. "Such a complete ass."

"Damme!" Abel exploded. "Damn, damn, *damn* if you're not loving all this. You take too many chances."

"Nary one of 'em not thought out, Abel. Who was it said, 'Fine, finished work is the mark of the professional'?"

"How would I know?" Abel Gant fumed. "If he was in your line, he's likely dead now."

"Look smart. We have to be off."

Jason unhitched the lathered team to wander off toward graze and water. When Abel retrieved Jason's bag and opened the pay pouch, he was speechless. Dumbly he scanned the accompanying manifest.

"Well, what?" Jason called. "What's there?"

"Jason, this . . . it's more than pay. There's money for the Dorchester quartermaster for supplies. Here, count it."

Jason riffled quickly through the bills, awed as Abel. "Near two hundred pounds," he whispered as if the money would disappear did he name it aloud.

"Right then," Abel decreed firmly. "No more chances. You've enough now. You've done it."

"Not quite."

"For the love of God and reason, Jason, enough!"

Jason fanned the banknotes in his hands. "One more."

"No, damn you." Abel stamped away to his horse, mounting with an effort as rheumatism twinged at his knee. "What in the world do you want, you fool? Not Bess. It's more than Bess now, isn't it? You grow more arrogant and reckless each time, and that girl dies a little every time you ride."

His old teacher looked flat frustrated, but Jason knew his mind. None outside the hardened shell of his own suffering, not even Owen Jones, could understand. All of this was for Bess, for Abraham, for the three of them together, and no harm in taking pride in a skill he never thought to acquire, or a bit of fun in the game. "One more, Abel. One more fat as this. I'll wait and be cautious, trust me. I'll let Roddy Hallow wear out horses and men looking until I'm ready. But I'll never be poor again. My father will never wear chains again or call some unworthy scut master. And by Christ on Tree, my Bess will never have to eat tripe."

Afraid and excited all at once, Bess felt a fluttering in her stomach as she went about her tasks that day. She was part of Jason's business in St. Andrew now, already bad as Rose Allen what with giving change a penny short whenever she dared. Not with Abel or any respectable customers, merely layabouts like that dirty pig Jocko Sullivan who was sober no more often than he washed and always tried to paw at her or pat her bottom, so he deserved it.

Still, that barely comforted Bess Whateley's Anglican conscience. Stealing was a sin, a blot on the soul. Jason did what he did for reasons of the heart and told her as little of that as he might. For herself she whispered her confession in Lady Chapel each Sunday and hoped Mary, if she couldn't intercede, would at least understand. Aye, she was deep in it now. When the soldiers came to post the new reward, she heard one grumble about wagon detail to Blandford St. Mary day after next.

"Officers get paid regular while we can wait two months to see a penny."

So it must be a deal of money. That tortured Bess with an agony of indecision. Should she tell Jason, haste them perhaps that much closer to Virginia? Or see him dead on the road or hanged? Or keep silent and have him alive that much longer in her arms?

Would it be so much to him to forget Virginia and settle here? No, he'd never. Jason said they needed more money, and what use to deny him? Gentle with her always but hard as a pistol ball when his mind locked on a purpose. With misgiving she passed him the place and time and melted into his arms when he kissed her.

"Then watch for me by moonlight, Bess."

"Promise me you'll come."

"I'll be in for supper. Ask your mum to save me a Bath cake."

No more than that. From dawn the next day and all through the dragging hours, she went about her tasks so taut and silent that her mother asked if she were ill. If 'twere only that.

Bess helped in the kitchen, washed the ale mugs, folded the linen, speared the ham with cloves, pounded her fear into the bread dough. Summer twilight faded slower than ever before, and it seemed to Bess, when she stole a moment outside, that night would never come, nor the cold, contrary moon ever rise.

Watch for me by moonlight.

And then at last to see him shining there in the inn doorway, Abel Gant in his wake and the two of them calling for supper. Her fear dissolved, but the hours, creeping all day as if all clocks conspired against her, now stood still as Bess lived for nothing more than closing time and the chance to run to him. In her happiness she pinched not a penny, not even from Jocko Sullivan, just gave silent thanks to Mary and promised the pence left her that night to the church poor box in gratitude.

She endured the century before her father called time to the last lingering drinkers, then she quickly cleared the tables and flew out into the kitchen yard where Jason waited. He must have been astonished at her ravenous kisses devouring his lips again and again, her hands feeling for the smallest hurt. Were there—? Did they—? Was it very dangerous?

"No, sweet," he managed before she stopped his mouth with another hungry kiss. " 'Twas a lark, girl. I bought them drinks—"

"You bought—the soldiers?"

"Right buckets. And when they climbed out for a Jericho, they were kind enough to leave me the coach and its profit. And a rich one it is. Oh, Bess." Jason hugged her close and led her by the hand out into the moonlit lane. "We can go soon, soon, *soon*. Before the leaves fall. And I almost forgot." Jason put the velvet ribbon in Bess's hand. "Fancied this in a shop in Blandford St. Mary. Red—'twill look dashing in your hair."

They wandered up the short lane to the church, past the darkened rectory and into the cool quiet of the churchyard, where moss-grown gravestones marked their passing without complaint from the old residents. On two sides of the graveyard, yew trees grew close together above the oldest graves, whose granite slabs were far too worn to read.

They had kissed and clung before but tonight was different in the fevered way Jason trembled as he caressed and kissed her throat and down into the cleft of her breasts. Her body burned with new pleasures wakened side by side with new fears, knowing she rushed toward a brink, fearful but joyous as well.

"Will you be with me tomorrow?" she whispered against his cheek.

"Tomorrow and the next night, all this week and the week after." In the shadows Bess could barely see his face but he was smiling. "The weather bodes good, Bess. And we'll be married before we sail."

"Here, Jason. Here in St. Mary's by Reverend Cobbe."

"Where else? With Abel and your mum and dad standing with us and all Whitechurch turned out to see."

Bess writhed herself tight to his body. "If you mean that—"

"No lies between us, you said. We're for wedding."

She pushed him away to search his face in the darkness under the yews. "Then no more business in St. Andrew. Promise me we'll wed and sail with what there is now."

"One more, Bess. One more fat and easy as today."

She stepped back from him, adamant. "No, Jason."

"I'll wait for it," he plunged on. "The right place and time, well planned as Christmas dinner."

"No."

The force of her denial brought him up short. "It . . . means so much to you?"

Means? There were no words strong enough. Bess could only press herself to him, clutching him so fiercely in her need that he must feel her nails through the broadcloth of his coat. Wanting him breathed the message to her pounding heart sure as a death warning. *If I give myself to him now, he can never leave me. This is the time, I know it.*

"If you want it so, Bess," Jason said finally. "No more."

She had dreamed of their first coming together in just this place, and how Jason would possess her tenderly while she hoped to know how to answer him with all the love she felt and only a little fear.

When Jason, trembling, pulled her down onto the soft, leafy earth, she breathed in his ear, "It means that much."

"From this night on."

"No, wait. Let me up."

"Don't be afraid."

"I'm not," Bess quavered with only half a lie. She trembled herself now, but her hands were swift on the fastenings of her dress. "Put down your coat for me."

Only truly frightened for a moment, then she bathed in the sweet, warm thrill of their bare flesh pressed together, and his hands were gentle stroking down her back from shoulders to the hollow of her back and her thighs. He didn't hurry, more reverent than hungry. At last his hand between her thighs found the spot that lighted a slow fire, and as it grew to rushing flame, the image of Rapunzel glowed in her mind before Bess forgot all but now and Jason over her.

Anne Whateley pushed the bolster away and turned over. Almost too warm to sleep well this night. She'd be another hour listening to Jedediah snore softly beside her before she could doze off again.

When the staircase creaked she thought it just the old house settling for the night, but then the sound came again. A careful footstep. Then Anne heard the soft closing of a door.

Lord, it's Bess. She remembered their daughter wasn't about when they darkened the downstairs lights. They gathered she'd gone up to bed. No, she'd gone out the back door on some errand. . . .

And then what? What business has you coming in at this hour, girl?

Anne Whateley started to do two things at once, wake her husband and get out of bed herself, then paused. She knew her daughter's heart. Right, Bess lit like a dozen lamps when Jason was with her, and Mr. Quick was a gentleman, the best Bess could find to suit, and high time. They seemed to have an understanding between them, and what if tonight they went a might beyond what was called proper? No more than she and Jedediah did once or twice before their banns were spoken. The only thing—

The child was always one for stories and dreams, and dreaming still she is. Bess feels things so deeply, like the time her hound puppy died of a fox bite. She never took any of the shire lads serious, always wanted something more, always building some fashion of a dream like sand castles on the beach at Bournemouth. I hope Jason is all that for her. When she loves, her kind will always love too hard.

Jedediah snorted, reared up, and crashed over on his other side. She wouldn't tell him about this. What good would come

of that? Much as he liked Jason, her husband would feel bound
to confront him with proper look-here-what-are-your-intentions
nonsense. Bess was a woman now, ripe for marriage, and Anne
had seen how Jason treated her, never for a moment taking the
girl for granted. The house would be emptier without Bess, but
that would pass in time. There were some who might wink and
say the way to a man's heart lay through his stomach. That
helped, but real lovers knew shorter and surer routes.

*Should I go in just to see if the child's all right? No hint of knowing where
she's been, just a kiss good night like when she was little. No, she's grown, Anne
Whateley, so let her be. Whatever's passed between them, close your eyes and
go to sleep.*

But she lay long awake nonetheless, worrying without truly
knowing why.

Bess sat by her window in the dark, brushing her hair and gazing
out over the peaceful Dorchester road bathed in moonlight. She
thanked Jason silently for not rushing her. Time stopped while
he found her, and it was not just hunger; Jason loved her. Come
tomorrow, Sunday, he would speak to her father. Above all he
promised no more business in St. Andrew. Done then; they were
finally shut of it all and nothing from here on but happiness.
What if they had to work and scrimp a bit in America? Was it
any more than both of them had done growing up?

Bess laid the brush aside and shook out the thick ebony waves
of her hair, letting them stream over her shoulders and back, soft
as Jason's hands caressing her. There'd been a little pain for her at
first, but even that was fading. She drew the red velvet ribbon
between her fingers. Tomorrow she'd plait it as a love-knot in
her hair for him to see.

Before she fell asleep, Bess recalled the image of Rapunzel and
the prince climbing up her long tresses. Feeling somewhat

wicked, she giggled at how ridiculous the picture seemed now when she could still feel Jason inside her.

Bess woke slowly on Sunday morning. As she stretched deliciously, she thought, *I'm different now. I'm changed forever.*

She slid out of bed and dropped her nightgown on the bed. The morning was already warm enough to sponge-bathe from the water pitcher, but before dipping the sponge, Bess passed her hands slowly over her breasts and stomach down to her loins, recalling how Jason touched them last night. With delight she could still detect the faint scent of him on her skin. She poured her basin half full and washed quickly. Jason would be coming to take her to church, but chickens must be fed, eggs collected, and the two cows milked before that.

She dressed, remembering Jason's gift of the red ribbon, and took more time than her tasks would really allow plaiting it into her hair. In the kitchen she gave her mother a more effusive good morning than usual and, as she virtually danced out into the kitchen yard with milk pail and chicken feed, missed Anne Whateley's faint, secret smile.

As she perched on the milking stool, squeezing the cow's udders, Bess considered that absolutely nothing could spoil this day of all days and barely heard the loose hay rustle behind her as someone entered.

"Jason?"

When there was no answer, Bess knew who it was before looking. Tim Groot stood there in his old gray wool shirt that he never seemed to change, staring at her with the same dull intensity.

"Oh, it's you." She went on milking, hoping he'd go away and wearily sure he wouldn't. Tim could bore her to death in her sleep. Even in *his* sleep.

"You got a ribbon in your hair."

She expected Jason any minute and had no time for the likes of Tim today. "I'll say this for you, Timmy. You never miss a thing."

More silence broken only by the rhythmic squirts of milk splashing in her pail. Maddening sometimes how Tim mulled over everything before framing an answer.

"How'd you come by that?"

"By what then?"

"That 'ere ribbon."

"From Jason. He saw it in a shop down Blandford St. Mary. Thought I'd like it."

Speak of dim. Why did she go and tell him where Jason went yesterday? Well, she reasoned hopefully, Tim wasn't shrewd enough to pair that with any robbery.

"Saw you with him last night."

"We all did. He was in with Abel."

"I mean after. Up the lane."

Tim's words were stained with innuendo, and Bess wondered how much he knew or saw before deciding she didn't care in the slightest now. "Go get cleaned up for church. Must I tell Papa what a bother you are?"

"You been with him."

"We only walked out."

"You been with him."

The pent fury of him turned Bess about, surprised to see, in his usually inexpressive face, something like emotion. "You've a bad mouth on you, Tim Groot. Go away."

He didn't move. "It ain't right and you know that."

"No such thing. Leave me alone, I said."

"He ain't right," Tim persisted. "It ain't the way things should be."

With a resigned sigh, Bess lifted the pail clear of the cow's feet and rose. "And what do you think is right?"

"You and me. You should know by now."

The damned stupid man could drive a nun to drink. "Well, for-give me, Master Groot. I must have missed that when you and God were putting my life in order." She wanted him gone and Jason here *now*, and where was he? Tim drove her beyond caution. A body had to pound him over the head before anything sank in. "It was never you and me, Tim, whatever you got into your head. You might as well know. Jason and I will marry."

Again the dull stare, then a slow shaking of his head. "No."

"He'll be asking Papa this very morning, and Reverend Cobbe will read the banns. You'll hear."

Tim twisted away, his back to her, his voice tight. " 'Twas always you and me, all these years. I ain't fancy like him or good with words, but . . ."

He trailed off into anguished silence. Bess tried to close gently a door Tim had too long kept open in his hopeless hoping. "Tim, I'm going to marry Jason, and there's an end. I wouldn't cause you pain, but put it from your mind now and for good."

"Devil I will," he choked.

"You'll see."

When she moved past him, his back was still turned. Bess saw the white knuckles of his clenched fists but not his eyes blurred with unaccustomed tears

Why must Tim vex her so? Why wouldn't he see how things stood and leave her be? More, the hour for church drew nigh and still no Jason. Which meant no bespeaking her father today and no first banns. Bess walked disconsolately between her parents to St. Mary's, Tim a few sullen paces behind as always. She would ask to sit so one of her parents was between her and Tim. She didn't like the look of the ostler today.

Bess barely marked the service, and when they stood to sing with the wheezy old organ, she moved her lips to the words, but the hymn was only discord to the desperate prayer in her heart.

Jason had promised to be with her. Where *was* he? Now that she'd given him all a woman could, was he going back on his word? Her heart caught on the terrible possibility. Had he taken her for a fool after all, enjoyed her and then gone off forever to Plymouth or God knows where? Or worse, broken the other promise and now lay in prison or dead on some road?

She dare not think of that. Jason lived and could never be false. Besides, she reasoned with feminine practicality, there was no Dorchester coach of a Sunday. He had a horse, but that old cob did well to make it from Cheselbourne to Whitechurch without needing a rest. She lingered behind her parents after the benediction and prayed on her knees in Lady Chapel. *Mother, make him come. Please let him be waiting for me. If he doesn't come, I'll hate him full as much as I love him now. Yet let him be safe. He's a clever one with a swift wit but not always wise, and he can't outwit a bullet.*

Shaken by the force of her emotions, Bess hurriedly murmured the usual beseechments on behalf of her parents, then walked alone and troubled out of the church only to find Tim waiting by the door. Bess drew her breath through clenched teeth. She didn't need this, not today. "What is it then?"

"I'll see you home."

"No need."

She started away but Tim caught her wrist hard. "What you said this morning—"

"Let me go."

He held her fast. "That about marrying him. It ain't going to be, Bess Whateley."

"May God damn you!" Suddenly savage, Bess twisted free and scooped up one of the whitewashed stones bordering the path, holding it high and threatening. "You listen, Tim Groot. Don't trouble me today. Not today, you hear? And you'll not touch me again or I'll tell Papa, and he'll sack you sure. Now shag *off.*"

Brimming with furious tears, Bess dropped the stone, snatched up her skirts, and ran down the churchyard path, cursing Tim for being there, damning Jason for not when she needed him most—

Only to see him standing near the inn's front door, smiling and talking to her parents as if he hadn't kept her in an agony all morning. He opened his arms as Bess hurled herself into them with a million silent thanks to Mary.

"I'm sorry a thousand times, Bess."

"Where *were* you? I waited and waited—"

"Well, I was just telling your folk."

"And look how I wore your ribbon just for you."

"Flat truth? I'm ashamed to say I overslept."

Bess wondered whether to kiss or kill the impossible man. "You—what?"

"So he did," her father confirmed.

And then that charmingly innocent smile of his that could wring forgiveness from the Devil. "No excuse, love, but here I've been asking of your dad."

"Inside, both of you," Jedediah invited with a twinkle. "I'll not stand in the hot sun to give my daughter's hand. Inside for a glass of the best."

Bess searched her parents' faces. They looked anything but dubious. "You've asked?"

Her mother nodded. "He has, like a proper man."

"And has my permission," Jedediah decreed, quite magisterial. "Your mother and I have thought it out before this." He clasped Jason's hand on a bargain. "Bess could do no better. Now let's drink to the wedding."

Yet they hung back when the Whateleys went in. Bess crushed her mouth to Jason's fiercely and then bit his ear.

"Ow!"

"There's for you, Mr. Quick." She hooked a possessive arm through his. "Do you know how afeared I was when you didn't come? How long it took putting up my hair with your ribbon? And you, you lout, lie abed on a day like this? 'Struth, I'd say go to the Devil, save I'm sure he'd take you."

"Bess, darling," Jason murmured close to her ear. "It is a lovely truth that you wore me out last night."

She ducked her head not to show how pleased that made her. "I would blush, but I'm too angry."

"When you know how much I need you?"

The tension of the terrible morning melted out of Bess. She wilted with relief and fatigue, wanting only to be held in his arms or find a soft chair and not move for the rest of the day. "I know, Jason, but I've not had the best day God ever sent me."

"The rest will be better. Come, your father's waiting."

In an expansive mood, Jedediah produced a bottle of Spanish sherris and poured liberally. " 'Tisn't every day I give away a daughter. To Bess's happiness and yours, Jason. And health to you both."

"And fine, sturdy children," Anne Whateley amended, wondering mildly if one were not already on the way.

"Thank you, Papa."

"And I thank you, sir."

"None of this 'sir,' lad." Jedediah clapped Jason on the back. "You'll be calling me Father soon enough."

The word stuck in Jason's throat while Abraham Quick wasted in servitude. Was he ill? Was the blighted bastard who bought seven precious years of his life working him too hard and fast toward death as a common laborer?

Jason raised his glass to Mr. Whateley. "I could find no better."

The wine went round again. Jason offered to pay for the wedding, but Jedediah Whateley would have none of that. From first to last, Bess's wedding would be his pleasure, by God.

On their third glass the talk fragmented. Jedediah waxed sentimental to Jason over his daughter and inquired of his prospects in the colonies. Bess and her mother talked of a trousseau. Anne's own gown, packed away for years in lavender, might well be cut down for slender Bess, but they'd be off to Dorchester for patterns and fabrics and a whirl of happy things to do. A September date was set for the wedding, and then they would sail for America at the soonest date afterward.

Wine-warmed and happy, Jason leaned back against the bar,

only half listening to Jedediah. All through the grim year that saw his father filthy and in chains, the hair's-breadth months with Owen Jones, the life-or-death chances taken on the road, to this incredible moment holding out to him a shining new existence. He couldn't begin to share this with Jedediah. The man simply would not understand as Bess did.

And yet last night, taking her maidenhood, he'd given in return his promise to lay the Golden Fleecer to rest. She wanted that more than anything. Certainly Roddy Hallow wouldn't mind if that thorn were removed from his side, thirty-five guineas or no. But something about the promise bothered Jason, and all the more because he couldn't tell *why*. Poverty for him had not lasted long, true, but like an adder's bite, struck its poison deep, and under his vow of *no more* sounded the insistent litany of *not enough*.

He really should listen to Bess and Abel. They had enough to make do until he found Abraham, but . . .

One more. One more fat as the last.

"Jason?"

"Mm? Sorry, I drifted off a bit. Must be this excellent wine."

"I said you must stay for a bite now and supper later."

"Supper gladly, but Abel has the rheumatism in his knees again, and I promised to lunch with him."

"Bring him back for supper," Bess said, taking his face in her hands. "You are promised to me now. In every way, Jason Quick, and you must keep your vows."

"So I will," he said and suddenly meant it all in a rush of joy. "You here and your father and mother. I didn't believe I could ever be this content."

"Listen to him," Bess jeered. "Merely content?"

"Happiness is moments, love. Like this. Content is longer and deeper."

If Bess was too young to appreciate the distinction, Anne Whateley could. "You're older than your years, Jason."

"I had to be, Mrs. Whateley."

When he took his leave Bess caught him at the door, whispering a world of meaning in his ear. "Promised, I said. As you love me, Jason."

As he loved her? Happy and feeling almost innocent, Jason whistled his way to the stable, nothing on his mind beyond the wonder of a girl who loved him, and to persuade the Dewlish apothecary to open briefly so he could buy poultice makings and vinegar for Abel's rheumatism. As he stepped out of the sun into the stable's shadow, he was struck a stunning blow on the back of the head and sent sprawling to the stable floor.

"Get up, lily-boy," the toneless voice pierced his dizziness. "I'm about to teach you good."

Jason blinked, struggling to clear his head. He recognized the ostler's voice. Tim must have used his bare hand, and that more than twice enough. A club swung with such strength would have smashed his skull. Unlit Leicester Place flashed darkly across memory: Dim faces hovering over him, fists and heavy boots breaking his ribs. His vision still swam as he managed to rise to one knee, hands in the dirt steadying him. Tim Groot hovered two paces away, fists up, coiled to attack.

"An . . . an historic moment, Timmy. I'm not easily surprised."

Tim's reddened eyes were pure hate. "I taught that Evan Bromley, and him twice your size."

Jason backed toward his horse. "From behind, I imagine."

"You fancy son of—"

Tim never finished the sentiment. As he sprang, Jason flung the handful of dirt and chaff in his eyes. Tim stumbled, wiping desperately to clear his sight. He heard the high-pitched neigh of Jedediah's frightened mare and then, clearly, the sharp click of a pistol cocked.

"You've taught me your lesson," Jason said coldly. "Never turn my back on a snake."

His eyes were still gritty but Tim could see a little now. Jason was mounted, the pistol leveled at him. "Back away, Mr. Groot. Clear of the door, if you will."

The ploy and the pistol snatched from his saddlebag had been sheer instinct. Looking down at Tim, Jason could not find it in his heart to hate the ostler, but no man would break his bones again. "No need to ask the why of this, but if you try it another time the law will deal with you."

Tim's ropy arms raised, trembling and tense, then chopped down in a torment of frustration. "You got no *right* here."

"If you mean Bess—"

"I seen you with her up the lane."

Jason turned his horse toward the door. "And she's suffered your attentions more than once, I gather. A real piece of work you are, Timmy. Bess and I are to marry in September. You'll hear the first banns read on Sunday next. Accept that or not and be damned to you."

Never spoke the word to her, never thought it out, but he did love Bess, and Tim had wept hunched down in one of the empty stalls, pounding rage and loss into his bony knees. He wasn't used to *feeling* so much, but now he was sick with so much churning inside.

He didn't believe Bess when she told him—then, word by horrible word, her standing there talking back to him calm and serious, he had to, and belief turned too real and bright when he thought of her and that Quick going up the lane last night. Tim didn't want to see that in his mind. They would marry. Bess said it first and then Quick. Married in a month. He had to accept but couldn't ever. His rage didn't bleed out with his tears but grew and heated as his fists drummed on his knees. He felt the impossibility, what they said was going to happen but couldn't, not if Tim Groot had a say, but what could he do? *Would be* was one wall, *could not* another, hemming him helpless as a close-hobbled horse in a barred stall.

He wasn't dumb like Bess thought he was. Damned snip, she always had airs like she thought she was so much better than him or anyone else, nor her folk didn't help much, mother always telling her how pretty she was. So she was and worked hard, but so did everyone else in Whitechurch. Just that old Gant filling her head with tales of princes and princesses and what all. Sometimes Tim wanted to shout at her flat out: *It ain't like that. Ain't no people like that, just us, and this is what we are. You'll marry me and birth my babies and help me in the Shilling, and that's all there is.*

A long mile from stupid was Timmy Groot, though nobody looked at him twice or asked his mind on any matter. He wouldn't have hurt Bess's lily-boy bad enough to fetch a sheriff, just a right hiding like he gave Evan Bromley, enough to make Quick remember. What ate at him as much as Bess betrothed was the way the bastard tricked him with dirt in the eyes and the pistol that surprised Tim more than scared him; it threw him off balance. Quick with his small white hands with nary a hint of honest dirt under the nails, you wouldn't think of him owning a pistol, let alone carrying one. But there it was.

Good job this was Sunday with no coaches or trade. He had enough to think on without others to hinder him. Tim clawed up straw from the stall floor, grasping and hurling it away to the slow, deliberate beat of his thoughts. Married in September, was it? A month and some away. Come what might, one way or other, that was not about to be.

No question of fair play with a man like Quick who took Bess up the lane before marrying. *His* Bess. What could be done? Tim thought so hard that concentrating became a pain between his eyes. Bess with her head full of nonsense and Quick on his high horse from the first night he came. Suppose a body shot that horse out from under him? Tim folded long arms around his knees, glowering and searching beyond the stall gate for answers. Quick threatened to have the law on him? How could a man turn that law around and get someone he hated so deep in trouble that Jason Quick would have no chance to marry anyone for a long time?

Come to that, now: What did he or anyone really know of the man? He came out of the night into the King's Shilling, just passing through to Plymouth. And didn't Tim himself point out to that sergeant how Quick was the only stranger about? Quick always wore fine clothes and had plenty of money without turning his hand to a lick of work, always buying things for Bess like that foolish bit of red ribbon.

Whateley's old carriage hack nickered in her stall. What with the morning's tribulations, Tim hadn't grained her. Besides, he was tired of thinking so hard, but short of murdering Jason Quick himself—by damn he would if he dared—he had to do something soon.

Granted the Lord worked in mysterious ways, but Tim never expected prayers angry as his to be answered so quickly. The following morning, Monday, was hot and astir with coaches rolling in from Blandford or eastbound from Dorchester, the inn humming like a hive with travelers, Bess running from the outside tables to bar, kitchen and back, and Tim with his hands too full of horses to notice if she ignored him or not. About one of the afternoon when he was sweating and rank as the coach teams, a private soldier trotted his lathered gelding into the stableyard and dismounted gingerly, handing the reins to Tim.

"Half a mo'," the soldier rasped, obviously spent. He flexed his shoulders with a gasp of effort, dropping his head down on the saddle in exhaustion.

"I'm Bell, Fifty-fourth down St. Andrew," he mumbled. "Christ but it's hot. Give'm some water, not too much, but walk him first. I need a beer."

"Been riding some then?"

Bell didn't look up or move at all. "Some and then some." He straightened slowly, stiff as an old man with the ague, and pawed a printed sheet from his saddlebag. "All morning up and down the shire posting these. Damned reward rises faster than Dorchester can print 'em."

Tim couldn't read letters, but the £40 leaped out in large type. "Reward?"

Bell thrust the poster into his face. "Don't it say? Forty pounds on the Golden Fleecer." He winced again. "Jesus and Mary . . ."

Bell wilted once more against his saddle, half turned away from Tim, who now saw the dark stains on his red coat. "You got blood on your back."

"Don't I just," Bell muttered tightly. "Ten with the cat o' nine and ordered to ride today just to salt the lesson in. Walk the horse."

He lurched away toward the inn door. Tim turned the gelding into the lane and walked it twice to the church and back, allowing it half a bucket of water before the soldier returned. Private Bell seemed a little better for a bite and beer. When he gave the ostler tuppence, Tim judged him a halfway decent fellow. Too many didn't bother.

"There's for your trouble," Bell said. He laid a reluctant hand on the pommel, in no haste to mount again.

Tim guessed the tuppence earned a friendly word. "What they flog you for?"

Bell looked like a young man aged too quickly in days. He put one foot in the stirrup but hesitated, steeling himself for what mounting would cost his flayed back. "Three of us on detail down Blandford St. Mary Saturday to fetch the officers' pay. Ruttin' Fleecer foxed us, caught us off guard. Got away with the money and coach, even our muskets."

Two images flickered in Tim's mind, the shadowy shape of the highwayman and, more vividly, the unimaginable sum of forty pounds. A man could live a year on that and show Bess Whateley how Quick wasn't the only one with money. "They give you ten lashes for that?"

"Ten?" Bell sucked in breath and heaved himself into the saddle. "You muck up bad enough, they'll give you a thousand. Seen it myself. Man died halfway through. Soames and me were lucky. Just ten apiece. Danny Winner got twenty and his stripes torn off, poor sod. Well—got two or three of these to deliver yet. Not they'll ever catch the scut."

A few minutes after Bell departed, Bess hurried out with Tim's lunch wrapped in linen and a mug of ale, barely looking at him before scampering back to work. Tim munched thyme-seasoned chicken while trying to remember what the sight of her vaguely recalled to mind. Something she said. He was halfway through his ale when the thought focused clearly. Her red ribbon. She said Quick bought it for her in Blandford St. Mary.

Tim chewed the thought and his food slowly. Saturday, the soldier said; the Fleecer robbed them on Saturday, and Bess told him yesterday Quick bought her ribbon in the same place. He frowned over the remains of his meal. Damn, she didn't say just *when*. Could have been any time in the last week. Quick often took the coach to Blandford Forum.

Except . . .

Except Tim never saw Bess wear the ribbon until yesterday morning a-milking.

Well, now.

Tim's frown lightened to a faint smile as he congratulated his own cleverness. He couldn't point a finger at Quick for sure, nor could even he believe lily-boy and the Fleecer one and the same. But the man carried a pistol and was in Blandford St. Mary on or close to the same day as the Fleecer. Close enough, perhaps, for the provost to be sniffing about, calling Quick down St. Andrew or even Dorchester. Enough to trouble him considerable with questions. That would take a tuck in any wedding plans, and Bess and her folk thinking twice about marrying Mr. Jason bleedin' Quick.

Tim finished his ale, quite pleased with himself.

"Squad—shun! Shoulder arms. Right—wait for't, you donkeys—turn!"

The drill corporal's commands pounded out over the barracks square as Sergeant Roddy Hallow and Private Daniel Winner walked toward Hallow's quarters. Their progress was too slow for Hallow's long stride, but every step pained Danny, whose only stripes now crisscrossed his raw back. Court-martialed for negligence, broken and stretched over the flogging rack for ten laid over ten. As for Billy Bell and Francis Soames, they'd head every fatigue list, standing guard and mucking out latrines until their enlistments expired.

Major Sedgewick's orders, not Roddy Hallow's. The corporal in charge of pay detail should have been more careful, but Danny Winner was a friend for all of that and needed fresh ointment to his back. This being Sunday, the surgeon and his orderlies off post, Hallow would do a friend's office in private.

"No need for any of 'em to see, Danny. You been shamed enough."

In his quarters he let Winner lie on his belly on the bunk while he applied the ointment gently as possible.

"I want to be there when we get him," Danny Winner prayed fervently. "I want that little bugger personal."

"That's a place you paid for. Least you got a good look at him."

"Ah, what look? A wig and most of his phiz wrapped in a toothache bandage—ow! Go easy, Roddy."

"Sorry, Dan."

"One thing sure," Winner said. "He's a young one. Too young for a rum business like that. Toff accent. You know: veddy-veddy."

And smart, Hallow reaffirmed grudgingly. The accent was surely false as all the others reported by witnesses as the voice of the Fleecer, who must be like to one of them weird lizards Hallow heard of that changed to whatever color it rested on. Most highwaymen didn't last long. Sedgewick would be hanging one in a week or so, which was about as long as the fool had lasted on the roads around Dorchester before they caught him. That kind was greedy and spendthrift alike, too loud and flash, throwing money around on public houses and whores soon as they grabbed it. But now in early August a week and some had passed without a hint of the Fleecer anywhere.

"He's layin' doggo, Danny."

"Think he's gone from the shire then?"

"Could be, but if he's still about, he'll come out. Likely he don't fancy hot weather no more than us, and then we'll get him, you and me."

Winner passionately craved the comfort of that prediction. "If he's gone, no forty quid."

Hallow would turn Catholic before losing that. Every man in the St. Andrew detachment and some in Dorchester barracks wanted a piece of the reward. Some must go to Danny, that being only fair, but added to sergeant major's pay, the balance would set Roddy Hallow up for the comfortable rest of his life.

He finished with Winner's back. "There. Up you go and into your shirt."

Hallow held the garment open while Winner eased into it as if his back might explode if he exerted too much force. Someone rapped at the door.

"Come," Hallow ordered.

The opened door revealed Private Soames sweating in full kit. "Eh, Danny. How's your back?"

"How's yours?"

"Like I'm fried on the Devil's own stove."

"What is it, Soames? I'm busy," the sergeant prompted.

"Fellow out here from Whitechurch, Sarn't. Says he has to speak with you. 'Bout the robbery."

Hallow and Winner exchanged hopeful glances. Folk had been questioned everywhere but none had come forward before. "Get him in here."

"All contributions welcomed with thanks," said Danny Winner.

Hallow recognized the young man who slipped in and hovered before them, uneasy in this strange place of authority, his hands twisting a hat already shapeless with dirt, sweat, and time. "You're the ostler at the King's Shilling."

"Aye, sir. Timothy Groot."

"Well?"

"That forty pound go to anyone catches the Golden Fleecer?"

As if this stableman who couldn't even look Hallow in the face was apt to such. "Fancy getting it, do you?"

Tim wrung his hat again. "Not sure, mind . . ."

Winner sighed and turned away. "A world of help at the start."

"Could be I know who he is."

Hallow waited. "Well?"

"Like I said, I ain't sure."

The state of Winner's back was not conducive to tolerance. "Think you might know before we throw you out?"

Tim's eyes darted nervously from Winner to Hallow and dropped again. "Jason Quick."

Roddy Hallow guffawed. "Quick? That sickly toff from London? He's a droopin' little blossom. What put that notion in your noodle?"

"Nothin's right about him," Tim mumbled. "Doesn't work but always got money."

"Little lads like him live off their fathers," Hallow said. "Plain starve did they not. Right then, you think it's him. Ever see him ride a big Cleveland bay?"

Tim did not. Only a plain old cob.

Winner remembered something else. "Does he dip snuff?"

"Never saw that neither," Tim admitted, already discouraged by their disbelief. "Nor a pipe."

"For a man who thinks Quick is one thing, I'm getting a lot of the other, Ostler."

"He lives down Cheselbourne but sups most every night at the

Shilling," Tim insisted, adding morosely, " 'n walks out Sundays with Bess."

"Who? Oh, right." The landlord's girl, Hallow recalled. Sweet piece, that. He hadn't made his rank being dense. He marked the ostler's manner and tone mentioning the girl. Perhaps Quick was poaching what this stableman considered his preserve. Who wouldn't? That still didn't make Quick the Fleecer. "Well, what else does this desperate character do? Throw his money around, brag somethin' chronic?"

The ostler was beginning to look more uncertain, even miserable. "No. Quiet like. Some nights he plays chess with old Gant from Dewlish."

"Probably sews too," Winner quipped. "What else?"

Hallow knew Quick's soft kind. "Whatever money he's got is on his back. Enough schooling to put on airs, but he'd faint at sight of a gun."

Tim's head came up in sharp denial. "No, by damn!"

"What?"

"We had a—a set-to in the stable. He threw dirt in my eyes, 'n when I could see, there's a gun in his hand."

"Mm?" Hallow worked yellow teeth over his lower lip. After the pay robbery Major Sedgewick was proper frothing at the mouth. Right now any suspect was better than none to show him Roddy Hallow was far from idle in the matter. "All right, Ostler. We'll look into Mr. Quick. Now you cut along home."

Tim stood his ground. "Sir, there's somethin' else, and this for sure. Bess said he was down Blandford St. Mary last week."

"When we were robbed?" Winner shot at him. "Saturday a week?"

Tim nodded too eagerly. "Could have been."

"Not good enough," Winner said.

" 'Struth, sir. Bess Whateley told me Quick bought her a red ribbon in Blandford St. Mary. Nor I never seen her wear it before that Sunday." Tim drew himself up with all the dignity he could muster, raising his right hand. "Lord strike me dead."

"All right. Go on now." Hallow reckoned the ostler had told all he knew of value, and his presence in the room did not sweeten the close August air. "We'll talk to Quick."

The ostler still didn't budge. The hat writhed in his hands. "That 'ere forty pounds. How much of that would I get?"

Hallow shrugged. "Hard to say. Much as you deserve, I reckon. If you're right. Danny, show'm out."

When he closed the door after Tim Groot, Danny Winner grinned coldly. "Just a good honest citizen doin' his bit. Whew! Bet that one ain't washed since I was last to church."

Hallow picked up Winner's uniform coat and held it open. "On you go. Think hard now, Danny. Didn't you get any sort of clear squint at the Fleecer?"

"None of us paid him much mind. Buck teeth, homely and foolish like all them bought subalterns. Dipped snuff real elegant."

"Think you could look at Quick and say for certain?"

Danny Winner was sure only of the torture crawling like fire over his back, eased a little under the ointment but still bad enough to make donning his coat an act of penance. "I just *said*, Roddy. I don't know."

They had to know soon. One more foray by the Fleecer and Sedgewick wouldn't wait to break Roddy Hallow, and that would be his lot. He still couldn't pair the image of Jason Quick with the Fleecer, even with the ostler's story of the gun. More men in Dorset owned pistols than did not, and as Hallow measured men, Quick lacked the sand in his craw for robbery. Nevertheless he'd be off to Dorchester to see Major Sedgewick when he could. And tomorrow or so—casual like, nothing official—he and Danny would happen in at the King's Shilling for supper.

About five of the clock two evenings later, Hallow and Winner drove a carriage and team the three miles to Whitechurch and the King's Shilling. Tim hurried out of the stable, bobbing obsequiously to Hallow. "Just lead them in out of the sun," the sergeant directed. "Maybe a bit of water."

"Yes, sir. Right this way, sir."

"Is Quick here?"

"Inside, sir."

Roddy Hallow couldn't help disliking the ostler. His loutish subservience barely masking his eagerness to do in Jason Quick faintly disgusted the older man. "Don't call me sir," he said curtly. "I ain't no officer and wouldn't be one for double pay. Which is his horse?"

The cob stood in the last stall down, staring placidly at nothing. "His gun's in the saddlebag," Tim volunteered. "I looked."

Hallow reached into the bag and withdrew a silver-mounted pistol.

"That's the one," Tim pointed. "That's the very one he held on me, God's truth."

With a glance at the priming pan, Hallow cocked the weapon. "Like this?"

He took aim at Tim's chest and pulled the trigger. Tim's body instinctively contracted as the hammer fell on the pan with a sharp clack. "Cor! Watch it!"

"Why? Ain't loaded." Hallow flipped the gun, catching it by the barrel. He sniffed at the priming pan: not fired at all recently. "Most like empty when he turned it on you. Come on, Danny."

Serving tables in the inn yard, Bess saw the soldiers drive in and ducked inside at her first opportunity. Jason sat alone at a corner table in his shirtsleeves, absorbed in an after-dinner game of solitaire. He signaled Bess with his ale mug. She drew it quickly and set it before him.

"Careful," she murmured. "Soldiers. That big sergeant."

"Roddy Hallow." Jason turned over a red five and placed it on a black six. "Lovely chap. Not to worry."

But Bess couldn't help herself. Soldiers always made her nervous, and Hallow's lot were little better than the dregs they jailed or hanged. She worried all the more today with Jason here. Bess prayed fervently that he'd kept his promise, that the Fleecer was gone forever. She made a swift, whispering circuit of the other customers—"Soldiers"—for those who wished to leave for their own reasons. One or two quickly paid their reckoning and slipped out through the bar's side door.

Bess's stomach twisted tight when she recognized the man with Hallow, the one on the pay detail to St. Mary. Lord, he would know Jason sure. *Please no, God, please.* She held her breath as they went to stand directly over him. Bess busied herself wiping down an empty table nearby but listened sharply.

Hallow set the pistol before Jason. "Evenin,' Mr. Quick."

"Ah. Provost Hallow, and a fine evening indeed. A bit hot."

"Your pistol, I believe."

As Bess watched covertly, the other man moved casually to place himself directly in front of Jason, boxing him in.

"Oh, that was in my saddlebag?" Jason seemed surprised. "Lud, but I forgot it was there."

"The ostler said you flashed it on him."

"Had to, sorry. He attacked me, frightened me half to death, but I bluffed him down."

Bess could have kicked him. *Why?* she demanded fiercely. *Why did you leave the damned thing in your bag?*

"Was it empty then too?" Hallow pressed.

"Sink me, I suppose so." Jason shrugged with careless innocence. "Last time I tried to load it, the demmed thing went off. Almost blew my foot off. Don't even know why I bought it."

Winner produced a snuffbox from his vest pocket. "Why did you, if we might ask?"

"I was advised so for traveling from London."

"Expensive piece." Hallow's finger traced the silver-inlaid initials. "Who might A. D. be?"

"Haven't the faintest, Sergeant. Bought it from a pawnbroker in Queen Street, London."

"Word o' caution, Mr. Quick." Hallow sounded friendly

enough, but Bess read the sharp vigilance in his eyes. "A man of your delicate nature best leave it empty or sell it. And don't go scaring any more ostlers."

Winner tapped his snuffbox, opened it, and took a pinch to his nose, politely offering the box to Jason. "Have a dip, sir?"

"Thanks but no. My mother never objected to spirits in moderation, but she regarded tobacco as the Devil's weed."

Winner canted his head at the solitaire cards. "Eh, you've put the knave of clubs top've the spade queen."

"Oh? So I did." Jason laughed and wiped his forehead with a handkerchief. "Can't keep my mind on anything when the weather's this warm."

"That's all, sir. Sorry to trouble you. Danny, find us a table." Hallow signaled to Bess. "We'll have supper, girl. Heard you set a fine table here."

Bess forced a smile and curtsied. "Finest in the shire, sir."

They chose a table across the room. As soon as Bess took their supper orders to the kitchen, she returned to Jason, swabbing the table edge with a cloth. "They looked at you very queer, love. You've not gone back on your word behind my back, have you?"

Jason turned up and discarded a ten. "I have not."

Still Bess felt uneasy. "You promised. Don't be foolish now when we're so close to what we want."

"Bess, my bride-to-be, mother of my children—do you see the black knave on a black queen?"

"That's careless too."

"No, that's cheating, but it is the worst sin on my soul since my promise to you." Jason captured her hand in his. "Where can we meet tonight?"

Bess gave the table a last flick of her cloth, not to be put off with charm. "You great fool, why did you leave the gun where they could find it?"

"Bess, I flat forgot." Jason turned up another card. "But a good job I had it when Tim came at me. I don't think he wants to come to our wedding. What about tonight?"

Bess sighed. What with running back and forth in the heat all day, she felt distinctly gritty. "Oh, I'll be hot and wilted and smell of the kitchen."

"You'll be roses." Jason pursed his lips to her in a silent kiss. "Where?"

"Churchyard I guess."

"Aye, bring a blanket then, pray for no rain, and I'll make such love to you as will make your beautiful head swim."

"He's courtin' the girl for sure. Old Whateley said they're to marry next month." And that, for Roddy Hallow, summed up the questionable value of their visit as he drove the carriage home toward Milborne St. Andrew through summer twilight. "You got a good look at him, Danny. Still not sure?"

Winner's back was a fading misery, but he thanked Hallow silently for avoiding the worst ruts in the road. "He's the same age, right enough, and he was sitting, but he seems a mite taller than the one at St. Mary. That 'un kind of stooped a bit. And the shape of Quick's face is different. Then the snuffbox."

"What about it?"

Danny Winner was rather proud of that ploy. "Roddy, I've dipped snuff for years, and it stains anything white. You mark that lace jabot on Quick? Clean as a bride's nightgown. He don't use it habitual."

Maybe the trip had been worth it, Hallow concluded, even if he was no surer one way or the other about Jason Quick, and the stupid ostler's suspicions he put down to jealousy over the girl. He wished he'd commanded the pay detail himself, being a man who remembered names, faces, and conversations. Quick said he did his banking in Blandford Forum. Close enough to the village of St. Mary. Hallow had thoughtfully sent a request to Major Sedgewick for an officer with full provost authority to find Quick's bank and note the size and details of his account. Probably that wouldn't prove anything either—but no stone unturned, as the saying went.

That night, as Jason loved Bess under the churchyard yews, Roddy Hallow found it too hot and his mind too busy to fall asleep easily. Major Sedgewick was due to inspect his detachment the following day and sure to demand his progress in tracking down the Fleecer. The matter had grown larger than any guessed. Since the pay robbery, officers of the Fifty-fourth, including the colonel and Major Sedgewick, had not seen a penny, and the quartermaster went begging for winter equipment.

Hallow sighed windily and turned on his back to stare morosely at the ceiling, tired of turning the problem over and over with no solution in sight. Gloomily he had to admit that Jason Quick was no more likely a suspect than the poor bumbling sod due to hang outside Crown Court in Dorchester day after next.

To hell with that for now. Sedgewick would find Hallow's detachment turned out sharp, every man's kit spotless, coatees, vests, and breeches brushed, brass shined, shoes and muskets clean enough to lick cream off. Quarters swept out, latrines emptied, guard details turned out fine enough to honor the king. Satisfied there at least, Hallow closed his eyes and let his thoughts drift at last toward sleep. He chuckled softly at the last image from the day: a private down on his knees in the guard room, baiting traps for mice that stubbornly refused to leave or be caught. Alternate bits of cheese, one for him, one for the mouse, one for him . . .

He woke in the small hours as the guard relief tramped by his open window. Hallow blinked his eyes into focus, then suddenly sat bolt upright in bed.

"Yes," he exulted to the darkness. "Yes."

Some part of his mind must have worried at the problem in

sleep. He swung long legs onto the floor and reached for the whiskey jug kept close to help him doze off, but now he was wide awake, hearing the receding tread of the guard, thoughts not racing but clear, methodically arranging the parts of inspiration like building blocks. Fortune dropped a bundle in his lap, and Roddy Hallow had to go to sleep to find it, a plan to keep Sedgewick off his back until a better mousetrap came to mind. And it just might work.

He poured a little water into the whiskey, sipped and smiled with self-satisfaction. Two weeks and more, almost three without a sign of the Golden Fleecer. If Jason Quick was their man — *Right, and I'm King George*— he would have to be caught in the act like that fool at Dorchester, and so they would.

Forty pounds . . .

The next afternoon was hot and humid when Major Sedgewick inspected the ranks, but the sweat rolled down clean, close-shaven cheeks. Only one man was faulted for squirming while at attention.

"You there!" Sedgewick barked. "Stop fidgeting. Name?"

"Private Winner, Daniel, oh-one-six, *sah!*"

"Why can't you stand still?"

"It's his back, sir." At the officer's elbow, Sergeant Hallow refreshed his memory softly. "Flogged and broken for negligence. Your order, sir."

"Oh. Yes." They moved on down the rank.

Sedgewick poked into everything without finding too much fault, though it was clear to Hallow the major had other matters on his mind. When Sedgewick suggested they retire to the relative cool of Hallow's quarters, the sergeant was sure of it. But this time he was prepared.

"Deuced hot." Harold Sedgewick slipped off his wig with visible relief and removed his coat. "We can dispense with formality for the time, Roddy. Sit down."

"Thank you, sir." Hallow remained standing out of habit.

Sedgewick cast his eyes about. The room was cooler than the

parade square but still close and whining with flies. "Er . . . may I trouble you for something to drink?"

"Whiskey and water, sir," Hallow offered, glad for an excuse for a drop himself. "Takes the curse off the heat."

"Splendid." While Hallow poured two glasses, Sedgewick scratched vigorously at his short, coppery hair. Light-complexioned, heat bothered him more than darker men. Hallow remembered he'd been down with it twice on Gibraltar. "Your men are well turned out, Roddy. They look smart. Now—"

He took the offered drink from Hallow, who puzzled at the sudden relaxation of class barriers between them. Unnatural by his lights. He felt distinctly awkward when he should muster all his persuasion. "Your very good health, Major."

"Thank you. Oh yes, on your request I sent Lieutenant Greenleaf to Blandford. Regent's bank has an opulent twelve pounds odd on account for this Quick."

"That's all, sir?"

"Quite all. If he's the Fleecer, he must keep the swag under his bed."

Another dead end but no real surprise. " 'Twas worth a go, sir."

"Yes, yes." Sedgewick set down his glass. "The commanding general is appalled by the business at St. Mary. When the general is displeased, our colonel is unhappy with me, and where can I turn but to you?"

Hallow braced himself for an arse-chewing—but perhaps not with the trump hand he was ready to play. "Major, I can catch the Fleecer."

"Gratifying. Why haven't you?"

" 'Cause we're goin' about it all wrong, sir. What's the name of the man going to swing in Dorchester tomorrow?"

"Uh . . . Parsons. Yes, Enoch Parsons. A pity he leaves a widow."

"How old would you make him?"

"How old? Demmed if I know. Near to forty or beyond. Said he was out of work and desperate."

"But he ain't the Fleecer," Hallow said firmly.

"Oh, really? Many folk around Dorchester are sure he is. Court was jammed with 'em."

"That's the one thing Danny—Private Winner—was sure of. Our man's a young one. But let 'em all think what they will. Parsons is a bleedin' godsend."

"What on earth—?"

"He'll swing anyway," Hallow rushed on. "Let him hang in West High Street with a sign namin' him the Fleecer."

"Roddy, come *on.*" Sedgewick batted a fly away from his perspiring cheek. "What good there? The real Fleecer will know for a start we've bungled."

"So he will, sir." Hallow drained his glass and straddled a chair in front of the major. "And I'll have the reward posters took down. If the bastard's gone from the shire, so's our problem."

"And if he isn't?"

"He may feel safe enough to have another go if the bait's rich enough." Hallow lifted the jug. "Another tot, sir?"

"Thanks, no. Bait?"

"Young and smart, that 'un. He's laid doggo since St. Mary, nor he don't bother the Royal Mail anymore. No, Major, it's my thinking he's a johnny what calculates profit oughter be big as the risk. Like pay boxes." Roddy Hallow paused to give his point emphasis. "Real fat ones."

Sedgewick studied him silently, but Hallow couldn't divine his thoughts. Like all his rich class, Sedgewick had that frosty-eyed aloofness about him, even though distance had been supposedly put aside. But he surprised the sergeant, holding out his glass.

"Believe I will take a drop more, Sergeant. You've good taste in spirits. And just what sort of bait had you in mind?"

Hallow did new honors with the jug for both of them. "For a start, sir, I'll need you to be writing something for me. Something official and proper."

Quickly he outlined what had taken him an hour to refine

before dawn and felt vindicated thoroughly when Sedgewick not only agreed but admired his thinking.

"Provost Roddy, you are a far more efficient policeman than I ever dreamed."

Damned right. Hallow stoppered the jug with inward glee. He would make sergeant major yet. "My thanks, sir. My old dad, rest his worked-out soul, was a laborer down Bournemouth. Sweated cruel hard for four shillin's a week. More'n once some counterfeit got put in his hand, and we went that hungry. I'll take the Lord on faith, sir, but nobody else."

Sunday again. Jason woke and stretched, feeling capital. Sundays had resolved to a pleasant ritual: breakfast with Abel at Dewlish, church with Bess, and the rest of the day for the two of them together. Jason lay, hands behind his head, enjoying the memory of Bess after services, kneeling alone in the Lady Chapel, opening her heart's secrets and deepest wishes to the mother of Jesus. She never shared these communings with him, and Jason was possessive enough to be curious. Did Bess find some fault with him worthy of heaven's consideration? Foolish question. She loved him completely, and after all a woman's secrets enhanced the magic of her.

He usually took only tea on waking, a safe choice since tea was one of the few things the Crown and Thistle kitchen couldn't desecrate. Rose was late with it this morning. He was up, washed, and mostly dressed before, without her usual rap, the door flew open. Rose stood there, no tea tray in her hands but a whiskey and a dangerous glint in her eyes.

Her rude familiarity annoyed Jason. "I didn't hear you knock. Has the custom lapsed? Is my tea hot?"

Rose glared. "Bugger your tea."

Lord, what now? "Isn't it a bit early for spirits?"

"Bugger that too. Little enough I'm paid for all I do, so I'll have a bit of my own back when I choose."

"Quite. The landlord should do penance for his wretched cuisine."

Rose leaned back against the door, but hardly relaxed, her voice tightly controlled. Her whole mien seethed like a kettle close to boil. Her eyes never left his. "You're the slippery one, Quick," she breathed with venomous wonder. "Slippery with truth as you are with words. Guess who was in for a drop and a chat last night."

Jason sensed a confrontation he would rather avoid. He'd known Rose Allen's passion and anger alike, both elemental as a storm. "Can't imagine."

"Timothy Groot."

"Indeed. No doubt he mentioned our misunderstanding."

"Didn't he just." Rose took an ample swallow of whiskey and wiped full lips on the back of her hand. "I wouldn't think a little toff like you would have the stones to put a gun on a man," she admitted with a tinge of contempt.

"It wasn't loaded. Never is."

"Guess what else he said."

Jason buttoned his linen waistcoat. "What is it, Rose? I'm off to see a friend."

Her eyes gleamed coldly. "Right, and I know who. Bess Whateley."

"Abel Gant in Dewlish."

"But sweet Bess after, I'm bound. Tim said you're to marry her. Said your banns been read twice already. And not a word to me. Fancy that."

So that was the matter. Abel had the truth of it, Jason thought drearily as he shrugged into his coat. There were times when no man, be he wise as Solomon, could deal with women and their oblique sense of justice. *They can leave you, Jason, but God help you if you walk away from them. They cannot bear rejection.*

"The banns have been read. That's the way things stand."

"The way things stand," Rose simpered in imitation. "That weepin' story of the London girl dying of consumption. 'Oh, Rose, so much of me died with her.' And you let me make a fool of myself—You're a dirty, lying coward, Jason Quick."

"I met Bess later. Met her and fell in love with her."

"That milky little bitch?" Rose flared. "What's she got I ain't?"

"What I need," Jason affirmed quietly. "What passed between you and me—I am grateful. There was never any desire to hurt you."

Through her clenched teeth: "You lying bastard!"

"If you will," Jason conceded, wanting to be gone and done with this. "Never mind the tea. I'm late."

"Bloody well fetch it yourself from here out." Her voice broke on the curse. "*Damn* you."

While he felt nothing for her, Jason sensed pain under Rose's fury and realized truth even as he spoke it. "You're strong as a ship's cable, Rose Allen. You'll find someone. You'll get on."

Rose emptied her glass neat as a man would and drew herself up with a kind of dignity. "Stronger'n you think, Mr. Quick. Yours ain't the first bed I've warmed, or the best. But Rose Allen don't forget anything done to her. Not the smallest thing."

Not the pleasantest way to begin a Sunday, and Lord knows he held no brief with Rose. Nevertheless, planted there, accusing him with every word and look, she reminded Jason vividly of Malcolm Beedle. His thoughts churned cloudily as he tossed a sixpence to the gnarled old stableman who saddled his horse, not hearing the fellow's mumbled thanks. He rode the short mile-odd to Dewlish with questions without answers haunting his mind.

If Tim told Rose of the wedding and their fight, how much had that pit viper insinuated to Roddy Hallow? The sergeant and Winner had a good look at him this time. He'd heard how the corporal was broken and flogged. Though outwardly calm and offhand, Jason had been shocked at the sight of Daniel Winner with the darker V on his faded coat sleeve where the stripes had been. Did the man suppose? Guess?

As Jason rode he half resolved to change residence to Dewlish or even Whitechurch now, to sweep the irritation of Rose Allen from his life—but then, he reasoned, only a few weeks remained before he and Bess married. Roddy Hallow could search for the Golden Fleecer till Judgment Day; they'd be gone forever. Moving now would entail needless expense from the less than four hundred pounds tucked away in Abel's chicken house. A tidy bundle to be sure, but with no idea of colonial prices, they would need every penny. Traitorous, but his mind misgave the promise to Bess. Aye, he was done with the Fleecer, free and glad of it. Still . . . one more pull, carefully selected and planned and fat as Blandford St. Mary, would remove his last compulsive concern over enough money.

No. He'd promised. Done and done.

But the thought persisted.

Jason cantered through Sunday-quiet Dewlish, turning off onto the barely visible and seldom-used footpath that led through a stand of trees to Abel's perfectly obscured cottage. He reined in by the tumbledown shed that served as a stable. In the stall next to his teacher's cob, the magnificent Cleveland nickered in recognition as Jason led his horse in.

"Good morning, Jones." Jason fed him two big carrots plucked from Mrs. Whateley's garden, and pressed his face to the animal's forehead. "You look keen. Abel's feeding you well. Did you miss me?"

Jones crunched contentedly at his treat.

"Need a bit of a run, you do, for all this inactivity since we turned honest. Might as well before we both retire." And only fair that he return the bay to the squire at Milborne St. Andrew. Jones would be found one early morning tethered conspicuously, perhaps with a polite but anonymous note of thanks.

"We've lived well, Jones. I've profited while you left every army horse to swallow our dust. You can go home with my thanks, friend."

"Jason? I say, is that you?"

Abel loomed in the entrance, silver hair sleep-tangled, shirt-tail hanging loose over his breeches. "I overslept, but the most amazing thing has happened."

"What's amazing?"

"Wonderful!"

"What?"

Abel positively bubbled with his news. "For you in all events. I took the coach to Dorchester, you know, for my money from London. The baronet is as punctual as he is honorable. In truth, the most profitable adultery I ever—"

"Abel—what?"

His friend came back to earth. "The Fleecer is dead."

"Of course. Did I not promise Bess?"

"No, no." Abel contradicted excitedly. "*Officially* dead. Hanged and still swinging in the breeze in West High Street, deceased as Methuselah."

Jason could only stare while trying to comprehend the impossible. "Who . . . who was he?"

"I made a point of his name. Enoch Parsons, as if I could forget. Caught attempting to rob a coach outside Dorchester."

But more—and here the most marvelous luck for Jason—the man had been identified as the Golden Fleecer by a large placard nailed to the gallows post, charging him with the late affair at Blandford St. Mary and numerous robberies of the Royal Mail.

Relief and pity alike flooded through Jason. "That poor man."

"And God rest his unfortunate soul," Abel agreed, "if one has no sense of irony. Hanged alike for what he's done and what he hasn't. Justice half served but half miscarried."

He bucketed a measure of water from a barrel and presented it to Jason's cob. "Give thanks to Providence and let the Fleecer rest in peace."

"Yes, Abel." Whatever God's cryptic design, all things worked for his salvation. "Be assured of that."

A black shame nonetheless that Parsons swung for Jason's crimes as well as his own writ large for the world to mistake, but there it was. Because one felon took his last breath, Jason and Bess could breathe full free at last. He filled his lungs with summer air sweet with honeysuckle and the future.

"Yes, Abel."

Closing time Monday evening, and Jason had promised to meet her. Bess hurried through the last clearing-away in the bar and dining room, then scampered out to see, in the moonless night, the darker figure waiting by his horse just beyond the stableyard in St. Mary's Lane. She ran to him, arms open, full of the impossible news just heard.

"Jason!" Bess crushed her mouth to his in a long kiss until she had to break off for breath. "Is it true?"

"What, love?"

"I heard tonight from Mr. Jellicoe, who was to Dorchester. He said a man's been hanged for the Fleecer."

"Yes," Jason confirmed soberly. "So Abel said."

Bess hovered there in his arms, too confused for clear thought. Somewhere in the fact was good news for them, but—"I can't but feel it a sin on our souls, Jason."

"Oh, Bess." His light laughter silvered through the dark. "What's to be done then? Tell Hallow it's all been a ghastly mistake?"

"Oh, be serious!"

"I am. Just as easy to hang two as one."

No, God wouldn't do that to her, not now. Still, her faith prompted, such things went hard come Judgment.

"The man was a thief himself, Bess. They caught him robbing a coach. Abel called it an irony."

"What's that?"

Jason gathered her closer. "Something that's saved us. We're free, Bess. We won't have as much money—"

"We'll have enough," Bess declared, firm in the truth. She hadn't helped manage a busy inn for seven years without learning every possible thrift. "Scrimp here, save there, we'll have enough even for your father."

"By God we will," Jason laughed again, infected with her happy determination. "And we'll be married and off to Plymouth quick as Jack Robinson. God's mercy on that poor fool in Dorchester—"

"We must both pray for him," Bess whispered against his chest.

"—but the Fleecer is dead."

Rose fumed silently as she pinched her second whiskey from the bar in the Sunday-shuttered Crown and Thistle. She helped herself regularly when the landlord and his wife were at church. Never enough for the old penny-shaver to notice, not that she didn't earn that much and more.

Angry as she was today, the drink didn't mellow her mood, only turned it blacker. She paced through the public rooms of the empty inn, hating the late August heat, the cursed condition of her life, and most of all Jason Quick. God damn him, she *was* that strong, stronger than him or his stupid, puling Bess. But she was twenty-five—twenty-six soon enough—and whatever seeds she planted in the soil and hopes of her life never came up. Rose gazed darkly about the empty rooms. Not that young anymore, and the only complete happiness she'd every known died on a muddy road with a bullet in his heart. Would something or someone ever come to rescue her from the stifling hopelessness of her life? Whatever did or did not come, a woman had to get on the best she could in a hard world.

"Bloody Quick," she seethed to the walls. "And ain't he slick?"

Slick enough, easy on her eyes, and eager enough to tumble Rose Allen when she offered. Then what turned him, what could possibly turn him from a full woman like her to that little

Whateley bitch? God damn him anyway, she swore to the shutters and droning flies.

She kept telling herself that she was strong enough to take this blow like all the others, but where would it end? As her temper honed on the whiskey, Rose wanted to hurt Jason somehow, invade his life and *take* from it. Some of her own back like the pinched drinks.

"Slicky Quicky," she snickered with whiskeyed whimsy. "But Rose takes the trick."

She could think of more descriptive names for Bess and had, but Rose Allen was no fool to tell all she knew or show all she felt.

"Listen, Willy," she whispered as the drink erased time for her. "Listen more'n you talk." Over and over she lectured her lover on that. "A man learns when he listens, 'specially in your line o' work."

But Willy Boston never listened. Life was a trumpet challenge, and Willy blared back in its face. Rose was made of shrewder stuff. When Tim Groot had come in the other night with a face disagreeable as his nature, muttering of the wedding over his first ale, Rose felt the news as a physical blow but betrayed no more emotion than a face painted on china. She never liked Tim much but let him lean close with his air of secrecy.

"He wants to marry her next month. Maybe," Tim amended. "If nothing happens meanwhile."

Rose set his second ale on the bar. "What could happen to a gentleman like Mr. Quick?"

Tim favored her with the condescending look of a man knowing much more than he spoke. "Gentleman is he? Folk about here—decent folk, that is—might be surprised at Quick. There's more about him folk oughter know."

"Flashed a gun, you say?"

Tim oozed masculine self-assurance. "We had a difference, y'might say. I knocked him flat, I did, but he pulled a pistol."

"He'd have to. A man like you would kill him."

So Tim might have, but Quick tricked him cowardly with dirt in his eyes, and when he could see again, that gun didn't even shake in the bastard's hand. When Tim cooled down, he asked himself what business would a toff like Quick have carrying a pistol in his saddlebag and looking for sure like he knew how to use it.

Another ale appeared before Tim Groot as Rose patted his hand and charged him only half price. Flattered, Tim enlarged his story to its daring sequel. He took himself down St. Andrew to the provost sergeant.

"You've seen the sergeant, tall and mean. But when he heard what I had t' tell, he sat up sharp and called me Mr. Groot. Treated me like quality."

"And so he should. You're a sharp one, Timmy." Rose let her eyes sweep over the ostler in warm appreciation. "What did you tell'm then?"

Tim winked at her. "Enough, I did. Enough for the provost to come to Whitechurch asking questions of Mr. Quick. Enough so's I might come into a piece of money one of these days. And then I'll be drinking of your best."

"Get away," she scoffed good-naturedly. "Only thing you'll come into is shit on your boots."

"That's all you know, girl. Ever strike you queer how Quick's always got money? Oh, he's worth some but not how you'd expect."

"Go on," Rose urged. "Tell me. Ain't we always been friends?"

"You'll see, Rose. Aye, y'just might see. And Quick just mightn't be marrying soon as he thinks."

Rose had dismissed Tim's posturing with contempt. He was a fool any woman over fifteen could lead on a leash eight days out of the week—but drinking now in the deserted inn with no sound but the whining of flies, she recalled his insinuations and just how little she knew of Jason Quick. There had always been something secretive to the man under the polished surface like a mirror where a woman might see herself in the flattering light of his charm, but little of him.

Oh, isn't he good at that? A spurt of fresh anger took Rose as she turned suddenly and climbed the stairs to Jason's room, determined without knowing why, but she had to wound him back. In the room she glimpsed his razor lying by the wash basin and flicked it open. As the blade caught the light, for one red moment Rose wanted to attack his fine clothes and slash them to ribbons. She resisted; he'd know she did it. What else? She turned about the room, lips moving with silent vengeance.

Few lodgers kept their rooms tidy as he did. On the stand by his bed, the books were neatly arranged, leather backs facing out. In the wooden hamper, shirts and jabots were folded precisely. Not a careless man at all.

Rose turned down the bed coverlet with a flicker of sensual memory as her hand slid over the pillow where once they'd lain together. Best *he* ever had. Her fingers slipping around and under the pillow felt something like leather. His wallet. When he brushed out past her this morning after their argument, he must have forgotten it. Fine pigskin lined with silk. Rose opened it and her breath caught. She couldn't read the flowing copperplate script on the money, but the numbers were opulent. A ten-pound note, not crumpled from handling; the thick paper felt and smelled new.

Rose sat on Jason's bed, studying the fortune in her hand. No one carried such a sum handy; she'd never seen one in the Crown and Thistle or the King's Shilling. It would be impossible to change anywhere but a bank. Her instinct was to slip it into her bodice, but Jason would know straight off 'twas her, and no need for her to get sacked again. She refolded the note in the wallet and slid it under the pillow, wondering how much Tim Groot really knew or was he just blowing, and how this might work for Rose Allen.

You hurt me, Jason Quick. Only right I pay you out in kind.

So much for feelings. Come down to it, how much did she

really know of Jason? The son of a prosperous London stationer, he said, gone to America and leaving Jason well provided. He came to Dorset in early spring—March it was, in foul weather, and took his supper for a week in the Crown and Thistle before moving in. That was poor Willy's last week of life.

No . . .

That was his last *night*, and Jason was there drinking brandy, then all on a sudden he ordered a pot of strong tea. She remembered because she brought it thinking him too handsome for his own good and tea a silly way to cap off brandy unless he wished to be awake half the night.

A cold snake of a thought slithered into Rose's mind.

That afternoon a soldier came from Milburne St. Andrew to take down the reward poster. The Fleecer had been caught and hanged, he said. So much for Tim's piece of future money, but Rose might still do for Jason Quick. She bought the soldier an ale with her own money, passed a significant word or two, and led him up to Jason's room.

> . . . and he said the girl was fair hot to show him the wallet with the new ten-pound note from B. of England. While I would not have said so before, I now think J. Quick most likely suspect.

Major Sedgewick put the dispatch aside and regarded the hot, dusty rider who had brought it from the provost sergeant. Unlettered Hallow had dictated the note to a corporal clerk, who had preserved the sergeant's flavor in writing. The girl was "fair hot," but the evidence remained circumstantial. Quick lodged at the inn and conceivably had intimate dealings with the serving woman before being betrothed to the Whitechurch girl. Jealous women, Sedgewick reflected, could often hang the cleverest criminal. The end of the dispatch, laboriously signed by Hallow himself, swayed Sedgewick to decision.

The money might well come from the pay robbery. Regent's Bank, where Quick has his account, issues its own notes.

Roddy Hallow might not be able to write much more than his name, but he was a bulldog who got his teeth into something and hung on. Part of the sergeant's zeal was undoubtedly wanting revenge for a good friend, the broken corporal. The major took no pleasure in having the man flogged, but that was past. He handed a sealed envelope to the waiting courier.

"This is to be read only by Hallow's clerk in the sergeant's hearing alone," he directed. "I repeat, alone."

The envelope contained the shrewdly thought and worded order Hallow requested and a note from Sedgewick urging careful planning. By way of congratulation, the major stuffed a bottle of fine brandy into the dispatch case to be presented with the letters.

When Hallow's mystified clerk read the dispatches to him behind closed doors, the sergeant offered him a measure of the brandy coupled with a warning cold enough to freeze beer.

"Corporal, you never read these to me."

"But—but this order doesn't make good sense, Sarn't."

"Never mind. You never saw them, right?"

The clerk understood. "Oh. Right."

" 'Cause if one word gets round, your stripes are gone quicker'n Danny's and your back will be laid as raw."

One word? That's all it would take, the clerk realized. Because as these orders read, they seemed to be begging for a robbery.

Roddy Hallow settled back in his chair with cold satisfaction. He'd warned the clerk, well and good. "Now read the orders again. Slow and clear."

Of course the word would get out. Roddy Hallow would see that it did.

Bess reveled in freedom and happiness bright as the moon that turned the heath to silver and the ancient hill fort into a wedding cake baked from magic and dreams come true. They walked toward the causeway, arms about each other, while Jason's cob, turned loose to graze, was free himself to meditate on his equine ancestors who might have charged up or down its disputed heights.

Nothing could diminish Bess's joy this night. They were so close to the end, so *close*. In two little weeks of excited fittings and pinnings she would walk down the aisle of St. Mary's in her mother's wedding dress, proud on her father's arm, to where Jason waited. From Dorchester he'd brought their passage papers to Virginia, and Bess made him read over and over the particulars: a good cabin on the *Beverley*, Captain Robert Allan master, for a voyage of two to three months.

"Or longer, they said," Jason added. "Depending on weather. Lud, I hope we don't get seasick."

Bess had no notion of the malady. To her the *Beverley* by its gilded name was an enchanted swan boat that would glide westward before gentle breezes all the days of their voyage. Her father, likely at Anne Whateley's urging, had already engaged Alice Sims to replace Bess at serving, only fifteen but quick to learn, giving Bess a largesse of freedom to be with Jason much of the time before they married and sailed.

Brimming with futures himself, Jason took Bess by the Royal Mail to Dorchester, where he bought her a large new reticule for traveling, and then to a stationer's to show her a map of the ocean and their ship's intended route. Captain Allan would sail a southerly course and take on fresh water in the strange and won-

derful islands called Azores or Canary, avoiding northern
storms. Bess followed Jason's finger as it neared America and the
large bay between a ragged peninsula and the mainland. Chesa-
peake they called it, with Alexandria at the end. To Bess the
names rang with pure romance.

Jason always talked of land and growing tobacco, but there in
the stationer's shop, Bess saw tenderly how he examined the different fonts of type, passed his hands over quires of new paper,
and pleasurably inhaled the smell of ink and leather bindings
like perfume.

He loves these things, she thought in a thrill of contentment. *He
touches them the way he touches my breasts.*

Two weeks more to the wedding, fourteen short days and only
twenty-one until they sailed.

They reached the highest level of the old fort and dreamed
out over a world already theirs.

TO PROVOST SERGEANT RODERICK HALLOW, 54TH FOOT
(DETACHED). MOST SECRET.
**Pursuant to orders rec'd from Cmd'g Gen'l Sir William
Trelawney, KC, CBE, I am directed to advise you of
officers' pay procedures for September which, of neces-
sity, and on the considered advice of the Paymaster
Gen'l, will depart from normal practice for reasons of
security and to the extent described below.**

"Tonight." Bess whirled about, giddy under the moon.
"Tonight I want to bathe in moonlight. I want to drown in it.
Jason, Jason, let's do that."

Deliciously mad, already stimulated by their lovemaking to
come, Bess slipped out of her dress and petticoats, bare in the
milky light pouring over her, arms outstretched in invocation to
her God and perhaps, deep in her blood, to an older goddess
sleeping under the hill. There had never been such moonlight; it

washed over her shoulders and breasts and silvered Jason's white
skin as he dropped his clothes away and caught her in his arms.

> Officers will be paid for both September and arrears
> for August. In addition those moneys intended for the
> Dorchester quartermaster will be included and supple-
> mented with funds for new field equipment and ord-
> nance. The total sum of five hundred pounds will be
> transmitted from the Bank of England, half in five-
> pound notes, the balance in smaller denominations.
> Gen'l Trelawney demands emphatically that there be
> no possible repetition of the Blandford blunder, there-
> fore transmittal procedures will be as follows.

They had never made love with such closeness. Jason would
not let her mouth go, and in a fever of tenderness, Bess mounted
astride him, her unbound hair an ebony river cascading about his
face and throat. She bent low over him, trembling in her passion
as they tore at each other, their cries carrying on the night wind.
For a while then they lay clasped together, spent, but this jeweled night and their joy made them gloriously mad. They ran like
young deer along the worn, ancient earthworks, spinning about
like pagan dancers, chasing and catching each other, collapsing
in laughter to earth again as Jason feasted on the flesh and scent
of his woman, deeper and muskier now than the first time he
loved her. In her answering his passion now, it was as if their separate essences and very blood combined to permeate the smooth
flesh of her with a third presence out of the two of them.

Bess stirred in his arms with a sleepy little yawn. "Ought to be
going back."

"No. Not yet, dearest."

"It's late. I'm sure Mum knows where we are, but I have to help
with Alice in the morning. Jason?" Her fingers laddered up his
smooth chest. She was glad, among other riches she claimed in

him, that Jason wasn't hairy. "I know you want cropland in Virginia, but . . ."

Lying with his face between her breasts, Jason responded drowsily. "Um?"

"I was thinking. Wouldn't a good shop do as well? A stationer's wouldn't cost half as dear as land, and your father would love it much as you would."

"You don't want land?"

"I want what you want, big ninny. But really want what you want, so you're truly happy."

He elbowed up over her. "Now what's this then?"

"I saw you in that shop. Oh, land is fine and being gentry is fine, but the shop's what you know. It's what you love."

"Won't bring half the money of tobacco."

"Won't cost half as much for a start. Damn, Jason. Money, money, money! Where's the shame in just having enough if we're happy?"

"Being poor, girl. You never went hungry, and you aren't going to. Money is the only real power. A king without a penny is just a man in satin breeches with empty pockets."

"Stuff! We'll prosper at whatever we do if we've a care to expense. If you think I'm going to send out your washing to some slattern 'stead of doing it myself—"

"Not married yet and already you're doing my wash?"

"Enough pennies make shillings."

"There's profound. I wish I'd said that. Lud, if you're not on like a wife."

"And you like a careless husband. I'll be going through your pockets, so I will, to save what money you've forgotten before the wash."

The paymaster's courier will meet ours at Regent's Bank, Blandford Forum, at noon of September eighth. Whomever you select will dress in mufti and drive a small open trap drawn by one horse. The older and plainer his dress, trap, and horse, the better. Driver's appearance will in no way suggest he is aught but a local citizen or farmer of modest means. He will carry two concealed pistols. The bag containing the funds will be hidden under the seat. At Thornicombe he will detour across Charlton Down to Anderson, thence to Bere Regis and by this roundabout route to Milborne St. Andrew, where an armed escort will bear the bag to Dorchester.

You will appreciate the reasons for such seemingly reckless procedure. No highwayman with an eye to profit will waylay a rustic wagon, but in this apparent carelessness lies our security. Secrecy is all important, for if we again lose such amounts through misadventure, the entire regiment will be disgraced even to the possible loss of our colors.

Harold Sedgewick, Provost Major, Dorch.

Hallow's troubled clerk carried the secret like a bomb about to explode, more willing to be dragged behind a horse than utter one word. He hoped the scheme would work, but the orders robbed him of sleep. He lay awake, his lips silently forming the fear again and again. In his prudent opinion, Major Sedgewick had gone round the bend, and Sarn't Roddy too.

"Beggin' for it," he whispered to the ceiling. "Make a bollocks of this one, we'll all be shipped to the colonies and never see England again."

Bess stretched her slender length and sat up, gathering the torrent of her hair into some kind of order. Bless her wise mum who must notice but never mentioned the stray twig, leaf, or smudge on her clothes after nights glorious as this. "I hope we can find your old horse."

Jason yawned. "After this carnage, I'll be happy to find our clothes."

"What if the Faerie stole 'em?" Bess dreamed to the moon gone far across the ocean of night since they climbed the hill. "We'd be a sight in Whitechurch right enough."

Suddenly she clung to him again, fierce in the depths of her love. "By the living, loving God I love you, Jason. By Him and by all the gods men and women prayed to on this hill through all time, I love you."

"And I," Jason whispered into her hair. "It is late. See? Our lovely moon is going down."

PART III

"One kiss, my bonny sweetheart. I'm after a prize tonight,
But I shall be back with the yellow gold before the morning light.
Yet, if they press me sharply, and harry me through the day,
Then look for me by moonlight,
    Watch for me by moonlight,
I'll come to thee by moonlight, though Hell should bar the way."

Only ten days to their wedding and seventeen until they sailed. This evening Bess reveled in sharing supper with Jason in his favorite corner of the King's Shilling, while plump little Alice pit-patted back and forth between the inside tables and those in the yard. Wide-eyed, moon-cheeked, with prominent front teeth her broad lips could never quite cover, Alice reminded Jason of a startled squirrel.

This evening with its pleasant hint of autumn coolness, most of the custom preferred to dine outside. Besides Jason and Bess only five or six farmers and their wives occupied the dining room. Suddenly Alice rushed in from the yard and, with a quick word to Mr. Whateley, hurried to Bess.

"There's soldiers," she blurted. "One's so drunk he fell out of the wagon. They're comin' in. Will't be trouble, you think?"

Her words were barely out when Daniel Winner shouldered through the doorway half dragging a larger soldier. Winner lugged the other private to an unoccupied table, dropped him in a chair, and slammed down a leather dispatch case by him. The inebriated soldier's head sank onto his arms as he mumbled incoherently for whiskey. A reassuring wave to Jedediah Whateley from Winner: "Just my mate Frank Soames. Nothin' for him, but I'll take an ale."

Jason recognized both immediately. As Winner approached him, the demolished Soames turned his bleary, baleful gaze on Jason.

"Eh, you're the young fellow we questioned," Winner declared in friendly recognition.

"I am, sir."

"Hope we wasn't too much bother."

"Not at all. And you would be—?"

"Private Daniel Winner, Fifty-fourth. Somethin' about a pistol?"

Jason raised a testifying hand to heaven. "Believe me, I am reformed since. Never mind his ale, Bess. Mr. Winner, please take a brandy with us."

"I will, thanks." Retrieving his pouch, Winner took a seat opposite the couple, glancing back at the inert Soames. "Best pay Frank no mind. He's a chore to manage sober and a bloody mean drunk. Pardon me, ma'am," he added in deference to Bess. "We're couriers back from Blandford. Old Frank goes missing for more than an hour, and when I find him he's like what you see. So bloody far gone—pardon, ma'am—he fell out'n the wagon in the yard yonder."

As Bess rose to fetch Winner's brandy, Jason's eye flicked over the dispatch case and back to Winner. "Miss Whateley and I are to be wed in a few days."

"Well! That bein' the case," Winner offered expansively, "I'll buy the next. She's a fair lass."

"Thank you. We're off to America as well."

Winner smiled affably but had noted Jason's quick glance at the pouch. "So many goin' off, won't hardly be a corporal's guard left to stand by the ruddy king."

"That will not trouble me, Mr. Winner."

"Nor me. My folks be Whig."

"And mine."

"Your health, ma'am." Winner raised the glass Bess set before him, swallowing a larger gulp than the connoisseur in Jason would deem prudent, and swiveled about to survey the slumbering Soames. "Now then, if Frank will take a quiet nap, I'll have me a rest. A long drive to Blandford and no shorter back. Seems me and him get every fatigue no one else wants this month. And the road no smoother'n a rock pile."

"I said *whiskey*, gahdammit!"

Their cordial moment was shattered as Soames reared up suddenly, pounding on the table with a ham fist. "Din' I say whiskey? Wassit take t'get a drink round here?"

"Easy, Frank," Winner called over. "No drink for you. You've had enough."

"T'hell with you, Danny Winner. You ain't corporal no more." Soames lurched to his feet, peering belligerently about. "Sick of't all, I am."

With an apologetic sigh—"Lord, he's on again"—Winner rose reluctantly to confront his friend. "I said easy on, mate. No need to disturb these good folk."

"Sick of it!" Soames trumpeted to the startled room at large. "An' mostly sick of bein' first name on every fatigue bloody Hallow dreams up, like prancin' off to Blandford 'cause some bleedin' paymaster got clever ideas."

Winner's voice cracked like a whip. "Frank! Shut your mouth!"

"You sod off," Soames cursed mushily, advancing on Winner. "You bastard, 'twas you dropped me'n Bell in it for a start."

"Jesus," Winner breathed with a regretful nod to Bess. "Sorry you have to see this, ma'am."

Soames swung wildly at Winner, who ducked nimbly and countered with a neat right to his friend's jaw. Soames fell forward heavily as a sawn tree. Winner bent quickly and let the man wilt over his shoulder. "Sorry," he apologized to Jedediah Whateley hovering in the bar entrance. "Happens all the time with him. Just can't hold it. Could y'spare a bed where he can sleep an hour or so?"

"I'll see to it." Bess jumped up and led Winner with his somnolent cargo up the stairs to her own room. Below in the dining room, Jason sipped his brandy and regarded Winner's forgotten dispatch case. The drunken soldier had babbled intriguingly, something about the paymaster. . . .

By the light of a single candle, Francis Soames, able at last to lie on his back without agony, placed large hands behind his head and grinned at Daniel Winner. Soames possessed two qualities beyond price to Roddy Hallow in this mission, a jaw solid as Stonehenge and an uncanny tolerance for whiskey. Able to drink any man of the Fifty-fourth into oblivion, Soames was presently sober as a Muslim.

"Ah, y'did smashin,' Frank," Winner admired from his seat on the window ledge. "Sorry I had to bless you so hard."

"You're goin' soft, Danny luv. Hardly felt it."

"Fancy our toff down below. Says he's off to Virginia once they're wed."

"Bloody hell he is," Soames denied. "It's him, Danny."

"You sure? I warn't."

"I am. Saw's eyes. Different expression from that bloke at Blandford. Keener like, but the same man."

"Then let's hope he takes the bait like a proper little fish."

"He'll take it," Soames prophesied vindictively. "If I 'ave to push his face in it. He owes us for what we took at the floggin' post."

"We'd best stay here a bit," Winner said. "Like Roddy said, give temptation a chance to work. Think of forty pounds, Frank."

"I will that," said Soames, remembering too vividly how he almost broke his teeth biting on the leather when the cat laid his back open. "What's 'is name again?"

"Jason Quick."

"Not quick enough," Francis Soames muttered fiercely. "Bugger the bastard. Bugger!"

The urge drew him like a lodestone. Soames's slurred "paymaster" put a rowel to Jason's mind as his eyes went again and again to the dispatch case within his reach. As farmers heeded weather signs year round, it behooved a highwayman, active or retired, to know the business of local provosts.

No harm in a quick look. While the other customers huddled over their suppers, muttering of the soldiers' fight, Jason slid his hand smoothly into the pouch and removed the single folded sheet of paper. The words *Most Secret* leaped out at him. Rapidly but with attention to detail, as Abraham taught him to scan script or print, Jason studied the order through, then returned it to the pouch. He savored his brandy as rising excitement stirred his vitals.

The eighth of September. Five hundred pounds.

No, be wise. Heed Bess and Abel.

Yet even as he so resolved, part of his mind meshed wheels and gears like oiled machinery under a skilled hand. *He'll turn off at Thornicombe across the downs. Not much chance for surprise but good clear ground for escape and no escort until St. Andrew.*

Jason could only admire the scheme. A risk only on the surface but efficient as Abel's subtle two-bishop checkmate in chess. Were he Paymaster General himself, he could not have dreamed a more audacious deception, or one that so cried out to be challenged. Find where they are, be where they aren't.

Bess appeared from the stairwell and returned to Jason, shaking her head. "He's far gone, that soldier. Unconscious as a stone."

She would have sat but just then her mother called her from the kitchen. The sight of Bess coursed a pang of guilt through Jason when he remembered how solemnly she took his promise to her heart. To break it troubled the core of his Protestant soul that had no cushioning sophistry. His promise mattered. Bess mattered.

Aye, Bess is good and Bess is wise. The shop was far sounder a plan than farming tobacco, about which he knew nothing beyond its profit in London. So rapt in his dream of being a landed gentleman, he never once paused to consider if that was really what Bess wanted for herself. But the wheels turned in the back of Jason's mind. September the eighth. Four days hence. Not much time to decide.

But with five hundred added to what we have . . .

The prospect gleamed. With such capital he and his father could expand far beyond pamphlets and broadsheets to a proper bindery annex. There couldn't be that many bookbinders in Virginia yet. There would be an apprentice to cut and stack paper, cut quills ready for sale, sort used type and manage the counter for the skilled and flourishing establishment of Abraham Quick and Son.

Five hundred pounds.

Best start the night before. Less than three miles cross country to the Dorchester road, and from there to Thornicombe a mite over four. Jones would take that for mild exercise.

Trail the wagon by perhaps a quarter mile when it comes in sight. Make sure there's no escort; that's easy on open downs. The driver's pistols would be under the seat, and if Jason came up fast . . .

He forced himself to banish the thought, imagining Bess when she knew. But must she? He couldn't easily conceal the venture from Abel, but what if Bess thought he was merely off to buy her wedding ring, as he'd told her? No, she would know the truth straight off or soon enough, and how would she look at him then? Faith and trust were natural and deep in Bess, who confessed to the Virgin Mary every penny filched in their cause. Could she ever trust him again? He saw her soft mouth parted in disbelief, then the hurt and her whole mien darkened with disillusionment, perhaps never to clear again.

Jason burned with a sudden, irrational anger at the girl. Damn!

In so many things Bess was yet a sheltered child. She couldn't imagine the cruel way of the stinking world when one was poor.

Jason paid his score, kissed Bess good night, and started to leave. Then, thoughtfully, he gathered up the dispatch case and climbed the stairs to knock at Bess's door.

The answer came after some pause. "Aye, come in."

Jason entered the dimly lit chamber to find Soames prone on the bed, mouth agape, dead to the world. Winner lounged in the open window casement. "Aye, what?"

"I'm bound home, sir, but you left your pouch."

"Sweet Jesus!" Winner shot off the sill as if propelled from a sling, snatching it from Jason's hand. Quickly he turned back the flap and peered within, then shut it again. "What with Frank here, I flat forgot. You're a gentleman indeed, sir. My thanks."

Jason bowed modestly. "Only good manners. Give you good night."

When his footsteps receded down the stairs, Soames inquired without moving or opening his eyes, "Think he 'ad a look inside then?"

Winner countered with his own question. "Still think he's the Fleecer?"

"Not a matter of thinkin', Danny. I know. The voice, too. Me eyes 'n ears are better'n yours, always were."

"Well, I put it to you," posed Private Daniel Winner, once and hopefully future corporal. "If you was the Fleecer right enough, wouldn't you?"

Soames snorted and turned over on his back. "Could I read, wouldn't I just."

Another day and night slipped by while Jason struggled between conscience and opportunity. He would, he would not. Abel Gant noticed his distraction, trouncing him at backgammon where Jason usually won. Bess sensed his preoccupation as well and, womanlike, feared that Jason had serious second thoughts about wedding her. In God's eyes they were already married, and both had certainly made the most of it. Was he tired of her? Didn't he want her to go with him after all?

"All men scare so before the wedding," Anne Whateley tut-tutted her daughter's apprehensions. "Your old dad was a pitiful sight the day we married."

"No fear," loyal Abel comforted Bess. "He's been in a fog, true, but it's not that, I'm bound. You're all he thinks about, but God's truth, I haven't the faintest notion where his mind is."

Despite its compunctions, that mind circled and narrowed about five hundred pounds only three days away, now two. Now tomorrow. And over and over, Jason's thoughts returned to the spectre of Roddy Hallow. Suppose, he conjectured, suppose Hallow didn't believe they'd done for the real Fleecer in hapless Enoch Parsons, God rest his poor, inept soul. Suppose the provost was still out there, searching, biding his time.

No, he's a stubborn bugger but not that subtle.

To his surprise and perverse amusement, he found he actually missed Hallow's hovering presence. Even more unsettling, despite his utter joy in the treasure of Bess, Jason was restless and bored. Not money alone after all, but the game itself that drew and enthralled him: the excitement, the planning of every detail, even the chase and escape, Jones plunging under him, arousing in its way as loving Bess under the moon. The fear-thrill coursing through his whole being with every life-or-death throw of the dice. Like the flush of liquor through a drunkard's blood, the game had become a physical need in Jason.

Finally, with the English genius for moral compromise, he reconciled need with conscience. He would dress normally save for hidden pistols, hat, and mask, and indeed buy Bess's ring in Blandford Forum. There he would confirm the courier's wagon at Regent's Bank. That done, an easy ride to select his vantage point on Charlton Down. If instinct misliked anything, he would abandon the pull and ride home. So he promised himself as he brought out the four pistols and laid them on the table to be cleaned and loaded. Looking up from his book, Abel watched first with alarm, then a sinking heart, as Jason swabbed out the barrels and priming pans.

"What in the world are you doing?"

With casual innocence: "Fancied I might take Jones for a run."

Abel closed the book firmly. "Business in St. Andrew?"

"Just to Blandford for Bess's ring."

Abel knew his pupil far better than that. "You promised her."

"I've not broken it yet."

A long silence before Abel spoke again. "You're mad. You'll be married in a few days, gone in a few more. When will you stop, man?"

"Just going to have a look. Reconnoiter, as it were. Piece of cake."

"Piece of cake," his friend echoed with a tinge of disgust. "By God but you do love it, don't you? I've watched it grow in you like a sickness you won't cure. You'll be fleecing passengers on the ship, so you will. I see some difficulty in escape, but you'll have a jolly go while it lasts."

Jason raised his head. They stared at each other as the rusty works of the mantel clock sourly clanged half-nine. Jason rammed a patch and ball into the first pistol. "I'm off to buy a ring, you old hen."

"With pistols?"

"There's desperate men on the roads."

"Don't cozen me, boy," Abel warned sternly. "I lack the honesty to be that gullible. You—ah, balls!" he exploded, flinging his book away. "Please, Jason. Whatever this is, it's not worth the risk now."

Jason took up the second pistol. "Old friend, enough. Stay out of this."

"You swore never to hurt her. Just what in hell do you think you're doing now?"

"Abel, you're putting me in the dock before the crime. I may not do anything at all. If not, I'll be home with her ring." Jason looked up at Abel. "If I do, it will be the last. I've thought it out clearly. The risk is minimal and the prize worth all."

Abel felt helpless and close to tears. He rose abruptly and jammed his battered tricorn on his head. Over his priming, Jason asked, "Where are you off to then?"

"By rights to church," Abel growled, yanking the door open with the force of his frustration. "Someone has to pray for you."

The door slammed behind him.

Abel saddled his horse quickly and galloped through the summer night toward Whitechurch and the King's Shilling. He couldn't stop the fool himself; all the while he pleaded with Jason, those small hands never paused over the pistols. Bess might dissuade him, and she must.

He left his cob in the stableyard without a word to Tim and hurried into the Shilling, searching about. "Alice? I say, Alice? Where's Bess? I must see her."

The apple-cheeked girl knitted thick brows. "Is something amiss, sir?'

"No, just—where is she?"

"Above, turnin' out the beds with fresh linen."

Abel would have taken the stairs two at a time, but age denied him after the first bound. He clumped up to the second floor, puffing a little. "Bess girl, where are you?"

She appeared from one of the bedrooms, carrying an armload of linen sheets. "Abel. Is Jason come with you?"

"No." Abel moved closer to her, lowering his voice. "Trouble."

"What? Tell me."

"I think he calls it business in St. Andrew."

"No," she denied firmly. "He wouldn't. He promised me." But even as she spoke, something gave her the lie. "When?"

"Come back with me now. Make him listen to you."

Bess dropped the linen and flew down the stairs, Abel in her wake. One hurried word to Alice, then Abel was legging her up behind the saddle and, double-mounted, they dashed away toward Dewlish.

Long after ten by Abel's clock, they burst through his unlocked door to find Jason gone and his note by the table lamp.

> Abel—
> Have gone to Blandford for Bess's ring. Return tomorrow.
> —Jason

Abel saw the hurt and fear in her eyes as he read the note to Bess. "In the middle of the night," she cried out. "No, he's lying. Oh God, Abel!"

"Wait. Sit and rest." Seeing Bess frightened and confused as himself, Abel went quickly to search the stable for what his fears had already confirmed. Jason's cob was stalled, the bay gone. Back in the cottage he opened the chest that held the Fleecer's black habiliments, briefly relieved to find them there. But the black hat, mask, broad belt, and four pistols were missing.

"I don't know what to think," Abel admitted to Bess as she sank into a chair. He tried to soften hard truth. "It might be as he says, to buy your ring."

He did not mention the pistols.

"But it's not." Bess's voice carried the weight of her intuition. "All week so absent, so far away. Now I know why."

"Bess—"

"*Don't*—don't try to lie for him, Abel. He's already done that. After he promised."

Jason's friend had no answer for her misery. Throughout his own long life, both clever and fool, Abel saw the same terminal folly in his best pupil, the lesson age could never impart to youth. Standing behind Bess, soothing hands on her quivering shoulders, Abel remembered. "Reconnoiter: That was his word. Just have a look."

"At what? Where?"

"I don't *know!*" Abel hastily softened his tone lest she detect his own fear. "God knows, girl."

How could he give someone young as Bess what he could never instill in her rash young lover? She feared for Jason, but he'd wounded her faith. Abel Gant's very wise, very used soul ached for her. Before Jason came into her life, she'd been on the brink of surrendering to oafish Tim Groot, but so it fell out and Abel saw her blossom from girl to woman over the first truly magical year of her life, a rainbow in her heart but that young nonetheless. Eighteen's first love could be sweet or agony but never forgotten, indelible as a handprint pressed into soft mortar.

"He always wore black when he rode," Abel said. "Those garments are still here."

Bess wilted over the table, shading her eyes, head shaking with bleak knowledge. "They'll get him sure this time. He'll die. I feel it like a chill in my bones. Why this so soon before—?"

"Now, now. You'll make yourself ill this way." Abel took her arm, raising the girl gently. "Come, I'll take you home."

"I don't know how I feel." Bess's tone was flat with weariness. "But I'll not sleep until I know he's safe. Abel?"

"Aye, child?"

Her eyes fixed him steadily, and Abel saw truth in them. "I'm not a child tonight. Is this how it feels to grow up so sudden?"

Yes, Abel thought sadly. *We can grow up in a day, a moment, to a lonely place with no tale of Rapunzel to believe in.* "Always."

The unoiled clock ground out eleven. The slightly discordant strokes reminded Abel of a funeral knell. In Bess's youth and his age alike, this would be the longest night of their lives.

"Where is he gone, Abel? What is he going to?"

Long past one of the morning, Bess lay awake tense with fear for Jason and crushed by his broken promise. Or did he break it?

Bess thrashed over on her other side for the third time in as many minutes. If she only knew—then she lifted her head at the sound of shod hooves on the cobbles below her window. In the next moment Jason's soft whistle sent her flying out of bed to the open window. Below her, almost within hand's reach, he sat the big bay, his scarlet coat and buff breeches merely gray in the dark.

"Jason," she breathed in a rush of relief. "Where have you been?"

"Why, nowhere."

"Shh! Be quiet; you'll wake Mum and Dad."

"Nowhere," he said again, pushing the hat back from his face, and Bess could hear rather than see the careless charm of his smile. "I was just off to buy your wedding ring."

The truth chilled through her. He wasn't telling all. "At this hour?"

"And it struck me: Though I've kissed your dear hands a thousand times, I've no notion of finger size. Give me a ring to take for a match."

"I said *hush*. You'll wake the dead at St. Mary's." She wanted to believe him, but though he wore no pistols, he never used the bay horse for anything but business. Bess tried to keep her fear from showing. "It's St. Andrew, isn't it?"

His silence told her the worst. "Isn't it!"

"For your ring, Bess. Give me one to take."

She felt her desperation rising. Perhaps that good errand would stay him from worse. Searching her dresser top for a ring, her heart still denied what her mind could not. She leaned far out and down as Jason stood in the stirrups, and her long, unbound hair fell over his hands as he took the ring and buried his face in the ebony river.

Let me hold him back, Bess prayed. *Let all of me be all for him and enough this night.* "As you love me, Jason, don't do this. Don't go."

She sensed the ambivalence in her lover's silence before the honesty spoke. "Would I could lie to you, but I can't."

"Jason—"

"This one last time."

He couldn't know how that pierced through her. Bess drew back above him. "Aye, one last time. And you come asking me to send you off with a kiss and a prayer. Well, I damn well won't."

"I swear to you there's no risk at all this time."

"When was there ever none? Lying to me and now to yourself." She leaned down again, stretching to grasp his waiting hand as if with that alone she could hold him back. "Not even if I beg, Jason? Not even for me?"

His hand was hot about hers. "Trust me, sweetheart."

"You said no more. You promised." Bess clutched at his hand like life itself. "Jason, my heart misgives tonight. You've had the Devil's own luck, but that luck is gone; I feel it sure. Stay and I'll come down."

"No, Bess."

She must stop him somehow. She could never be strong where he was concerned, but now she must be the strength for both of them. "Let me come down," she entreated in whispered urgency. "We'll go to the churchyard as we did that first time, remember? And I'll make such love to you—"

"Bess, please," Jason hissed. "I can't. I have to do this."

"You don't. You mustn't. So often out on the heath when we came together, I was afraid I'd be with child before we wed. But take me tonight, Jason. Love me, and if God starts a child in me, I'll be so glad, for 'twill be born in America of the two of us. Our child, Jason. Let me—"

But he suddenly released her hand, turning in the saddle, alert. "Did you hear something?"

"Hear?" Bess heard nothing, all her being fiercely narrowed on the need to stay him.

"Bess, we need the money."

"*We* need?" she shot angrily at him. "Stop it! Damn you, it's you needing. Did you ever ask what I truly need? God's blood, but I could hate you for this—aye and that old man in Virginia.

Hate you, Jason. Whatever takes you from me tonight, don't say *we* need when all I need is you."

His voice came up to her like a prayer. "Trust in me, Bess. Trust me and good Jones here. This is a prize, the last and best. I swear by my love for you, tomorrow will end it."

Trembling above him, she heard his soft, reassuring chuckle. "This one is easier than picking flowers. There will be no trouble, but be there even a hint, I'll hide during the day and come to you tomorrow night."

Jason backed the bay and swept his hat wide in farewell. "With your ring, love. Watch for me by moonlight then. By moonlight I'll come to you though Hell should bar the way."

"Then come not at all, you *fool*," Bess choked through despairing tears. "If you go now, I—I'll not marry you."

"But you will," he promised in the darkness. "I'll be waiting at the altar and Abel with me, and Reverend Cobbe will join what none will put asunder. In life and death, my Bess, you will be with me."

Then he was gone, leaving Bess to hammering fear that banished sleep. Jason's luck was gone. They would take him, kill him this time. She stayed long by the open window, staring numbly down into the yard where he had been until the night's chill crawled over her skin. She crept back to bed to lie awake an eternity. Close to dawn she dozed off only to awaken with a start at the sound of a horse clattering about the stableyard.

"Jason?" She stumbled to the window heavy with the need for more sleep, to see Tim Groot trot her father's mare out of the yard. Dully she wondered where he might be off to at this hour. Her exhausted mind refused the question, and Bess sank down like a drowning swimmer into dreamless sleep.

Roddy Hallow swung out of the sergeants' mess toward his quarters, his mind beating time to his stride as he ran down the orders to be given and actions taken this day. He'd made a clever plan, even Sedgewick said so, but still with too many *ifs* for comfort. *If* Quick scanned the orders temptingly planted by Winner, and *if* he couldn't resist the prize, then they'd shear the Fleecer today, right enough. If he didn't—well, they could arrest him on suspicion, but then it would be rough Frank Soames's word against a well-spoke young gentleman in the dock, and what jury would believe a dung beetle like Tim Groot with most of Dorchester believing the Fleecer already cold in his grave? With no other evidence and a good barrister to defend him, Quick might easily go free to marry his bit of fluff. Hallow shrugged inwardly, sick of it all. Either way, Quick would be gone and good riddance.

"Sarn't Hallow! Half a mo'."

Daniel Winner trotted toward him across the parade square from the post gates. No, Hallow amended; *not* either way, not to Danny Winner, who wanted to finish the Fleecer himself and deserved that much.

"Aye, what?"

"Bloke at the gate wants to see you. That Groot from the Shilling."

"What in hell for? We've no time now."

"Can't wait, he says. About the Fleecer. Says he's sure now."

"So are we." Hallow squinted off at the ostler standing expectantly by his horse, and Danny Winner with the glint of a huntsman in his eye spoke what leaped into the sergeant's mind. "Seems our toff took the bait, hook'n all."

Finally. Hallow slammed a fist into his palm. "Good. High time we had a piece of luck. Bring that bastard to my quarters."

With a shrill whistle and wave, Winner signaled the gate guards to pass the ostler in.

Standing before the sergeant, Tim Groot appeared haggard, as if he hadn't slept much or at all. To Roddy Hallow's mind he still looked too bloody eager to hang Jason Quick. No mystery there: the girl. As a provost Hallow quite often disliked his informers more than his quarry. Groot was a mean-spirited man born with a grudge, the sort ever ready to bring suit against a world that owed him. With good fortune or ill, such men went angry and cursing to their graves. By contrast, save for the trouble of him and the feeling that Quick was always laughing at him behind a mask of soft manners, Hallow might have enjoyed a drink with the cocksure little rooster.

"Well," he demanded. "What is it now?"

"It's him," Tim said. "Quick's the Fleecer. Seen'm plain last night."

"Seen what?"

"Under Bess Whateley's window at the Shilling." No twisting of his hat this time. Tim's words were as hard with narrow right as the vindictive gleam in his eye. "He sat a big bay. Remember?" he appealed to Winner. "The bay horse y'asked about last time? Long after midnight it was, when decent folk's abed. They thought they was secret, but I heard 'em and sneaked out to listen. And 'ere he was."

Winner was skeptical. "A bay? Middle of the night and little moon, how'd you know what kind it was?"

Tim Groot knew what he knew. "Beggin' your pardon, sir. Think I don't know a fine bay over sixteen hands from that common little cob Quick rides usual? Looked like the squire's mount what was pinched last spring."

Behind him Winner's eyes made satisfied contact with the sergeants. "Go on," Hallow said.

Tim allowed he didn't hear every word, but Quick was off to Blandford right enough. "To . . . to buy Bess a wedding ring," he added haltingly. "But on 'nother matter, too. Somethin' Bess tried hard to argue him out of. Dead set she was, but him, too. Somethin' big, I'm bound. 'Last and best,' he said, and how 'ere was no danger. His very words. Then he rides off, leavin' Bess still in the window and weepin' hard. He's ridin' now."

When neither soldier spoke, Tim looked from one to the other, wondering if these hard-faced men believed him. "Swear

on Cross he is. And he'll be back at the Shilling tomorrow, heard
that clear. Morrow day or night. Heard that plain."

Hallow glanced away toward his gear hung on a wall peg. "We
know it's Quick. Right. Leave it to us."

Tim stood his ground, not about to be dismissed. "The
reward."

"What about it?"

"Some's mine by rights. Bein' honest men, you can't but own
to that. Din' I come here to tell you?"

"You'll see some of it." Hallow clearly ended the interview.
"You can go now."

Still Tim stubbornly refused to move. "How much?"

"What your help is worth," Hallow prophesied. "Go on now.
We've work to do."

Tim opened the door but turned with a thought that seemed
more than important to him, even vital. "I want to help catch
him."

"That's not smart," Winner advised. Tim didn't see his cynical
smirk. Rabbits couldn't hunt hawks.

Tim hovered in the doorwary. "It's just—"

Hallow snapped at him, impatient to be mounted and gone.
"Just what?"

"I were goin' to marry Bess Whateley. She were close to sayin'
yes afore he came. Dirty thief he is."

When the door closed behind him, Danny Winner appealed
to Hallow. "Brings tears to your eyes, dunnit?"

"Breaks my heart. We'll give him a fiver or so. Maybe in silver,
like in the Bible."

In Roddy Hallow's book, that was fitting. He slung the broad
belt and cartridge box over one shoulder. "You, Bell, Soames,
and five good marksmen. I said *good*, Danny. Some of this lot
couldn't hit Monday night with Tuesday morning. Light kit, just
powder and shot. Assemble in the square ready to ride. Trap
driver sure of the spot, is he?"

"Showed him just where on the map. He's sure." Danny Winner grumbled his way to the door. "Ready to ride, ready to ride. All the ridin' we do, ought to be in the flamin' cavalry."

Roddy Hallow pulled off his parade shoes and reached for the boots under his bed. He disliked riding as much as Danny, but this day would be the end. He'd be regimental sergeant major, and Danny might even get his stripes back with a word from Roddy himself. If Quick's blood was on those stripes, the Fleecer was a blessing after all.

The Royal Mail, Jason remembered from his first trip west, stopped overnight at an inn on Blandford Forum's high street. Horses were changed while passengers breakfasted, and then the coach went on to Dorchester. He rode Jones east through the small hours at a lazy pace, arriving several hours before the inn opened, saw Jones stalled and grained, breakfasted among the passengers, and booked a room for a few hours' rest.

In a narrow side street he enjoyed the most pleasurable part of his mission at a shop that bought and sold jewelry. The proprietor was a small brown bear of a man with humorous eyes and a scraggly beard crying for definition.

"A wedding? I have just the ring for a lovely girl. Show me hers please."

Jason produced the ring, which the owner slipped over a round, tapered rule. "Yes, young sir. I have a genuine creation in this size."

He placed on the counter a thick gold band crusted with diamond chips. Oh no, not at all. Thrifty Bess would scream at the extravagance.

"But why?" the proprietor reasoned. "Only eight pounds. At that price, in a manner of speaking, you are robbing me."

"God knows, sir, I would not dream of that." Jason firmly returned the creation. "Something simpler."

Several trays of rings were set before him, the value and virtue of each fulsomely extolled. Jason struggled in a miasma of uncertainty. He knew nothing of jewelry beyond what he and Owen occasionally pulled and as quickly sold for whatever it would fetch. At length he confessed his ignorance to the shopkeeper, but Bess's hands he did know.

"They're slender but strong, for she's worked with them all her life. And white and somehow always cool to the touch or kiss. If you know rings, sir, you've seen many kinds of hands. Hers are—yes, I would call them honest. To put a great gaudy band on such fingers would be placing a dustbin in the midst of flowers. No, her ring must be part of the loveliness that starts at her fingertips and flows like light through all of her."

"Eloquent," the shopkeeper said admiringly. "Young sir, I have written verse myself in my time. In my very young time. You have a way with words. Have you considered taking up the pen?"

"Not seriously. The pay is appalling. Wait." Jason broke off as his eye lighted on a treasure. He lifted the ring from the tray, wrought of two thin strands of gold braided together, as he and Bess were joined now and forever. "Yes. This."

"Excellent taste, sir. Simple but elegant and only three pounds including a lovely box."

Jason paid for his purchase while the jeweler closed the velvet box about the gold ring. "We're to be married on Sunday."

"For many years, I hope," the merchant blessed them.

"Oh yes. For all time."

"She must be very beautiful."

"Like spring she is. Like morning on the most beautiful day of your life. Surely you have felt so?"

The little man's expression softened with memory. "I wrote my verses to such a girl." Then romance congealed to resignation. "But then, alas, I married her. Good day, sir."

A church bell clanged eleven. Jason found a coffeehouse across from Regent's with a good view of the bank entrance. He waited, sipping at his cup, absently toying with his lace jabot. Well-dressed men went in and out, but they were not whom his practiced eye hunted. Ranging with Owen from Leicester Square to Covent Garden, Jason had learned to cull a pigeon from a crowd of profitless paupers as a shark smelled a single drop of blood in a lake. The man he waited for—

—now drove his homely one-horse trap to a stop directly in front of the bank and alighted. He crossed to the entrance and disappeared inside. A young fellow with a long-boned northern look to him, but the stamp of the barracks read clear. He moved too energetically and far too ramrod-straight for a farmer used to stooping a lifetime to his tasks with the economical movements that conserved a man's energy over endless toil. He was dressed in farm clothes and shabby shoes, but the the buttonless jacket was not weather-faded or dirty enough, the boots not daubed with dried mud. Nor would a poor peasant farmer dare leave his trap directly in front of a place of such authority for fear of having to move it for someone of quality who might berate him for presumption and the inconvenience. Nor would he gust into Regent's with such confidence. In all, only the old hack harnessed to the rickety trap had the melancholy, flyblown appearance of lifelong labor.

In a very few minutes the young man emerged from the bank carrying a small leather satchel. He leaped up into the trap's seat and turned the horse west again toward the Dorchester road. Jason paid his reckoning and rose with a philosophical sigh. Poor Roddy Hallow: If the rest of the day went as well, there would be pain and lamentation throughout the Fifty-fourth this week—but so went the harsh world.

He strolled back to the inn, paid for Jones's stalling, and set out at a leisurely trot toward the west road. When he caught sight of the trap in suburban Blandford St. Mary, Jason fell back another two hundred yards. The trap was merely ambling along. No need to get close yet. Once on the Dorchester road there were only a short two miles to the turn for Thornicombe.

On the highway the trap increased its pace. Jason waited until it disappeared round a bend before following, staying a good quarter mile behind. Only on the open down would there be sharp need for caution and picking his time.

Per his orders, the driver passed slowly through tiny Thornicombe and swung out across Charlton down. Jason kept his distance, watching the trap jolt across the uneven heath, sweeping his eyes back and forth across the horizon for any sign of an escort. The directive specified none until St. Andrew, bless their devious hearts, but he hadn't lived this long being careless. After another quarter hour, with no human or habitation in sight, Jason dismounted and led Jones at a southerly angle to his quarry. If by chance the trap driver glanced back, he'd see only a man walking his mount through the warmth of a September afternoon. Jason watched the trap crest a hill and disappear down the other side. He snaked the belt, pistols, and mask out of his saddlebags and slipped the black kerchief into a pocket, cantering Jones to a spot just below the rise. Armed and ready, Jason bent in a running crouch to the hill's brow, where he flattened out to observe his pigeon. Still no other soul on the downs but himself and the prize, and a lone kestrel, black against azure sky, gliding on the breeze.

From where Jason watched, the gentle north-to-south rise steepened as it curved sharply west, the trap moving now along its base. As he watched, the driver abruptly halted and jumped out of the vehicle.

What's this now? What are you up to?

He had gradually closed the distance as scant cover afforded. The trap was again only a hundred yards ahead; the driver bent to inspect the hack's left forehoof. Thrown a shoe or picked up a stone? No matter.

Now.

Jason masked his lower face, pulled the hat down over his brow, and mounted. Quickly he checked priming on his pistols and touched spurs to Jones's flanks. "Go, boy."

The soldier's back was to him, absorbed in his inspection. Jason held Jones to an easy trot; no need to announce himself too soon. At fifty yards he spurred into a gallop, closing the last distance, pistol out and cocked. The driver heard him now and turned about to stare as Jason pulled the bay up short, reins twisted about the pommel. He threw one leg over and slid to the ground.

"Good day, sir. And a fine day it is. Step back a little."

He knew the soldier's arms were hidden under the seat with the money—but, oddly, something tweaked his instincts. The man raised his hands but seemed hardly surprised.

"Thee'd be the Fleecer," the big redheaded soldier drawled in thick Yorkshire.

"So I am," Jason replied cheerfully. "No need for unpleasantness, sir. I'll detain you only a moment." But as he moved toward the trap, Jones snorted. The gut feeling grew stronger as Jason pulled the satchel from the seat box and fingered it open.

Jesus, he should have heeded his senses. Top to bottom the bag contained nothing but rags and newspaper.

"Thee's been much bother, Master Quick," the stolid soldier said in a tone too calm for his situation. "But now thee's fookin' well knit up."

At the sound of his name Jason whirled to see the man's hand come down to his mouth. The sun flashed on something shiny in his hand, then Jones snorted and shied at the whistle's shrill blast, but Jason was already sprinting for him as the nine horsemen erupted over the ridge to the north. He vaulted into the saddle and dashed away to the south.

Nine of them hot after him, but Jones could leave them far behind with little effort. Jason rode in a wide curve, gradually bearing west again, his mind pounding in time with the bay's swift pace. *Should have known. I should have known.* Too tempting a prize and too easy all along. How could he be so easily gulled? He cursed himself; flattered and lulled by his own cleverness, he'd underestimated Roddy Hallow, trusting one time too often the luck Bess knew had run dry.

Jason snatched a quick look behind him: His pursuers were still at a safe distance but coming on. Was that Hallow in the lead? Looked like him. Right then. Wear them out. He veered northwest toward the Dorchester road. Once across, there would be harvested fields, broken ground, and stone walls Jones could take with ease while army horses might balk at them. He'd have to hide all day, but where?

Thee's been much bother, Master Quick.

Christ, they knew him now. How did that happen? Why didn't he listen to Bess and Abel? He dare not go near Bess today but must go to ground somewhere else. Hide and bide his time. They weren't gaining on him at all, and his fear lessened a little at sight of the Dorchester road and the open fields beyond. With no sign of tiring, Jones shot across the road, sailing with ease over a four-foot stone wall. Just one more day's luck, Jason prayed. That would see him through, see both of them through, he and Bess. Steal her away in the night and on to Plymouth.

All right, Roddy. One last time we'll have a go.

They broke off the chase west of Higher Whatcombe when Billy Bell's horse refused a jump for the second time, and it was all Bell could do to stay in the saddle. The other horses were clearly done in. When Hallow ordered dismount, nine grateful, sweating men dropped to the ground. Bell stared wearily to the west that held no sign of the Fleecer but the bay's tracks, and those would vanish when Quick found harder ground. Lost the bastard again, and his flogged back still went tender under the heavy musket banging against it with every stride of his horse over the miles.

"Walls and fences," he snarled. "Fences and walls. Damn if he ain't done this a-purpose."

"Course he did," Danny Winner panted by his own spent horse. "Too clever by half, he is."

Roddy Hallow cleared his throat and spat on the ground. "Not this time."

"Same's before," said Soames, miserable as Bell. "We bloody lost'm."

"Hell we have. Don't be wet." Hallow looked over their played-out mounts. "We'll have to walk them some. Follow me."

He led his horse back toward the road leading south, his men plodding behind. They'd had an even chance of taking Quick on the downs. Hallow would have preferred to finish it there and clean. Dorset folk had no love for soldiery and would love them even less by this day's end, but an end it would be.

Trudging along before his horse, Danny Winner caught him up. "What's the plan now, Roddy? Where is it we're off to?"

"Where he's going," Hallow said, coldly sure of himself. "Where the whole rotten mess began."

At Whitechurch. The King's Shilling.

Bess kept glancing at the clock over the bar in the agony of her fear. Not come all day. If there was any trouble, he said, then wait until night. Something went awry, must have. They'd caught him. He was already dead, and her last words to him were bitter and denying. She should have stopped him, cried out, woken all Whitechurch to hold him back.

Blessed Mary, keep him safe. I'm sorry for letting him go with no more than a curse, only please keep him from harm.

The laggard hands of the clock crept toward four of the afternoon. This was the worst day of her life. To keep herself from screaming, Bess helped Alice swab the tables for the evening's business, and while the girl kept up a lively stream of chatter

about how she was walking out this month with a boy from
Winterborne Kingston, Bess gripped her soul by the throat to
keep from going silently mad.

By half-four the Shilling's bar and main room were serving
seven or eight local farmers savoring a pint and talk of the har-
vest before setting out home. Bess was drawing ale at the bar tap
when Alice glanced from a window into the inn yard.

"Preserve us, Bess. It's soldiers again."

Bess froze for an instant. Several men in the bar gulped down
their drinks, scattered their reckonings on the bar, and departed
by the side door. Roddy Hallow entered the main room, followed by eight dusty soldiers obviously fatigued and out of
sorts.

"Evenin'," the sergeant greeted an apprehensive Jedediah
Whateley. "Beer'n ale all round for my lads."

"Certainly, Sergeant, but I'd rather your men stacked their
arms outside."

"Not tonight."

"King's business," stated the one Bess knew as Winner.

Oh God, no . . .

"Anyone in the kitchen?" Hallow demanded.

"Just my wife," Whateley declared.

"Bring her out. I want everyone where I can see 'em."

When Alice scurried to fetch her, Anne Whateley came from
the kitchen to stand by her husband, wiping floury hands on her
apron, nervous as himself. "What is it, Jed?"

Hallow swallowed half a pint in one pull before stumping to
the middle of the room. "All of you drink up and leave now.
And you, Amos Pointer"—to a wizened little man trying to be
invisible in one corner—"Squire notions you've been poaching
his woodland again. Leave now before I remember you were
here."

"You heard," Danny Winner barked. "Hop it afore we take
down names."

Pointer and the other customers vanished speedily.

"Ah, Danny," Frank Soames admired. "If you don't sound like a corporal yet."

"We're your custom this night," Hallow informed Bess's father. "You two lasses come out from the bar. Which is closed," he added pointedly to his men. "No more tonight for any of us, clear?"

Jedediah Whateley found his voice and dignity. "Sergeant Hallow, what does this mean?"

"Means we need your house tonight. All night if need be. We're waitin' for Jason Quick."

"Lovely man," Winner muttered.

"That's him," Tim Groot crowed in the doorway. "What goes by the name o' the Golden Fleecer."

A cold hand wrapped about Bess's heart and squeezed, but praise the Blessed Virgin, they'd not caught him yet. He was still alive, but for how long? If he returned as he promised—*Blessed Mary, no. Keep him away. Got to warn him some way.*

Anne Whateley flatly refused to believe. "Jason? No, surely not. He's to marry our Bess this Sunday."

"We've witnesses," Hallow told her. "Soames here remembers him from Blandford St. Mary."

Soames lifted his face out of his beer, sporting a foam mustache. "And no mistake."

"And your ostler here saw'm the other night."

"Under Bess's window," Tim spoke up eagerly. "After a prize he was. I heard him say." He met Bess's bitter contempt with a smirk of poisonous triumph. "Told y'din I? Should've listened."

"This is mad," Whateley protested. "Jason Quick's a gentleman." A searing look at Tim. "Think I'd give my daughter's hand to just anyone?"

Hallow jerked a thumb at Bess. "Ask the girl herself."

"So I will. Bess?"

Her world crumbling around her, Bess forced herself to meet

her father's questioning eyes, but the words wouldn't come.
"I . . ."

"Bess," he entreated gently. "For your mum and me."

"She'll deny it," Tim yelped.

Whateley exploded. "Shut your lying mouth before you're
sacked. Can't take his word, Sergeant. A stableboy with no more
wits than the horses he tends. I'm your father, Bess. Tell me this
isn't true."

Her fear, the terrible truth, the weight of it all crumpled Bess
down onto a bench. They were all staring at her. No future for
her and Jason now or ever. Sunday would never come, nor their
children in America, but there was still his life to be saved.
"You're a right little toad, Tim Groot."

"Told you, din I?" Tim's voice broke on an agonized squeak.
"Din I . . . ?"

"Girl, look at me." Whateley moved to stand over his daughter. "What do you know of this? The truth now."

No use lying now. Bess fought to compose herself. "I know my
Jason. He is what he is." She appealed to her mother. "I'm sorry,
Mum, but so am I. Yet Jason never harmed a soul or took tup-
pence from any man of this village. Never."

Her mother was a study in confused compassion. She could
say nothing.

"And here he was," Billy Bell observed. "Under our noses from
the first."

Bess's mother hurried to gather the girl in protective arms
while the soldiers just looked stoic and tired. Alice Sims experienced a heart-fluttering thrill. There she was not an hour past,
going on about her fellow down Kingston while Bess, grown
suddenly much older and very glamorous in her sight, had not
shared a word about dashing Jason Quick. As lives went in
sleepy Whitechurch, Alice would live sixty-eight years with
seven children and twenty-one grandchildren but would ever
recall this as the most, possibly the only, exciting day of her life.

"All right." Roddy Hallow retook command of an ugly situation. "Sorry, Mr. Whateley, but we've our duty. The men will be havin' supper, whatever you've got. Make it quick," he ordered his detail. "And every man jack pay his score, hear? Danny, you, Bell, and Soames upstairs. Find a room with a good view of the road."

Hallow took Bess by the arm. "Take this lass with you. Don't want her slippin' off to warn Quick."

"Don't hurt my daughter," Whateley pleaded. "I'll be telling them at Dorchester if you do. Can't she stay with us?"

"No," Hallow refused. "They won't harm her—that's an order, Danny— but Quick'll be coming. Moonrise or moonset, he'll be here."

As Winner's detail led the forlorn Bess upstairs, Hallow found he could feel for her parents, mute there on the bench, the woman's hand clasped tight in her husband's. Suddenly Hallow wanted to spit out the whole dirty business. He wished he were back in St. Andrew drinking himself to sleep. Tomorrow night he would do just that. For the moment he found a fine target for his disgust. "You!" He pointed at Tim and then the door. "Get out."

The big one, Soames, put his soiled hands all over her as he sat her firmly in the rocking chair, but Bess chilled him with a look cold as she felt. Young Bell didn't bother her, but Winner frightened Bess. From the moment he pushed her into her room and closed the door, he took a seat on the window ledge, musket within reach, and rarely took his eyes from the road. He removed his tricorn and lolled his head against the wall. "Billy, Frank? Remember this sweet lass? She served us in the bar 'fore we went off on that damn pay detail down Blandford St. Mary."

His eyes slid to Bess: not cold like Soames's, but unforgiving. "And there we were, lappin' up the beer and goin' on about the stinkin' detail—what, where, and when. I'll lay a month's pay she remembered it all for her sweet Jason. Didn't you, girl? Know why Roddy sent us three up here with you? Plain justice. Every one of us got scars still red on our backs. They'll turn white in time, but we'll always have'm. All because of you and Quick."

She wouldn't give him the satisfaction of an answer, hands gripped together in her lap until the knuckles went bloodless.

Winner yawned and returned to his vigil over the road. "A hard ride and a long walk after. Jesus, but this's been one flamin' long day."

The man had no idea how long, beginning for Bess the moment Jason rode away from her. They came at half-four; must be going six now or even later. With no clock, Bess could judge time only by the fading light marching across the wall as the sun dipped lower. She wouldn't for her soul ask the time of Winner's men. She sat silent, trying not to let them see her torment. Soames stretched out on her bed that was too short for him by more than a foot. Bell sat on the floor, musket between his knees, staring at nothing with the dullness of fatigue.

The air had changed. With the sun down, warmth was gone from the day, leaving the room in gathering shadow.

By moonlight I'll come to you . . .

Winner stirred and stood up to relieve the cramp in his limbs. "Frank, light the candle there." In answer to a timid tap at the door, Winner threw it open. Anne Whateley stood there with a laden tray. "The provost said to bring your supper. Chicken barley soup, bread and butter."

"Good." Winner indicated the dresser. "Set it there."

Only Billy Bell remembered manners as he took his portions. "Thank you, ma'am."

"Doing what I was told, no more," Anne Whateley clipped, the wish clearly audible in her tone that he choke on it. "Bess, dear, here's some for you."

"Not hungry, Mum." As if she could eat with her stomach in a knot all day.

"Best have some," Winner advised, slathering a chunk of bread with butter. "We could be here straight on till morning."

The hungry men gave their attention to food and missed the silent woman-meaning that passed between mother and daughter. As Anne bent to kiss her, Bess whispered, *"What o'clock?"*

"Past seven."

With another kiss her mother departed. Bess tried to swallow a few mouthfuls of soup as darkness deepened beyond the candle's glow.

Time crawled by. Bess forced herself to sit still, but her heart and mind rioted. Winner kept his position in the window, musket trained into the night. Soames and Bell flipped pennies for heads-or-tails. Alice Sims crept in timidly to carry away their dishes. Her footsteps faded away down the stairs and all was quiet again. Bess strained for one sound in the unnatural silence beyond the open window where Winner waited like a cat at a mousehole.

Don't come tonight, Jason. Break this one last promise and live. Live for me, for I've no life without you.

She heard it then, sharp against the silence, the *tlot-tlot* of a single horse nearing on the road. Bell and Soames took up their muskets as Winner crouched ready at the casement. Near and nearer, now slowing and turning into the inn yard. Bess bolted out of the chair, shoving Winner aside—

"Jason, run! They're here, the sol—"

A big hand clamped over her mouth as Soames hauled her away from the window. Bess lived rigidly through a hell of waiting for the sound of Jason's horse to wheel and gallop away, but none came. He must have heard her. No shots, only deadly silence; then after a time, the thump of a heavy man stumping up the stairs. Roddy Hallow loomed in the open doorway.

" 'Twarn't him, just one of Whateley's reg'lars name of Jellicoe wanting supper. Turned him away. Did I hear the girl yell out?"

"She did," Winner admitted with some embarrassment. "We weren't lookin'."

"Well, *look,* damn you all. Watch her. If that'd been Quick, we'd've lost the bleeder again. Tie that wench to her bedpost and put a gag on her. Jesus."

Hallow turned and thumped back down the stairs.

"Tie her with what?" Bell wondered.

"Knot up one of her petticoats," Winner ordered. "Not the one she's wearin', Frank. Fetch one from the dresser."

"Got to excuse Frank," Billy Bell murmured in gruff apology as he gagged Bess with one of her hankerchiefs. "He ain't quite housebroken around women. I'll not tie this cruel tight, but you be quiet."

With the gag secure, Bell made sure Bess could still breathe freely through her nose, but that was all. As Soames twisted her arms about the bedpost behind her, she gave a muffled protest of pain.

"Hurts her, Danny," Bell said. "We'll tie'm in front. Just as sure."

"We'll make good and sure." Winner slipped his musket between Bess's hands and body, the muzzle hard just under her breasts. "Now pull it tight—that's it. This ain't our usual way, girl, but you ain't usual neither. Sarn't says you're dangerous as Quick. And we've had the manners flogged out of us."

Soames grunted. "Right enough."

"They got ten apiece with the cat, Miss Whateley. I got twenty."

Winner's eyes slid away from hers, remembering a nightmare. "After ten, y'can't stand up. You just hang there till they finish and cut you down. When I could think again, I knew Quick would be mine when we caught him. Had t'be. Now listen, girl."

Winner clearly took no pleasure in what he said and did, only cold determination. He spoke softly as he knelt to the musket's hammer. "Quick's a fine shot, not only true but fast. Better'n me. But I'll have him. Just give me one good shot."

He cocked the musket. "Against king's regs, but I filed the hammer lock some. You move a mite too much or too fast, it's liable to go off. So be quiet," Winner advised, patting Bess's cheek. "Be still."

With the musket muzzle below her breasts, Bess could see the road far too moonlit bright beyond the window.

Jason sat on the ground, badly needing rest. By his shoulder, spent Jones drooped his head to graze the thin grass that grew under the trees across the road from the Crown and Thistle. Jason had been running all day, watering the horse at streams when he could but with nothing to eat since breakfast a hundred years ago, though fear and tension killed much of appetite. Now, when he must think clearly through this last, longest day, fatigue dulled his brain. Jason wrenched his thoughts from chaos back to order.

He had a hundred pounds hidden in his room. Nothing else mattered among his belongings, but the money was vital. Were there soldiers inside waiting for him? He'd held this position for an hour with no sign of them, but he couldn't see the stable. The time must have gone nine by now but near bright as day with a full moon. He'd meant the moonlight to be an added jewel for Bess this night when he whistled under her window, but now light was his enemy. He'd be seen far away on such nights.

Time to move. The Crown and Thistle had a brisk custom; snatches of song and laughter drifted out to Jason. The stairs to his room were just to the right of the main entrance. Perhaps he could slip in and up without notice.

He tethered Jones to a stout bush and packed two of his pistols away in a saddlebag, thankful he hadn't needed them all day. All the same, to be safe, he rebuckled the broad belt beneath his coat, concealing the other two weapons, then moved unhurriedly across the road into the lighted stable. He could see no army horses or saddles.

As he entered the crowded inn only one person took notice: Rose Allen's eyes widened for a moment, then turned inscrutable. Jason forgot her, taking the narrow stairs two at a time.

He moved rapidly about the chamber. The wallet with its hundred pounds was still in its latest hiding place at the bottom of the clothespress. Jason stuffed the note into a pocket and chose three shirts to fit inside a saddlebag, tossing them onto his bed to be rolled. Absorbed, he didn't hear the light step on the stairs.

"Your money's safe and all the rest."

Rose lounged in the open door, quite at ease and sure of herself except for eyes hard as death. "Course I showed it where 'twould do the most good."

"Must have wounded your sense of profit to put it back." Jason turned back to rolling the shirts. "Go on, Rose. I've no time for you."

He could feel her cold stare boring into his back. "Jason Quick," she hissed through her teeth. "Mr. Jason bloody Quick."

"Not now, I said."

"Not ever, my fine Jacky. I swore to kill the scum who did for my Willy, and here you are."

"Your Willy killed an innocent man in front of me. He robbed me, and when I tried to get my money back he shot first."

Silence behind him. The saddlebag would hold one more shirt. He yanked it out of the clothespress. Against the doorjamb, Rose was unmoving.

"I even went down Dorchester to cheer when they hanged the wrong man. And hel-lo? Here was Mr. Quick all the time. And to think I let you touch me. I'll watch you swing off and laugh."

Jason hastily rolled the shirt into a tight bundle, aware of time flying. "A bit late for scruples. As for watching me die, you'll have to queue with all the oth—"

"*Kill him!*"

Jason froze not at her voice but the flat sound of the musket hammer cocked behind him.

"Turn around, Quick," the male voice ordered. "It ain't Christian to shoot a man in the back."

"Or anywhere else, pray God." Jason turned his head slightly, easing his right hand toward the pistol belt.

"I said turn aroun—"

Jason fired under his arm as he turned, the two explosions as one. He caught only a glimpse of the soldier's mortally surprised face as the musket ball ripped through Jason's left sleeve, deeply scoring skin and flesh. A young man too nervous to aim and squeeze properly. The soldier dropped like a stone with the stain spreading over his white uniform waistcoat where Jason's bullet had found his heart.

Rose screamed as Jason advanced on her. "Get out, woman."

As he slammed and locked the door, heavy footsteps pounded up the stairs. Beyond the panels, Rose's voice quavered with fear and shock, though still vicious. "You're done, Jason!"

His left arm going numb, Jason couldn't look at the dead soldier. "So are you, Rose, but there's always London for a girl like you. Find a woman called Long Jane in St. Martin's Court. Tell her I said you've a sterling talent for her trade."

Pounding now at the door that wouldn't hold long. Forget the shirts; he'd have to climb out the window with only one good arm. Gripping the edge of the sill, Jason hung by his right arm, then dropped heavily to the ground. He got shakily to his feet and stumbled across the road toward his horse.

Help me, Bess. I didn't want to kill him. He was only a boy. I never wanted to kill anyone, only to find my father and the wonder of you. God, give us one more miracle tonight.

Jason hung on to the pommel as his head swam with shock that turned his limbs cold and shaking. Courage washed out of him completely, unable to hold back the tears that welled suddenly. Better if the soldier had shot true, better for Bess and Abel—

Stop it. Put your foot in the stirrup and ride.

The luck of the Quicks would hold long enough, had to. Jason hauled himself into the saddle and turned Jones southeast toward Dewlish.

By late afternoon the news had spread through little Dewlish, buzzing among the customers in the one small public house. Abel had gone distractedly through his daily tasks, scattering feed to his hens, collecting eggs, and graining his horse. By sunset he could no longer stand not knowing and rode to the inn. He was quickly warned off in the stable by the hunchbacked old ostler.

"Stay away, Mr. Gant. There's two soldiers in there just bidin' their time for Jason Quick or anyone who knows him."

Posted as well at the Crown and Thistle, the ostler knew for sure, and probably the King's Shilling, too. Without another word, Abel walked his cob out of the stableyard through thickening dusk toward home.

He had little appetite but heated the remains of his mushroom and leek soup. The works of the old mantel clock had wheezily struck ten when Abel heard the muffled knock at his door. Three times a fist thudded against the wood, slowly, the sound of exhaustion.

"Jason?" Abel answered the door as swiftly as fifty-odd years and the onset of rheumatism allowed. Jason wove on his feet in the doorway, steadying himself on the jamb. "Abel, I'm hurt."

"Love of God. Here, come sit."

He helped Jason to the table, inspecting the blood-soaked coat sleeve. "I've linen and alcohol. Can you move the arm?"

"Yes. Didn't hit bone."

"Easy off with the coat now."

"Do I smell food?"

"There's soup and a cold mutton joint."

"Let me have some. Please, I haven't eaten all day."

"You're white as paper." Abel worked the coat off Jason. "Pity I must do this to a fine shirt."

He tore the bloody sleeve away from the long laceration, then fetched clean linen napkins and a bottle of alcohol while Jason wolfed down soup and savaged the mutton. "That's fine napkin," he regretted. "Shame to waste it on—*ai!*"

Jason's arm turned to fire as the alcohol seared into his raw wound.

"I've a weakness for good linen," Abel remarked over his cleaning. "Borrowed from the best inns in dear old London."

"By a dear, larcenous old heart." Jason winced as Abel pressed a fresh swab to his arm. "But bless you, for I'd nowhere else to go. God help me, Abel. I had to shoot a man tonight."

His friend received the confession with fatalistic calm. "You knew 'twould come to that one day."

"Did I?" When Jason closed his eyes, red memory turned and fired, and the young soldier went down and down. "Thrift, Abel. God's banked my misfortunes and paid me interest today."

"Miracle it is you're not dead."

"He was slow and more frightened than me."

"I heard in the village. The soldiers are out all over the shire, likely at the Shilling by now."

Jason seemed not to hear. "They tricked me. There was no money. Just an ambush." His head drooped forward. "But Jones made 'em eat our dust. Give him some grain and water before I ride out."

"Ride? How?" Abel tore another napkin into strips and bound a clean dressing to the wound. "You've got to stay the night and rest."

"Got to get Bess away tonight."

"Damn it, you're not thinking—"

"I am."

"You are in no fit condition to ride."

"Has to be tonight," Jason persisted stubbornly. "How long before they track me here to you? Harboring a fugitive? You wouldn't appreciate the Crown Court cells in Dorchester. No,

I've more chance this night than the morrow. After midnight. Those at the Shilling, if they're there at all, will likely be drunk or asleep or close to both. Let me up."

Jason lifted himself with difficulty from the chair and stumbled toward Abel's bedroom. "Wake me at half-eleven."

He sagged down on the rumpled bed as his teacher regarded him with frustration and a vast pity. "All the rest is coming apart, but not Bess and me."

Jason lifted his wounded arm. "Lovely bandage. Where would I be without you? Remember: half-eleven. We'll . . . trust my luck one last time."

And we'll skirt round Dorchester and make for Plymouth by easy stages. No one knows us there. We can hide until . . .

Too burned out to think anymore. The black curtain covered his mind in merciful sleep.

Bess had lost all sense of time. Minutes dragged by like prisoners chained in a file. The men's casual talk fragmented, then ceased altogether, one resting on the bed while the others remained at their window vigil. They took turns going to the privy outside but never considered Bess at all. She was too embarrassed to ask but would rather die than use her chamber pot in front of them even if they let her.

Her whole body ached from being forced unnaturally erect for hours against the bedpost, but over and over she prayed to the Blessed Virgin to keep Jason away. She told herself a hundred times he wouldn't come. He must not.

The inn was quiet now. Hallow had allowed her mum and dad to go to bed, and no voices drifted up from the soldiers below. Billy Bell went down and returned with leftover tea from the kitchen. "All there was, Danny."

At the window Winner yawned. "What's the time?"

"Gone twelve."

"Damn cold tea," Soames grumbled. "Think Roddy wouldn't grudge us one real tot through a long night."

They drank the tea and went back to waiting.

Wait away, Bess challenged with cold satisfaction. *He won't come now.* By this hour Jason would be tired and resting, perhaps at Abel's cottage, and when he woke he'd be too wary for stupid, dull men like these to snare him.

She tried to relax her body. The petticoat binding her had loosened a bit, but every time she tried to ease herself away from the hard bedpost, the musket muzzle jabbed cruelly into her breast. Even that could not lessen the relief flooding new strength and confidence through Bess. She would weather this night; they both would. The soldiers would not stay forever, and Jason would pick his time shrewdly. They would be all right.

Bess found she could twist a little away from the weapon's muzzle, this way or that. If only she could ease her back and legs for just a minute. Better to think on Jason than her body's suffering. Beside his other business he had purposed to buy her ring for Sunday. What would he choose then? Not too dear for price, Bess hoped. Flat foolish to wear all their fortune on her finger. Poor dear Jason worked cruel hard in his way for every pound but had not tuppence worth of common sense in the spending. Not too plain, either, but a ring fitting and right as their love.

That love had changed her as deeply as the flow of her courses—Nature's Wand, Mum called it—which had taken a thin stick of a girl and carved suddenly a woman in Bess's looking glass; some said the prettiest in the shire. In little more than half a year she'd gone from a desperate girl in a life with no more future than one could chip onto a tombstone, to a woman with a deepened soul, and not one moment of it regretted or wrong since Jason came.

And I'm sorry, Dad, for how you looked at me and must have felt when you knew, but it can't be changed.

He was hers. She possessed him completely. Making love on their hill, she couldn't writhe herself close enough to him but always lost herself in the one they became. His body was a hunger in her, and his soul had made her wiser. Enchanted at first with the glamour of him, now she knew his flaws, and they were nothing beside the good of the man. He came from London trades-folk with their new notions and bewildering machines, never content just to be what they were born but always eager to rise. Last night in that one moment of spite she could hate him and his father alike. *Mother Mary, you've heard my prayers and how many times this day I've repented that.* But that was the fire in Jason that drove him on, and now she loved him for the obsession, noble as any story Abel ever spun for her. And Jason never looked at her but she could see the honest need and wonder in his eyes, unbelieving of his fortune in her.

The bonds about her wrists still held tight, but she could move her back a mite away from the bedpost and side to side. Behind her Billy Bell dozed on the bed, breathing loudly. Soames and Winner drooped over their weapons. Bess arched her back as far as she could to relieve the ache and forced her mind into the future.

They would marry in Virginia—no, on the voyage out. She'd heard how a ship's captain could do that. Jason would buy his father free. Bess could see him with that done at last, like a burden of stone lifted from his back. There would be the shop in a house they owned outright, and she would care for them and give Jason children. No matter how many; they'd prosper right enough in America away from the king's laws and soldiers. Their children would be dark-complected as they were, perhaps with a tinge of her dad's red hair in one and Mum's light blue eyes in another, but every one well turned out and quick at learning as their father. Jason would see to that.

That was a new thought to Bess, to think a child of hers would be able to stand in church and read the words in a hymnal instead of mumbling from memory like most of Whitechurch, or even open for themselves the Scripture of the blessed King James.

She would want the first boy to be christened Jason, the first girl Anne Mary for her mother and Our Lady. Then Jedediah or Abraham for another boy, and perhaps a second girl might be Caroline after the queen—

No, Jason was flat right in that. They'd had enough of foreign queens who spoke English no better than parrots, and kings who wouldn't stomach an honest Whig Parliament. Bess's second daughter would be named . . . would be . . .

Help me, Mary. I'm so tired.

Don't give in to it. See your children.

Before the learning, feeding at her breast and for a while beyond, they would be hers to hold. So often young wives came to the inn with newborn babes tucked close on their shoulder, the infant's cheek against the mother's and held with a protectiveness Bess knew always without having known when she asked to hold the child for a moment. A baby's cheek was sweet and cool but somehow sent a new kind of warmth all through her. Those first months when they slept at her breast before wavering up to take their first unsure steps would belong to her. Perhaps if she ever came close to Jason's wit with words, she could tell him sometime when they lay together in deep Virginia night, and perhaps when he was wise enough not to need words, he might understand.

Billy Bell's snores wrenched her back to the present, the house around her so quiet Bess could hear the bar clock strike one below. She stretched her back; more give in her bonds, but the discomfort had become one large ache from knees to neck. Bess limped across the minutes of the night like crossing stepping-stones over fire.

Tlot-tlot-tlot . . .

Was it her fatigue or a sound on the night wind? Bess held her breath, straining to hear. Winner and Soames still dozed at the window.

Tlot-tlot-tlot.

No mistake. A rider coming, nearing at a cautious canter, now slowing to a walk. The two thoughts crashed as one into Bess's mind: *He didn't break his promise. They'll kill him.*

And then: *I can't let them. Sweet Mary, help me.*

Winner and Soames still didn't move. No sound from below stairs. They must hear in a moment. Now the horse entered the inn yard. She had to warn him, but the gag muted her. However much she screamed, Jason couldn't hear. Her head drooped in despair. Bess stared into the black hole of the musket muzzle and went a little mad.

By now her bonds were loose enough. She twisted this way and that. Nearer and nearer, the shod hooves were drums crashing in her ears. Now Winner stirred and shook Soames. "Frank. Billy. Look sharp. It's him."

Bell snaked off the bed to snatch up his weapon as Soames cocked his piece. All three men were crouched at the window now, their attention riveted beyond it. The *clack* of Bell's hammer drawn back was loud in the small room.

With the last of her strength, Bess strained forward and to one side. The swell of her right breast wedged tightly over and then past the deadly metal snout. There, she'd done it. She didn't want to die. Mary wouldn't allow anything so cruel now, but Bess quailed with fear. Perhaps it wouldn't hurt too much or wound too deeply.

Mother Mary, just my arm or even less with your help. He's got to know. Let me just reach the trigger.

She heard it then, his low, soft whistle. He must be directly under the window, only a few feet away. Soames leaned forward, tucking the musket into his shoulder. Straining for the trigger, Bess's exertion forced a muffled gasp from her, but one finger attained the cold little trigger. At the same time, Winner heard, turned and saw her—

"Girl! For Christ's sake *no!*"

Yes. Jason.

The force of Winner's reaching hands jarred her erect as the gun discharged.

That he'd lost Quick again into the night was a dull reality to Roddy Hallow, pale beside the few minutes after bolting up the stairs at the musket report. He found he could look into the shock-dimmed eyes of the girl's parents and be too sorry to speak. He could pity Danny Winner, tough as leather yet sobbing his heart out, choking and stammering over and over that the child did it herself, that she tripped the trigger just as he jumped to stop her. And Hallow, who had seen men riddled with so many bullets they seemed one great wound, found he could be sick and drained at the sight of Bess Whateley. His stomach stayed down but he had to keep swallowing with a dry mouth against something deeper than nausea.

His soldiers from below were staring at the body and poor Danny. Needing to reassert control, Hallow dismissed them curtly. "All right, all right. Downstairs, the lot of you. Nothing more to see. Come on, Danny."

Maybe they hadn't lost the bastard yet. Hallow considered. Winner and Bell were too shaken for what he had in mind. He took Frank Soames aside—stoney, stolid Soames who lacked the imagination to feel much of anything deeply. "Tomorrow when the inns open, ride to Cheselbourne, Dewlish, Kingston, all you can cover. Everyone's to keep an eye peeled for Quick. And Frank, I want every livin' soul in earshot to know what's happened. And no bein' polite about details, clear? Then get back here."

With any luck they could still end this today.

He never could find the words to tell Bess how he felt, nor any now for her death. The soldiers wouldn't let him upstairs. All

Tim saw was what two of them carried out of the inn wrapped in stained sheets.

He sat in the dark, hunched down in the farthest empty stall, fist jammed over his mouth to keep from howling, trying to get his mind around a thing too vast and impossible. Quick it was what did this. Took Bess away. Made her look at him like he was dirt. Killed her.

He cried over her once, more than a man should. The fist hard against his teeth trembled violently, but his eyes now were dry and terrible.

Early Saturday afternoon now, and they were to have been married on the morrow. That would have to wait. The Devil's own luck he had, so Abel said, not daring to ascribe it to angels, but if such it was, the angel had flown. Since Cheselbourne and the soldier he killed, Jason was too shaken to think clearly.

They'd been waiting for him. Stupid and arrogant to assume they wouldn't be there, but what fool fired the shot too soon that sent him flying away? And what of Bess? What had they done with her?

"True, it is maddening," Abel agreed as he cleaned Jason's wound and applied a fresh dressing. "But you've gone to ground and here you must stay while it's light."

"I must know she's safe."

"What you must do is rest and wait."

"Damn it all, I can't just sit here. I've got to know."

"Very well," Abel decided. "Then I'll go. Not to Whitechurch; that will be crawling with soldiers. I'll go to the Bull's Horn in Dewlish. I'll learn what I can."

Left alone, Jason paced and fretted. After one by the clock when Abel left. Going on three now. He tried to read but couldn't concentrate. Again and again he looked to the clock, whose hands hardly seemed to move. Finally, desperate to silence the questions whirling through his mind, he took up the pistol emptied at Cheselbourne and reloaded it.

Past three now. Where in hell was Abel? The Bull's Horn was no more than ten minutes' ride. Had Abel gone on to Whitechurch after all? Cursing liberally, Jason went to feed Abel's hens and bucket some water for Jones. He felt calmer now, able at least to order his thoughts. Somehow they would get out and away, and Bess would never have to wait for him again. He counted over their money again, tucked the notes away, and waited.

The time was close to four when, standing in the open doorway, he saw Abel riding through the trees at a lagging walk. His old teacher didn't look at him as he reined in, just slumped in the saddle, making no move to dismount. The reins slipped from his hands and hung loose.

"Abel?"

His friend dismounted stiffly, unsteady on his feet. Abel had imbibed more than one strong drink.

"Abel, what news?"

The reply was barely audible. "I don't know. It's—I heard at the public house. A soldier had been there and told."

"Will you look at me, man? Told what?"

Abel began to uncinch his saddle. "The host must have thought me an idiot. Had to tell me twice over. I couldn't grasp it all. Couldn't come back straight off, not without a drink or two. And all the way here, I didn't know how to tell you. Didn't want to tell you."

He closed his eyes tight, head leaned against the saddle. "Jason, I am so sorry."

"What?" Jason sprang at him, forcing Abel to face him with the tears running down his lank old cheeks. "Is Bess all right? Tell me. Is she safe? They haven't hurt her?"

"They took her to the church. To the sexton."

Abel was evading. Jason's hands dropped heavily to his sides. "Whatever it is, for the love of God tell me."

Abel gave up fumbling at the saddle and simply sat down on the ground. "She did it herself. The soldier said. He spared no details."

Head bowed almost between his knees, Abel mumbled out the rest. How Bess was bound to the bedpost, gagged to keep her quiet while the men waited for Jason. The musket at her breast. She must have worked at the bonds for hours until they were loose enough.

"That was the shot that warned you away," Abel concluded. "I knew she loved you. I didn't know how much until now."

Jason's mouth opened in a soundless cry. No, he would not believe. He couldn't. "Not until I see her."

"You can't."

"I will."

"Jason," Abel sobbed. "You don't want to. They can't even let her coffin be open."

Like a sleepwalker Jason turned and stumbled into the house, his mind red and whirling but his small hands steady as he buckled the four pistols about his scarlet coat. When he emerged, striding toward the stable, Abel was inside dropping his saddle on its rack. He saw with alarm the pistols and the silent, lethal energy in Jason's movements as he saddled Jones.

Abel tore his friend's hands from their task. "Stop. Have you gone completely mad?"

"Get *away*." Jason spat with taut fury, repelling him so hard that Abel went reeling. Jason sprang into the stirrup and saddle, and Jones was trotting out into the yard before Abel caught him up. He tried to grasp the bridle, but Jason wrenched his hand away.

"She died for nothing then," Abel wailed in his wake. "Jason, she gave you your life."

The big bay shot into a gallop through the trees, but Abel had seen the death in Jason's eyes.

She gave you your life.

His life. Was that all?

He didn't believe. He wouldn't until he saw his love with his own eyes, and any man who hindered him would die today. Jason's mind was ice, knowing one reality alone.

Jones plunged on across the fields of shocked corn, taking walls and fences with a madness equal to Jason's. They cleared the last broken field and dashed out onto the Dorchester road half a mile west of Whitechurch. Once on the deserted road, Jason slowed the horse to a walk and then a halt. He bent forward, panting, sick with the agony burning him out.

He had known passion that shook him with Louisa, that and so much more with Bess, but this was a different, poisonous seizure. He trembled with it. Nothing mattered beyond this hour, not one moment beyond this. All must go as this day fell out. If he found her alive, then hell take all else. If dead, he would tear the lid from her coffin and sweep his love up in one last embrace. Life? There was no life beyond Bess.

She's alive, his heart pounded out. *Will be. Must be. But not you, Hallow. Not today.*

"Right then." Jason straightened and gathered the reins. "Go, boy."

Topping the last rise some hundred yards above the King's Shilling, he should have paused to reconnoiter, but he was too far gone, swept on the fever-tide consuming him. He spurred the long-legged bay down the last distance, swerved sharply across the inn yard onto St. Mary's Lane. Some atom of caution should have noted the absence of customers about the outside tables. Jason saw nothing but the few yards left before the church—

—and the soldiers suddenly swarming onto the road, aiming their muskets, and the tall figure of Roddy Hallow raising his arm in command. Jason's lips went back in a snarl. He twisted the reins about the pommel, drew two pistols, and kicked Jones into a last run.

"*Hallow*—"

"Front rank—fire!"

The world tore asunder, its fragments ripping into man and horse. Jones went down, sprawling Jason in the dust. He didn't know if he'd been hit, felt only a merciful numbness.

"Rear rank—fire!"

Jason was jerked violently as the bullets struck him. With the arms of a broken doll, he aimed and fired both pistols before they dropped from his hands. He knew the coppery taste of too much blood pouring into his mouth. God damn him, Hallow was still standing, and behind Jason someone was screaming at him, not words but only lunatic sound.

"Reload!"

Jason rolled over weakly to see Tim Groot, his face a mask of madness, charging at him with the ax raised high. Breath came harder now, and what he could manage was half blood. He spat it out. He wouldn't have Hallow. That was too bad.

"But you'll do, Timmy."

At a bare ten feet he couldn't miss. As if Tim had slammed into a wall, he jerked crazily to one side as the two bullets ripped into his chest, stumbled two more steps and collapsed. Jason lay with his empty pistols and dying Jones convulsing feebly beside him. Bess was in the church. He could see the church. She was that close. Bess . . .

When Hallow ordered stand-easy, Danny Winner stared out at the carnage on the road. The ostler didn't move. There was his piece of forty pounds. Winner grimly admired the skill that dispatched him. Half dead, Quick was still too good with a pistol. Now he lay propped on one elbow, refusing to die.

Someone prodded Winner in the side. "It's your place, Danny," Hallow said. "Go finish him."

Winner cocked his musket and walked forward, closing the space between Quick and himself. Carefully: Even now the bastard might have a last trick up his sleeve, like an extra pistol.

But Jason's hands were empty. And damn if the son of a bitch didn't greet him with a blood-flecked grin. "Lud, Danny. You finally got it right."

Winner stood over him. The man was done. His own shot would be only a mercy.

"Please," Jason labored. "Did they lie?"

"Who?"

"Bess. Is she really gone?"

"Aye, she's dead." *And you did it,* Winner accused with a kind of pleading. *Not us. Not me.*

Jason's arm could no longer support him. He sank back heavily. "Doesn't matter then."

As he took aim, Winner's mind blinked with a double image. Jason waiting to die and another too-vivid death he couldn't prevent, stinging now and forever worse than the cat across his back.

"Sorry for all the trouble," Jason managed. "Nothing personal, really."

"No. It's personal." Winner pulled the trigger.

> *. . . wine-red was his velvet coat,*
> *When they shot him down on the highway,*
> *Down like a dog on the highway,*
> *And he lay in his blood on the highway, with a bunch of lace at his*
> *throat.*

Jason and Bess were buried in the cool verge of St. Mary's churchyard, not quite side by side as man and wife but close enough that the roots of the same sheltering yew caressed both.

Roddy Hallow saw a good share of the forty pounds reward. Major Sedgewick proving as good as his word, Hallow became regimental sergeant major before retiring, and indeed found his willing widow with a bit put by, though his was a Pyrrhic victory. The widow had a Puritan streak and hounded Roddy's declining years with tracts and exhortations against his pipe and bottle. Roddy stuck it for five years, then abandoned her and cheerfully drank himself to death with Frank Soames, whose liver proved less durable than his thirst.

Danny Winner won his stripes back, served with the Fifty-fourth in Ireland and later in the colonial campaigns of New York and Connecticut. Mortally wounded in the latter, he died in the arms of Billy Bell. Staunch British soldier that he was, Winner's last words were for King George, valedictory but unprintable.

Rose Allen never saw America but ran off with a handsome whiskey drummer less solvent than a churchmouse, who deserted her in London where, prophetically, Rose found her true calling as a white-stocking doxy plying the Strand.

Abel Gant lived quietly among his chickens and dusty books for ten more years. Dewlish remembered and respected him as a scholar of modest means who nonetheless never seemed to want for anything. On his death in 1773 he left an astonishing bequest of several hundred pounds to Jedediah and Anne Whateley, a sum to St. Mary's Church for fresh flowers in perpetuity on two graves, and an anonymous but gratefully received fifty pounds to the widow of one Enoch Parsons. Like his sorely missed Jason, Abel considered himself not so much dishonest as selectively principled.

In their age, with Bess gone, the Whateleys lost heart for their trade and sold the inn to the strapping young fellow from Winterborne Kingston who married Alice Sims and kept the name. The King's Shilling continued to be known for the best cuisine on the Dorchester road and had its share of legends, which, given English eccentricity, swelled rather than diminished its reputation. The inn and the adjacent church were firmly believed to be haunted, but as no guest or parishioner was ever frightened or bothered in the least, the presences, if they existed, were regarded in little Whitechurch with great affection and pride.

And still of a winter's night, they say, when the wind is in the trees,
When the moon is a ghostly galleon tossed upon cloudy seas,
When the road is a ribbon of moonlight over the purple moor,
The highwayman comes riding—
　　Riding—riding—

Jason waits at the altar of St. Mary's Church. He has a dim memory of waiting so before, perhaps many times, but no matter. It is always new and a joy as Bess glides down the nave, radiant in her mother's wedding dress. She puts out her hand for him to take, and Jason reverently touches the ring, two thin strands of braided gold, to each of her first three fingers and slips it onto the fourth.

There is no sense of time for either of them, though now and again faint voices echo in their world. Sometimes, waiting at her window, Bess can feel movement in the room and almost hear the voices of Alice Sims and others as they come and go. She doesn't heed them or mind. They have their place, but she has eyes only for the moonlit road beyond her casement and Jason coming to her.

And he whistles his tune under her window.

The Highwayman

PART ONE

The wind was a torrent of darkness among the gusty trees,
The moon was a ghostly galleon tossed upon cloudy seas,
The road was a ribbon of moonlight over the purple moor,
And the highwayman came riding—
    Riding—riding—
The highwayman came riding, up to the old inn-door.

He'd a French cocked-hat on his forehead, a bunch of lace at his chin;
He'd a coat of the claret velvet, and breeches of brown doe-skin.
They fitted with never a wrinkle; his boots were up to the thigh!
And he rode with a jewelled twinkle—
    His pistol butts a-twinkle—
His rapier hilt a-twinkle, under the jewelled sky.

Over the cobbles he clattered and clashed in the dark inn-yard,
He tapped with his whip on the shutters, but all was locked and
    barred,
He whistled a tune to the window, and who should be waiting there
But the landlord's black-eyed daughter—

Bess, the landlord's daughter—
Plaiting a dark red love-knot into her long black hair.

And dark in the dark old inn-yard a stable-wicket creaked
Where Tim, the ostler, listened; his face was white and peaked;
His eyes were hollows of madness, his hair like mouldy hay,
But he loved the landlord's daughter,
    The landlord's red-lipped daughter:
Dumb as a dog he listened, and he heard the robber say—

"One kiss, my bonny sweetheart, I'm after a prize tonight,
But I shall be back with the yellow gold before the morning light.
Yet if they press me sharply, and harry me through the day,
Then look for me by moonlight,
    Watch for me by moonlight,
I'll come to thee by moonlight, though Hell should bar the way."

He rose upright in the stirrups; he scarce could reach her hand;
But she loosened her hair i' the casement! His face burnt like a brand
As the black cascade of perfume came tumbling over his breast,
And he kissed its waves in the moonlight
    (Oh, sweet black waves in the moonlight!)
Then he tugged at his reins in the moonlight, and galloped away to
    the West.

PART TWO

He did not come in the dawning, he did not come at noon;
And out of the tawny sunset, before the rise o' the moon,
When the road was a gypsy's ribbon, looping the purple moor,
A redcoat troop came marching—
    Marching—marching—
King George's men came marching, up to the old inn-door.

They said no word to the landlord, they drank his ale instead,
But they gagged his daughter and bound her to the foot of her narrow bed.
Two of them knelt at her casement, with muskets at their side!
There was death at every window;
    And Hell at one dark window;
For Bess could see, through her casement, the road that he would ride.

They had tied her up to attention, with many a sniggering jest,
They had bound a musket beside her, with the barrel beneath her breast!
"Now keep good watch!" and they kissed her. She heard the dead man say,
Look for me by moonlight;
    Watch for me by moonlight;
I'll come to thee by moonlight, though Hell should bar the way.

She twisted her hands behind her, but all the knots held good!
She writhed her hands till her fingers were wet with sweat or blood!
They stretched and strained in the darkness, and the hours crawled by like years,

Till, now, on the stroke of midnight,
    Cold, on the stroke of midnight,
The tip of one finger touched it! The trigger at least was hers!

The tip of one finger touched it; she strove no more for the rest!
Up, she stood up to attention, with the barrel beneath her breast,
She would not risk their hearing: she would not strive again,
For the road lay bare in the moonlight;
    Blank and bare in the moonlight,
And the blood in her veins in the moonlight throbbed to her love's refrain.

Tlot-tlot, tlot-tlot! Had they heard it? The horse-hoofs ringing clear;
Tlot-tlot, tlot-tlot, in the distance? Were they deaf that they did not hear?
Down the ribbon of moonlight, over the brow of the hill,
The highwayman came riding—
    Riding—riding—
The redcoats looked to their priming! She stood up straight and still.

Tlot-tlot, in the frosty silence! Tlot-tlot, in the echoing night!
Nearer he came and nearer! Her face was like a light!
Her eyes grew wide for a moment; she drew one last deep breath,
Then her finger moved in the moonlight,
    Her musket shattered the moonlight,
Shattered her breast in the moonlight and warned him—with her death.

He turned; he spurred him Westward; he did not know who stood
Bowed, with her head o'er the musket, drenched in her own red blood!
Not till the dawn he heard it, and his face grew grey to hear

How Bess, the landlord's daughter,
  The landlord's black-eyed daughter,
Had watched for her love in the moonlight, and died in the darkness there.

Back, he spurred like a madman, shrieking a curse to the sky,
With the white road smoking behind him, and his rapier brandished
  high!
Blood-red were his spurs in the golden noon, wine-red was his velvet coat,
When they shot him down in the highway,
  Down like a dog in the highway,
And he lay in his blood on the highway, with the bunch of lace at his
  throat.

And still of a winter's night, they say, when the wind is in the trees,
When the moon is a ghostly galleon tossed upon cloudy seas,
When the road is a ribbon of moonlight over the purple moor,
The highwayman comes riding—
  Riding—riding—
The highwayman comes riding, up to the old inn-door.

Over the cobbles he clatters and clangs in the dark inn-yard;
He taps with his whip on the shutters, but all is locked and barred;
He whistles a tune to the window, and who should be waiting there
But the landlord's black-eyed daughter—
  Bess, the landlord's daughter—
Plaiting a dark red love-knot into her long black hair.

—ALFRED NOYES